The Perilous Road To Her

a novel

N. L. Blandford

The Perilous Road to Her

First Edition

ISBN 978-1-7776601-2-3 (Paperback Edition) / ISBN 978-1-7776601-1-6 (ebook) / ISBN 978-1-7776601-3-8 (Kindle Edition)

Permission to use material from other works:

Cover Image by 'kwest', used under license from Shutterstock.com

Author photograph by @PhotoHuch

Visit nlblandford.com

The Perilous Road To Her

LETTER FROM THE AUTHOR

In 2013, I wrote out the general outline of the story you are about to read. A story about a woman who so desperately loves her sister that she goes to inexplicable lengths to try and find her.

At the time, I knew the world of human trafficking would be at the centre of the pain our protagonist faced. I also knew that this was a topic that was not talked much about in 2013 and feared that readers may not want to explore the dark and violent world millions of people around the world face every day.

My fears about how this fictional story would be received not only by readers, but by victims themselves, kept the story inside of me for seven years. As a spotlight on human trafficking is growing brighter I felt now was the time to share this story. I have not let go of my fears but have used them to fuel the words you will read.

I debated putting a disclaimer on a fictional story about the physical, sexual and mental abuse the characters experience. It is fiction, after all. However, the worlds of fiction are in some way connected to the worlds of truth. As such, I want you, my reader, to know that if anything you read in these pages creates questions, pain or grief, you are loved. Take a break and rest as needed.

I encourage all readers to check out the *Resources* page at the back of the book, and do your own research, to learn more.

N.L. Blandford - April 2021

For my husband, Brian. My safe place.

&

For my sister, Lindsay.

There is no road I wouldn't travel for you.

CHAPTER ONE

MY PHONE MADE THE FAMILIAR SOUND OF A BIRD TO notify me I had a new text. I ignored it for a few minutes as I sat in the passenger seat of our black unmarked police car. I watched the tall office buildings that filled the Toronto sky pass by my window. I craned my neck to look up to the top of the buildings in wonder at the architects who first dreamed of making buildings touch the clouds. Did they know how society would change with the heart of commerce being held within their walls?

Most days gazing up at the infinite glass made me feel part of an exciting world of possibilities. Today the buildings overwhelmed me. A world of wealth, deception and greed which had captivated Claire, and turned her into someone I didn't recognize, lived behind those glass walls I had started to resent those walls. I finally pulled up the text.

'O - I need your help.'

"Of course, you do." I mumbled, locked my phone and rested my head against the headrest.

"Of course, you do what?" my partner, Detective Joe Cattaneo, asked.

"The usual. Claire 'needing' me. We both know what that means."

As we sat at a red light, Joe turned down his classic rock music and looked over at me. "For a big sister, she sure demands a lot from you. You know you only enable her by running to her every time she asks?"

"I know. But she's my sister. I can't just abandon her. Claire took care of me when we were younger and I guess it is my turn now." I said begrudgingly. "I just wish she would see what a shit show she has turned her life into and get it together."

"Do you want to go see her? I could turn right and head over there."

"No, keep going straight. She can wait."

I looked out the window and watched the traffic go by as I thought about the hundreds of times Claire had reached out for help. The calls were always requests for money. Money, she claimed was for rent or food but was always used for drugs. I knew where the money went but I couldn't stop myself from hoping maybe the next time would be different. It hurt too much to look into her broken eyes and say no. Every time I saw her I couldn't help but wonder what happened to the Claire I used to know. The caring person who was always looking out for others while still determined to make her dreams come true. She was the life of the party. She would make each person feel as though they were the only one who mattered in the moment they spent with her. She wasn't the strung-out shell of a woman she had become. I was startled from my thoughts by Joe turning on the siren. I looked over at him and he smiled.

"Welcome back. How about a homicide to take your mind off things for a while?"

Joe and I had known each other since the academy and had been partners since we both became detectives four years ago. They say your partners on the job are your family and I never understood that until Joe.

My previous partners were not keen on developing an actual relationship. Kyle was close to retirement and demanded silence. All day. After he retired, I worked with Gene who talked all day about nothing of importance. I would be lucky if I could recall anything he said during our time together. Having worked a couple of cases alongside Joe, before we were partnered, we quickly ran out of superficial things to talk about. During our second week together, we got into the nitty gritty of our private lives; no holds barred. After six months together, everything had been put on the table. From Joe's rowdy college days and fights with his wife, Sally, to my obsession with 90s television and Claire's drug problem.

On numerous occasions Joe has shown up at Claire's, in the middle of the night, to help me take her to the hospital after a night of heavy drug use. Taking care of Claire would be a struggle without Joe. I would be buried alive under the weight of it all.

Every weekend I thank Sally for her willingness to let him help me. I knew if I was her I would have a hard time seeing my husband run to help another woman. Sally isn't like me. She is her own woman, who knows what she wants, and is someone I would never want to hurt. It's sad to say, but Sally is the big sister I wished Claire would once again become. Joe? He is the brother I never had or ever thought I wanted. Turns out both Joe and Sally are the people I desperately need.

Most Saturday evenings we have a 'family' dinner where Sally always outdoes herself preparing a delicious meal. These meals are where I get most of my weekly sustenance from. I don't really cook and my food intake mostly comes from takeout. After dinner, everyone gathers in the living room and, in stereotypically Canadian style, watches Hockey Night in Canada. Everyone but Sally. Sally usually reads a book on the couch beside Joe, shaking her head and laughing at both of us when we yell at the television after a referee makes a call we don't agree with.

As we pulled up to the crime scene I looked over at Joe and a familiar feeling of gratefulness formed in my mind. I don't know what I would do without the support he and his family bring into my otherwise dismal life.

We got out of the car and made our way up the front walk of a small, white, 1920s home. The house reminded me of the ones you would see on the front of Christmas cards. Green shutters on the window, a red front door at the top of a small wooden porch wrapping the front of the house. The quaintness of the outside of the house did not match the inside. The few pieces of furniture were rundown, there were stains on the carpets, and the 1970's yellow and green floral wallpaper was peeling. We were about to head into the kitchen when the bird in my phone sang. I glanced at my phone before the message disappeared from my screen.

"O, I really need you!" I put my phone in my pocket.

Joe put his arm across the doorway to prevent me from walking into the kitchen. "Just call her. Then I don't have to hear that damn bird all day."

"Fine," I grunted. "I'll be right back."

"Well this guy isn't going anywhere." Joe joked as he nodded towards the body on the kitchen floor.

As Joe talked with the first officer on the scene, I walked out of the house and down to the sidewalk. I dialed Claire's number and the first ring didn't finish before it was answered.

"O - thank goodness. I, I, I am so scared. I just... I think I have really done it this time."

I couldn't tell if Claire was crying or on the verge of hyperventilating. I instantly went from annoyed sister to mother bear. "Claire, breathe. Can you do that? Take a deep breath for me." I heard a large intake of air through the phone. "That's right. Okay, now slowly tell me what happened."

"Well, you see Troy and I were at this party and we just wanted to have fun you know, and there was this new kind of stuff everyone was trying.

But we had no money, so I tried to sweet talk the man into letting me have a little but it didn't work. He just blew me off. As if he had no idea who I was! I mean I am Claire Beaumont, Claire freakn' Beaumont! He was such..."

"Claire, stay on point please; I am working."

"Sorry. Anyways, Troy decided that if we could just distract him we could take just a little taste and no one would notice."

"Oh, Claire you didn't?"

"It was just a tiny amount, minuscule really. Troy was chatting with the guy and I took a sample and slipped out of the room. I don't know how he figured it out, but next thing I knew, Troy and I are running down the street being shot at."

"Are you okay? Have you been shot? Where are you?" I silently cursed myself for not calling sooner.

"No, no I am fine, well, bruised but fine." Claire's voice trembled as she spoke. "But O, the guy and his men came to our place today, trashed it and beat the shit out of Troy and roughed me up a bit. Just a black eye and a couple bruises on my arms but Troy is hurt really bad. They said they would come back and kill us if we don't pay them for what we took, plus interest, by the end of the day. O - I hate to ask but can you help us out?"

I shook my head as I listened to Claire cry. She didn't actually hate to ask me for help, it happened all the time. I didn't know whether to believe her. She had fed me similar stories before. Hard up with no money to buy drugs, so they steal them. Then I have to bail her out to ensure she doesn't end up at the bottom of Lake Ontario. But something was different this time. Claire seemed genuinely scared and I knew what her fake tears sounded like -- this wasn't it.

"How much?" I asked sternly.

"$1500."

"$1500 is how much a taste costs! Claire what am I missing?"

"The guy seemed to think we took more than we did. Other people were sampling as well and they are now pinning it all on us."

"For God's sake Claire, you do realize I am not the world's richest cop, right? Where am I going to get $1500?"

"Please O - I need it by 7 tonight otherwise … well I don't want to think about the otherwise."

I looked at the house in front of me, and wished in that moment that I was the dead man in the kitchen. I hung my head, "Let me see what I can do."

"Thank you, Thank you!" Claire exclaimed.

"I can't guarantee anything Claire. So, you better have a backup plan." I took a deep breath to muster the courage to say my next thought. "And this has to stop. Me helping you out all the time has to stop. It is bad for you and for me."

"I know, I know. It will."

"I am serious. This is the last time. No matter what happens I cannot help you anymore." As much as I didn't want to admit it, Dad was right and I had to let Claire hit rock bottom. I had to stop trying to save her. "I got to go. I will call you later." I hung up the phone and let out a loud grunt of frustration as I headed back towards the house.

I didn't know if I was more frustrated with myself for letting Claire take advantage of me for so long, or the fact my drunken, abusive, and intolerable father had the answer I refused to face.

I hadn't spoken to my father since mom's funeral, two years ago, but six months ago I was desperate to help Claire. My best friend was on the fast track to death and I couldn't seem to stop it. When I called, all he could muster was, "There's no helping those that don't want help. Best wait until she hits rock bottom."

"What if rock bottom is death? We need to do something!" I cried.

"Sorry darling, but ain't nothing that can be done right now. She will bounce back, you will see. She's strong, our Claire is."

We had sat in silence for a few minutes and then I hung up. I realized where Claire and I got our persistent denial from.

I walked into the house, and Joe was nice enough not to ask what Claire was calling about until after we had finished our review of the crime scene, and were on our way back to the station. "What does she say she "needs" now?" he asked.

"$1500 -- otherwise she and Troy are dead for stealing what she calls a 'sample'."

"Wow, and how much did you give her a couple weeks ago, and a few weeks before that?"

"I know, I don't even have $1500 that I can afford to save for myself let alone give her. I am so frustrated!"

"Do you think you could get her into rehab this time?"

"We've tried that. You've been there. If she doesn't want to go, I can't force her."

"If it is as serious as she says and her life is in danger, maybe she will go this time. Even if it is just to get away from the danger."

"I don't know. Maybe. I will go see her and see if her story checks out first. If I don't see a black and blue Troy she is getting nothing. Then maybe I can take her to rehab somewhere far away from Troy."

The rest of the ride we sat in silence. Joe occasionally looked over to see if I was alright and I would give him a half-reassuring smile. It was only a few years ago Claire was on top of the world. The happiest I had ever seen her. Now she was the saddest person I knew and I was powerless to help her.

CHAPTER TWO

I PULLED UP TO CLAIRE'S RUN-DOWN APARTMENT BUILDING in Regent Park and felt my heart rate increase and my shoulders tighten. I knew the tension in my body would result in a headache after this conversation. I sat in my car for a few minutes, running over how I was planning on telling Claire that this time there was no money. No get out of jail free card. She would have to figure it out herself. Resting my head on my hands on the steering wheel, I knew I would never be able to tell her that. No matter how much I wanted to. I just didn't know what I could do. I didn't have $1500.

I got out of the car and walked through the gap where a door had once been. The building was dilapidated and the many broken windows easily transported the sounds from within to the street and vice versa. My eyes watered from the stench of piss and puke.

I stood outside the door to Claire's apartment and couldn't help but think that three years ago I was standing in front of a very different door. One made of high-end steel in an upscale building on the waterfront. The white stone walls, floor to ceiling windows, modern design and furniture spelled money and lots of it. Now her dingy brown and peeling walls spelled desperation. I knocked on the door and turned the handle.

As I opened the door, I was greeted by the additional smells of sweat, dust and mold. There were holes in the walls I didn't recognize, which either supported Claire's story or Troy had gotten angry again. Garbage was everywhere and the few dishes they had were piled up on their small counter with food stuck on them and flies circling. Usually when I encountered the destitute lifestyle of an addict, I rationalized how they could live as they do. But with Claire, the fact that her addiction's grip kept tightening made no sense to me. How could the strong woman I knew be so dependent on a powder? Why couldn't she snap out if it? My stomach started to fill with knots of desperation in response to Claire's environment.

Claire ran over from the couch and gave me a hug. "Thank you for coming," and she squeezed with what little strength she had.

"Where's Troy?" I peered into the bedroom but didn't see him.

"He went out for a bit. He'll be back soon."

"We should get going then."

"Going, where are we going?"

"Claire, I can't keep bailing you out with money. The only thing I can do to help you is to get you away from here. From all of this."

"How many times do I have to tell you, I don't want to get away. Everything is fine."

"You called me saying your life was in danger and you call that fine?"

"It'll all work out, it always does."

"It always does because I always give you the money!"

"This is it, I promise."

"Bullshit! How many times have you promised Claire? How many?"

"Look I know, I am a crappy sister but I don't have anyone else."

"You apparently have Troy! What is he doing to fix the situation that I am sure he got you both into?"

"Troy is a good guy. I don't know why you can't see that." Claire was always defiant when it came to the virtues of Troy.

"Can't see... Oh I see perfectly. You had an amazing life. The life you wanted since you were in high school. Then you met Troy and he took all of that away from you. You can't possibly tell me that you are perfectly happy living in this run-down shithole of an apartment."

"I like my life," Claire said with the stubbornness of a five-year-old.

"Well then you have two options, you stay here and enjoy your life without my help, whatever consequences that may bring. Or you come with me and I get you out of this city and get you the help you need."

"She's not going anywhere," said a deep voice behind me.

I didn't need to turn around to know Troy had returned. I heard him close the door and he walked over to Claire, putting one arm around her, and holding a plastic bag in the other. Troy was a tall dark-haired man who had traces of once being handsome, however drugs had turned him into sagging skin and bones. We stood staring fiercely at each other until he spoke.

"All we need is to get out of this jam and we will be fine."

"And how are you getting yourselves out of this jam Troy?"

"Look, our lives are at risk here. You're not going to just let us be killed, are you? Isn't it your job to serve and protect?" he asked with a sly grin on his face, as he pulled Claire closer to him.

I wanted to lunge at him and slap that grin off his face, but for Claire's sake I contained myself.

"I notice you are not looking very beat up Troy. What happened? Did you miraculously heal from all the wounds Claire said you received last night?"

Fury rose in Troy's eyes and he dropped the plastic bag, spilling a bottle of vodka, a crack pipe and a couple of bags full of white powder. He ran towards me and forced me up against the wall with his arm pressed against my neck.

"Listen here, bitch. You give us the $1500 we need to make things right with these people -- people you don't want to mess with -- or we send them to you."

The smell of Troy's breath made my stomach wretch even more and I heaved as I pushed his fragile frame onto the floor. Claire ran over to make sure he was okay and he promptly pushed her away, "I'm fine!"

Angry and frustrated I pointed to the spilled contents of the bag. "I see you can put money toward something other than saving your lives so I am out! I am not giving you anything! I offered a solution to help Claire and that offer still stands. But as of this moment you will not get another dollar out of me. You understand? You can send those people, if they even exist, to me if you want. But I can guarantee the moment they find out I'm a cop they are going to think you're rats and you really will be dead. So, the decision is yours."

Claire and Troy looked at me in disbelief. I had actually put my foot down and as far as they knew I meant it. I held my hand out to Claire, "Are you going to come with me?"

Claire's sad eyes looked at Troy and then at me. She took his hand and I wanted to shake some sense into her, but instead, I walked over to her and gave her a long, hard hug. "I love you sis. Even like this I love you. But I can't help you anymore." I let her go, gave Troy a grimacing look and walked out of the apartment.

CHAPTER THREE

WHEN I GOT HOME I TOOK A LONG, HOT SHOWER AND cuddled up on the couch with a tea. I paid no attention to the movie I had turned on. My mind kept wandering the paths of how Claire and I got to where we were today.

For as long as I can remember, we were inseparable. Where there was one, there was the other. Claire with her long legs, dirty blond hair, and blue eyes of mischief, followed closely behind by me with my knobby knees, auburn hair, and green eyes of wonder. When our parents called for either "Claire!" or "Olivia!" we both showed up, and usually out of breath from whatever adventure we had been having.

Our bond was formed over six different moves in ten years. With each move, we became the outcasts both at our new school and in our new town. At first, we tried to navigate creating new friendships and were excited for new adventures. However, during our third move in as many years, we decided it was easier to just stick together. What was the point of making friends when we would inevitably have to say goodbye? Rather than leaving a town heartbroken, we took with us the only friendship we ever thought we would need.

I then thought back to when Claire and I were kids playing in our tree house. We spent a lot of our time in that beautiful yellow tree house, after dad had eventually got fed up with moving and we finally stayed put. Uncle Steve, my mother's brother, and Aunt Josephine came to visit one weekend after we had settled into the new house. When they pulled into the driveway, Claire and I saw the truck bed was full of lumber. Curious, we ran out to say "hi" and inspected the contents.

While dad sat in a folding lawn chair, hurling instructions no one listened to, the rest of us spent the weekend building the tree house. The adults did the harder work, but Claire and I were right there getting sawdust and paint all over us. Afterwards, we felt accomplished, which was a rare feeling for Claire and me back then. We created our safe space with our own hands. Our favourite pastime was to stare up at the stars, through the small skylight, as we lay on the floor of the house. Every Canada Day we would watch fireworks from the roof of the tree house and proclaim our dreams to each other. The cute boyfriend, becoming a movie star, traveling the world and getting our own place together. The dreams changed as we got older but one theme that stayed the same was that we would always be each other's number one. We vowed no one would ever come between us. We wrote our dreams down and saved them in a blue shoe box inside the wooden chest in the corner of our tree house.

One night, when Claire was 13 and I was 11, during a drunken rampage dad decided Claire and I no longer deserved the tree house and declared, "Tomorrow I am tearing down that damn house. You're too old for it anyways. Best you two grow up and learn what a shitty world we live in".

Mom tried pleading with him to change his mind, but as always it ended up with a black eye. Claire and I ran outside and up into the tree house where we sat holding each other until sunrise. Dad was too drunk to climb the stairs so he stood below yelling at us until he needed another beer. After retrieving two more beers he didn't return. Claire wiped away my tears and tried to reassure me, "Don't worry Liv. He will forget what he said by morning. We will still have our house."

"But what if he doesn't. What if he really does tear it down?"

"Then we will make a new home." She said confidently.

"Should we move our letters just in case?"

Claire unwrapped her arms from around me and got the shoe box out of the chest. She placed it in front of us. "It's too dark to bury it now, but before Dad wakes up we will put it under the raspberry bush." We fell asleep with the box between us.

As planned, the next morning we buried our letters under the raspberry bush, but first we each put in one last note. Mine said that I dreamed of stopping people like dad from taking away things their children loved, and I didn't want to see Dad ever again. Claire said that she wanted to make a lot of money so that she could provide children their own tree houses.

We had just stood up from our dirt pile when Dad walked out, in the clothes he had worn last night, and with bags under his eyes. He was carrying a ladder and a crowbar. We held each other's hands all morning as he tore down the house, one board at a time. When the skylight shattered on the grass we couldn't hold back our tears any longer. Mom tried to get us to come inside but we refused. We wanted to stand and watch as Dad tore down every piece of the one happy place we had in our lives.

For years afterward, Claire and I would still tell each other our dreams but we never wrote them down. It seemed different with the tree house gone. We couldn't stop dad from tearing down the tree house, but Claire was able to stop him from using me as a punching bag. I don't know why dad never seemed to want to hurt Claire. It may have been that she wasn't afraid of him. I, on the other hand, was terrified and he knew it. If mom wasn't around, and he was looking for a fight he always came after me. Maybe it was because I was the spitting image of my mother. As if I was my mother, he would call me a whore and yell about having sex with other men. He chased me around the house until I was able to hide and Claire stood guard over me. We didn't know it back then, but Dad was right about mom's affairs. She sought comfort in those who didn't leave visible marks behind. Even if Dad's rage was founded, his expression of it was not.

After the divorce, Claire worked two jobs during high school so that she could get enough money to go to University and get away from Mom and her numerous boyfriends. As is typical with sisters, we started to drift apart when we were teenagers. Claire started to rebel and wanted to figure out who she was without her little sister hanging around all the time. I couldn't blame her, but those years were some of my loneliest.

By chance, Claire met a man at the coffee shop she worked at who was a partner at Mallenbow Inc. He offered her a job as his assistant, as his current one had gone on paternal leave. He said if she worked hard she could really be something.

Work hard she did. I hardly saw Claire for four years. On top of school she worked long days. Not only was she an assistant, but she got herself onto any project she could. After four years she had her own office, her own assistant, and there was talk that she was on the fast track to becoming an executive. After six years, at age 30, she became the youngest Chief Financial Officer Mallenbow Inc. had ever seen.

By then, I had moved out of Mom's apartment and found a modest one-bedroom unit of my own. Claire had tried to pay for a place closer to her but I couldn't allow that. I wanted to make my own way, and besides, if you are part of the police department and live alone in a high-end condo, people start asking questions. Not good ones.

It was at the party celebrating my promotion to Detective that Claire met Troy. We were at a pub by the station and he was playing pool. Claire spent much of the evening watching him.

"Who have you been staring at all night?" I finally asked.

"You see that tall, dark, and muscular man about to take a shot at the pool table? Do you know him?"

I looked over and immediately knew who she was talking about. "He's not one of ours."

"Really, well that's a plus for him. I only have room in my life for one cop." We chuckled and as Claire always did she took the bull by the horns and went over to introduce herself.

Troy was a construction worker for a non-profit organization building playgrounds and community spaces in underprivileged neighbourhoods. He had been with the company for five years and had just become a senior project manager.

The first six months of their relationship seemed to go well. Troy got Claire to spend a little less time at work which meant I got to see her more. After eight months Troy was pretty much living at Claire's place and they appeared very happy. Then I got a call from an officer at the Division 11 station letting me know they had just booked my sister for possession of cocaine. I laughed at the officer, thinking it was a prank. They reassured me it wasn't and had been responding to a noise complaint where upon entering the condo the officers saw drugs splayed across the coffee table. They did a quick search and found drugs in an elephant-shaped vase. It was then I knew the call was not a prank. Claire had brought that vase back from a trip to Thailand and kept everything but flowers in it.

I went to the station and saw Claire. She told me the drugs weren't hers but Troy had a record and one more incident would put him in jail. Troy told her that as it was her first offense she would probably get a fine, probation and community service. Claire told me she had been a recreational cocaine user for a few months but only at after-work parties. She promised it was nothing serious. I knew that there was no such thing as recreational cocaine use. But I felt I owed her the benefit of the doubt. I posted her bail and told her if she wanted to keep the life she built she needed to quit while she could. On the drive home we took a detour through Regent Park so I could try and show her what she could become. She didn't seem to care and in a few short years she would become a resident.

Troy was right: Claire received a $1000 fine and had to do 100 hours of community service. After a few months, Claire appeared to be back on the right track. She was still with Troy but there were no more parties at her condo. I had thought the arrest and cocaine were just a phase. Just Claire's reaction to our mother's untimely death by a drunk driver a month prior to the arrest.

My thoughts changed when Claire started talking as if everything she had built didn't matter. "What's the point? It could all be gone tomorrow!" she would wail into a drink. After the death of a loved one, some people would become more charitable, travel and become more focused on relationships. Not Claire. She always had to be different. She went down the road of destruction. She started to party with other executives at Mallenbow, but it got to a point even they could barely keep up. After while, her choice of 'friends' became anyone who would get her whatever she wanted, from drugs to sex and anything in between. I tried hard to get her to see how she was throwing everything away, but she wouldn't listen. I was starting to feel helpless.

Six months after mom's death, I once again found myself in an interrogation room with Claire. Except I hardly recognized her. She looked as though she hadn't bathed in a week and smelled just as bad. She was 20 pounds lighter than the last time I saw her, which put her at about 100 pounds soaking wet. Claire had been picked up trying to buy drugs from an off-duty officer walking through St. James Park after his shift. I convinced the officer I would take care of her if she was released with a warning. Thankfully, he agreed.

Over the next few months, nothing I did helped. I begged Claire to stay with me, so that I could watch over her, but she refused. She had no interest in cleaning up her life. Instead, Claire and Troy traipsed around town, spending all of her money on drugs and parties.

Then one night, at 2 a.m., I was awoken by a knock on my door. Claire stood in front of me, black mascara running down her face. Her clothes were torn and her hair disheveled.

"Claire, what's wrong?"

"Can I stay here tonight?"

"Of course, come in." Claire walked past the galley kitchen with the last three days' worth of empty take-out containers strewn over the countertop. She moved some magazines from my emerald green couch and took a seat. Comparatively speaking my whole apartment would fit into Claire's living room. It wasn't much. But it was mine.

"What happened? Why can't you stay at your place?"

"Before I say anything, I need you to promise not to freak out."

"Given that statement I am not sure I can, but I promise I will try."

Claire rubbed her hands nervously, "It's all gone."

"What's gone?"

"The money, the condo, my job."

"Wait, what are you talking about? How can it all be gone? What happened to your job?" I had so many questions but reigned them in.

"I bribed the intake officer to not tell you, and I am not sure how you didn't find out, but a couple months back I got busted again."

"Claire..."

"Please. Just listen. This time, though, they added a trumped-up charge of trafficking. I swear I wasn't. I was just sharing it with some friends but the cops claim they saw my friends give me money."

"You didn't take any money from your 'friends', did you?"

"No." She looked at me with pleading eyes.

"Claire, tell me what happened. I can't help you if you aren't honest with me."

"Troy may have picked up some cash off the bench"

I started to pace my tiny living room.

"Why am I not surprised to hear his name?"

"Look, it was stupid - I know. Somehow my boss found out and he decided that I would need to go. Even though I am not the only executive who uses drugs. Apparently, I was drawing too much attention to the company. He was afraid we would lose existing or future clients if anyone decided to Google me. The worst thing is, they only gave me six months severance! After everything I did for them. All those hours! I mean, I had ample opportunity to skim a little money from the company. But I didn't! All I got was a lousy six months' pay."

"When did this happen Claire?"

"3 months ago."

"3 months and you are just telling me!"

"I was going to fix it. All of it. I knew you would overreact. Besides, you aren't the big sister. I am supposed to fix things, not you!"

There was no point in arguing with her so I took a deep breath, "You said everything was gone, where did all of your savings and severance go?"

"This is where I don't want you to get mad. I was angry, so angry to be treated unfairly, that we spent it all. The trip across Europe included a lot of partying in expensive hotels. I don't remember parts of it but I know I spent a lot of money."

"And what about Troy, what was all his money spent on?" I had a feeling I knew the answer. Troy had been living off Claire since he moved in with her.

"Troy doesn't have much so I covered it. We got back a couple of weeks ago and there was a notice under my condo door asking me to leave. The board found out about the first conviction and pending case. They said they had a reputation to hold up. I had thirty days but I overreacted and had one last party. I was so high that things got out of control and we destroyed the place."

"That was a million-dollar condo, Claire, what were you thinking?"

"We weren't thinking, alright? We were just having fun. It was cathartic at the time to release some of the stress."

"How much stress did you release?"

"Well the light fixtures are no longer fixed to the ceilings and anything that could be destroyed was."

I couldn't believe what I was hearing. Claire had turned into our father. I felt the room start to spin so I sat on the couch and put my head between my knees as Claire continued. "The cost of the damages has taken up all the money I had left. All I have are a couple hundred Euros from the trip." I lifted my head and wrapped my arms around her. We sat like that for a while. They way we used to.

"Where is Troy?"

"He has gone to his parents to see if they can help us out a bit."

"And you have come here. Divide and conquer I see." I couldn't contain my annoyance. "Let me ask you this. When was the last time you used?"

"Why does that matter?"

"Are you high right now?" The lighting in my apartment was not great and I couldn't clearly see Claire's eyes.

"What? Olivia, I'm fine."

"Did you come here to get money so that you and Troy could score? I swear Claire!" I started pacing and tearing at my hair. "What is your plan to get yourself out of this mess?"

"I am not one of your suspects. You don't need to interrogate me. I just need a little bit to get by. I am going for a couple of job interviews tomorrow and I will be back on my feet right away. Trust me. You gotta trust me."

"I do trust you, I just worry about you. Wait here."

I went into my room to get my phone. I expected the money I was about to give her would probably be wasted but I wanted to have faith that maybe she would pull herself together. What kind of sister would I be if I didn't try and help?

"I just sent you $500. That is all I can give you."

Claire got up and gave me one of her bear hugs. "Thank you. I promise everything is going to turn around."

She sounded as if she meant it. At least that's what I told myself.

Claire slept on the couch that night and was gone before I woke in the morning. That was two years ago and I have kept bailing her out of her financial jams ever since. Every night I prayed she found her rock bottom so that I could work on getting my sister back -- The beautiful blond-haired girl who used to laugh at all my horrible jokes. I missed my sister. I hoped she missed me too.

CHAPTER FOUR

JOE AND I COMBED THROUGH BOXES OF EVIDENCE AND witness statements as we investigated our new homicide. Our desks were covered in papers and food wrappers. When we weren't out gathering more evidence to add the pile, we were methodically analyzing it. Anything of importance was added to the rolling corkboard that now resided beside our adjoining desks.

What we knew so far was that the victim, Alec Strauss, was 35-years-old and based out of L.A. His mug shots showed a dark haired, bearded man, who was 5'9 however he held himself as though he was taller. His dark eyes glared at the camera. He was part of a drug smuggling ring that used multiple avenues to move hard drugs across the United States and Canada. Mr. Strauss appeared to be middle management. From what we could find he had made his way up in the ranks and worked in shipping and procurement of new products. We didn't have access to his medical records, but the large scar under his left eye told us he had been in at least one serious altercation. What we didn't know was why Mr. Strauss was in Toronto, or specifically who would want him dead.

I was so focused on the complexity of the case a month had passed when I realized I hadn't heard from Claire. I tried to call her but her phone went straight to voicemail, which was odd as she never turned it off. I left a message asking Claire to call me. I would try again when I got home.

After a late dinner, I tried Claire again. Straight to voicemail. I reluctantly tried Troy; his phone rang a couple times and I had thought someone picked up but the call was quickly dropped. I called back and could hear muffled voices. I couldn't make out what they were saying but from their tone I knew something was wrong. I grabbed my jacket and headed to my car. I turned up my collar to stop the brisk spring wind from hitting my neck.

As I drove to Regent Park, I swore I would drag Claire out of that shithole kicking and screaming if I had to. Against protocol I brought my service weapon with me. Troy wasn't going to get in my way this time. Traffic went by in a blur of red taillights and I wrote one of our childhood notes in my mind; "My dream is that I get to Claire, get her somewhere safe, and keep Troy away from her."

I walked up the crumbling steps to Claire's apartment. For the first time I was thankful for the awful stench which awakened my senses from their exhausted state. I walked over bodies passed out and snoring on the stairs and in the hallway. I knocked on Claire's greasy door. No answer. Then I heard a quiet shuffle. I listened for a minute and heard it again. I instinctively went to put my hand on my holster as I slowly turned the handle, opened the door, and crept cautiously into the apartment.

I barely had time to register the footsteps when I was thrown hard against the wall. A hooded figure rushed past me. I quickly recovered, pulled my gun, and scanned the apartment but didn't see or hear Claire.

I ran out the door and down the hallway after the dark figure. Outside the front doors I could see the hooded figure running across the parking lot and entering a poorly lit park. They were limping and I was able to easily catch up and tackle them face first to the ground. I turned the body over and found Troy's terrified face looking up at me. He looked more haggard than ever. I sat on his chest to make sure he couldn't move.

"Troy! Why are you running? Where is Claire? I swear if you..."

"I didn't." His voice trembled and he stopped struggling, "I don't know where she is. I haven't seen her in almost a month."

"What do you mean you haven't seen her in a month? What happened?"

"One night she went out but she never came back."

I angrily pushed myself off of Troy, afraid if I stayed on top of him I would beat him.

"And you didn't think to call me?"

"I thought she went to see you and you had gotten her into rehab. I tried to call but her phone was always off. After that, I figured if she wanted me to know where she was, she would call." He tried to get up but I used my foot to push him back into the grass and pointed my gun at him.

"Don't move." I started pacing in circles around Troy while I ran through everything in my mind before I grilled him for more information.

"Is there anyone else she would go to for money?"

"I don't know. She was usually pretty successful with you so she never had to go anywhere else."

I felt like I had been punched in the stomach. Claire played me like a fiddle. She knew I wouldn't say no if she sang a sad desperate tune. I wanted to scream but I pushed it down deep and squatted beside Troy.

"There had to have been someone over the years that she got on with that she would think to turn to if I ever said no. Did you ever talk about that?"

"Not really. I mean there was this one guy that was always at the parties we went to. He seemed to give her more drugs than anyone else for the same price. I never questioned it as it meant more for me. But maybe she went to him."

Troy tried to get up and again I pushed him down.

"What was his name?"

"Ahh now I don't know."

"You don't know!" my anger got the best of me and I punched him in the groin. He screamed and curled up into a ball.

"Your girlfriend could be missing and you don't know this guy's name." I grabbed his hair and pulled his head back. "How about you think about that for a minute while I rest my gun here on your face" I pushed the barrel into his cheek. "Now what is his name!"

"Okay. Okay. I think it was something like Alec... Alec Stra-something Stram, maybe?"

"Alec Strauss?"

"Yeah. That's him."

"What does he look like?"

"Umm in his mid 30s I think, white, brown hair, beard and has a scar."

"Under his left eye?"

"Yes, how did you know?"

"That's not important. What is important is what would Claire think Alec could do for her?"

"Maybe give her a little something to tide her by. She was pretty strung out and desperate. She knew Alec liked her. He kept asking her to leave me and go with him to L.A."

I removed the gun from Troy's face and stood up. Troy clamoured to his feet but didn't run.

"Other than his involvement with drugs what else should I know about this Strauss guy?"

"He is not a great guy. I can tell you that. He always had women hanging off him, hot ones too, who seemed desperate for him to pay attention to them. Word was that he either paid for them to be around him or they worked for him if you know what I mean. He always had stacks of cash and drugs. It's what kept Claire and I around. He was practically giving it away."

"I swear if anything has happened to my sister I will bring you a world of hurt. Starting with this..." I used the butt of my gun and broke his nose.

"Fuck!" Troy tried to stop the blood pouring down his face and sweater but he was covered. "You're all talk. You're a 'good' cop, you won't do any serious harm."

I looked Troy dead in the eye and put my gun under his chin. He tried to back away but found himself up against a chain link fence.

"You are not the type of person people would miss if you happened to disappear. 'Good cop' or not I have 'friends' that would make it so you would never be found. So, on that note, is there anything else you think I should know about my sister, or her life, that will help me find her?"

"Look, she was the one who wooed the guys and made drugs and money appear. I was never good at that and I never asked questions."

"Are you telling me Claire pimped herself out for drugs?"

"I am telling ya, I don't know. But it wouldn't surprise me. We were desperate and you cut us off."

"Do not put this on me. If my sister... No..." I took a deep breath "You better get out of here before I use this." I pushed the gun further into his chin then stepped back.

Troy bolted out of the park as I sat on a bench, adrenaline coursing through my veins. My mind was racing with questions. Where was Claire?

What was Alec Strauss' involvement with Claire? Why couldn't I have just figured out how to get $1500? Did I force my sister to sell her body?

As I stared up at the face in the full moon I cried.

CHAPTER FIVE

THE MOMENT I GOT BACK TO MY CAR I CALLED JOE. I relayed what Troy had told me about Alec Strauss and told him to meet me at Strauss' house. It was 10 p.m. by the time I reached the house and I had to restrain myself from going in before Joe showed up. Thankfully, he wasn't too long behind me. We stood on the walkway looking at the house, both of us in our after-work sweatpants and old sweater ensembles. I saw Mrs. Norris watching us through the curtains of her front window. I waved.

"Troy really said Strauss' name?" Joe asked.

"Yep. Described him right down to the scar under the left eye."

"And Claire knew him?"

"It appears so. I pray she wasn't somehow involved in his death."

"And if she was?"

I nervously fixed my ponytail, "I can't think about that right now. I just need to find her. No matter what happened, she cannot be in a good place right now."

We broke the crime scene seal that was still on the front door and walked inside. We went room to room to try to find something that could point to Claire having been here. We had originally identified there had been a struggle in the living room which spilled into the kitchen where Mr. Strauss' body was found. The rest of the house had looked to have been untouched, therefore Joe and I had only done a cursory look and let the Scenes of Crime Officers do a detailed review of the property. But now I was desperate for anything that would give me a starting point on where I could find Claire.

As we were going through the master bedroom Joe called to me from the en suite. He was standing in the middle of a large newly-renovated shower. It was quite curious given the state of the rest of the house.

"Couldn't wait until you got home to clean up?" I joked, and Joe smiled.

"Didn't your sister use some fancy shampoo? You always complained about how the bottle cost the same amount as your monthly car payment?"

"Yeah, it cost something like $150 for a bottle. I never understood how someone could spend so much on shampoo. Why?" I made my way towards him and joined him in the shower.

"If Sally could see us," he joked. "Here" and he handed me a small black bottle of Oribe Gold Lust Repair and Restore shampoo and continued, "What are the odds Mr. Strauss used the same shampoo Claire did?"

"Small."

I opened the bottle and the scent made it feel as if Claire was standing beside me. I put the bottle in the kangaroo pocket of my sweater. "I am sure there aren't a lot of places that sell it. If Claire was here, and Strauss was buying her expensive shampoo, maybe it wasn't against her will."

As we exited the shower, I noticed something tucked behind the medicine cabinet on the wall. I gently and slowly pulled out a small piece of paper. I opened it up and gasped. It was Claire's handwriting.

"What is it?" asked Joe.

"It's a note from Claire," and I read it out.

O:

If you find this I couldn't fix things. Alec said he would help me get better, get back to who I was, but I heard him on the phone talking to someone about me. About sending me away to work. I know Alec works some girls on the side so I am scared that's what he meant. I tried to get away, but when I said I was going to go visit you he locked me in the bedroom and boarded up the window. He said you would only make my problems worse and that tomorrow I would start new. I don't know what is going to happen to me. I'm so scared O! I don't know why I think you will find this, but if you do please help me. I will do anything you want. Go to rehab, move away. Maybe we can finally get a house on a beach somewhere. Please just come get me.

Love C

Silence filled the room after my last word. Tears started to slowly run down my cheeks. "She was here."

Joe hugged me and then pulled out his phone, "I will call the techs and get them to comb this place again. Maybe there is something else that was missed. I will get them to bag everything." Joe reached into the kangaroo pouch of my sweater, pulled out the shampoo, and put it on the counter. Joe went into the living room to make the call. I sat on the toilet staring at the handwriting and asked the universe, "Claire, where are you? What have you gotten yourself into?"

Joe walked back into the en suite. "They will be here tomorrow. They are just finishing a multiple homicide where all hands are on deck."

"Tomorrow! Joe you know the longer we wait the less chance we have of finding her, it's already been a month." I could no longer control the tears and started to shake as years of pent-up anger and hurt poured out.

Joe pulled me off the toilet, held me in his arms and kissed the top of my head.

"I know. And you know the Superintendent will never sign off moving the team here tonight after the scene has been sitting for a month. Especially when he finds out your sister could be involved. He wouldn't want to be showing favourtism."

I shrugged my shoulders as I continued to soak Joe's sweater with my tears.

"Come on, let's get you home. It's been a long day and you need rest. Will you be okay alone or do you want to stay with us tonight?"

"I'll be fine." I straightened myself out and put Claire's note in my pocket.

"I know what your 'fine' means but just try and get a little bit of rest. We can go over everything again tomorrow." He looked me in the eyes, "Liv, we will find her."

CHAPTER SIX

NOTHING ELSE WAS FOUND IN THE HOUSE TO SUGGEST Claire had been there. The only other connection we could make between her and Strauss was that they were usually hanging around each other when they attended the same parties. Sources speculated Strauss was trying to branch out on his own and create his own drug network. They said he was in Toronto to try and round up prospective partners. His boss, George Compton, was not happy about that. Evidence was starting to point to Strauss being made an example for anyone trying to leave the flock.

Compton was the quintessential 1950's-style gangster. He even wore the pin-striped suits, trench coat and fedora. He did not give anyone a second chance when they stepped out of line. From what Joe and I could find, the LAPD had never been able to get Compton for so much as a parking ticket. So, we were both very surprised when Compton and his lawyer showed up at our station wanting to talk. Their only stipulation - we couldn't ask questions about his business. They were there strictly about

Strauss.

We weren't about to turn him down so we led them into a pale grey interrogation room. Compton placed his fedora on the table, slowly took off his jacket and placed it carefully over the back of a chair. He sat down, crossed his legs and placed his folded hands on his knee. His face had aged faster than the years he had been alive. He looked as though he was in his late 60s and not the 52 he actually was.

His lawyer, also meticulously dressed, looked over-worked and had tired green eyes. He opened his briefcase and took out an expensive silver pen and a notepad. Joe started the recording, everyone introduced themselves and got to the matter at hand.

Before we could ask any questions, Compton confirmed he knew Strauss and that he distributed drugs but added with a smile and a wink, "or at least that's the word on the street. I wouldn't know anything about that mind you."

I started the probe into Strauss' death, "The obvious question we have is, who would want him dead?"

"I was told that Strauss was trying to go it alone but to stand out from the competition was adding new products."

"What do you mean by new products?"

"I want it known I do not condone this line of work. I admit Strauss and I fought about it and it is why we amicably parted ways." He paused to ensure he had the power in the room and then continued, "The new product was girls. Way I hear it he always had girls all over him and he figured he could make a pretty penny off them. I may have also heard he was moving less drugs and focusing more on girls."

"You mean he was trafficking women?" asked Joe.

"I don't rightly know of course, but that is along the lines of what I may have heard."

"Is that why you had him killed, he was no longer doing your bidding?" I asked a little more politely than I wanted to.

Compton's lawyer immediately spoke in a soft but firm voice, "Detective, we said no questions about his business. Move on or we leave."

Compton waved his hand, "That's okay Sal, I will answer the question. I did not kill Strauss."

"Did you have him killed?" I followed up.

"No."

Knowing I wouldn't get anything else out of him, and not wanting to ruin the opportunity in front of me, I moved on. "Then I go back to my original question. In your opinion is there anyone who would want to kill him?"

Compton grinned, "I can't say I do know of anyone. But I hear that your sister may have been with him and is now missing."

"How did you know that?!" I exclaimed as I stood up, pushing my chair over as a result.

Compton's grin widened, knowing he had gotten under my skin. "Well now, if I tell you that I need you to do something for me."

Joe grabbed my arm, to prevent me from jumping across the table, and took over the conversation. "Nice try. She is not doing anything for you, no matter what information you may claim to have on her sister." Joe pulled me out of the room before I could even respond.

"Liv, you know what he is doing. Don't even think about it. We can find Claire another way."

"What other way? She could be in Timbuktu by now if Strauss was trafficking her."

He took both of my arms and looked at me affectionately, "We will find her. Go back to your desk and I will see if Compton has any other usable information, otherwise I will escort him out." Reluctantly I agreed.

I stood staring at our corkboard, the information all blurring together, until Joe showed up ten minutes later. He had gotten nothing further from Compton.

WE SPENT THE next few days combing through everything we could find on Compton and Strauss. We revisited all the evidence we had. Our guts were telling us Claire was likely no longer in Toronto. But we didn't know where she could be and had no evidence to support our hunch.

Superintendent Frey, not knowing Claire's connection to the case, was starting to push us to move on. As far as he was concerned this one was going nowhere, the victim wasn't generating any sympathy from the public, and no gang wars had broken out over it. We had one last move to try and keep the case open. Joe and I sat in the Superintendent's cramped, but immaculately clean, office and told him everything. To say he was not impressed would be an understatement.

After he was finished yelling at us about withholding information and conflicts of interest, he sat down in his chair, folded his hands on his desk and said "You don't have any evidence outside that letter. She could have decided to start a new life somewhere else."

"She would have told me if that was her plan. She would have at least said goodbye."

"I'm sorry but you need to move on. I am being asked questions about the time spent on this file. Now if they find out I wasn't aware of your sister's potential involvement, all of us are going to be out of a job. If you are concerned about your sister, file a missing person's report. Now shut it down and move on."

I wanted to fight with him but I knew I would get nowhere. Joe and I walked out of the office, defeated, and found Troy seated at our desks.

"You better have a good reason to be here," Joe grunted.

"I got something. A note. I think it's from Claire." His shaking hands passed me a small piece of paper.

"When did you get this?" I asked, reading over the note.

"This morning." Troy was visibly scared and kept looking around the room.

"Did it come in an envelope?"

"It was taped to my door."

"That's odd, why would Claire tape a letter to your door? Why wouldn't she knock or go inside?"

"Maybe Claire didn't deliver it." Joe stated as he looked over my shoulder, "What does it say?"

I read it out: *Help. In the house, lots of women who are hurt.*

"That's it, that doesn't give us much to go on," Joe said.

"This doesn't look like Claire's writing. How do you know it is from her?" I asked.

"Who else could it be from?" Troy replied.

He was right. As far as I knew, Troy didn't have anyone other than Claire. It would make sense the note would be from her.

"Why would they go to you, why not to me?"

"I don't know, I just found it and thought you should have it. I need to go." And he ran out.

"Odd," said Joe.

"Yes, but I am going to talk to the Superintendent. There has got to be something here."

"You know what he is going to say, don't you? 'What house, there are millions of houses in Toronto. You plan on checking them all?'"

Joe was right. The new note made no difference.

I spent my night staring at the ceiling above my bed, running through everything over and over. Then at 3 a.m., it hit me. "The house" not "a house" "The house". Could she mean that house? I got up, got dressed, and started to drive.

CHAPTER SEVEN

I SAT PARKED ACROSS THE STREET AND DOWN A FEW DOORS from a run-down bluish grey house. The last house Claire and I lived in with Mom and Dad. The shingles on the roof were peeling and the blue paint had turned grey from the sun and dirt. The windows were boarded up and the fence had all but fallen down. It didn't look anything like the house I remembered. Even with the hardships suffered while living there, looking at it now, I was reminded of the colourful flower garden mom carefully curated, the succulent raspberries and all of the adventures Claire and I took in the backyard. Looking out my car window I felt loneliness, longing, and dread for Claire.

I hadn't seen anyone come or go from the house for the two hours I had been sitting there, when suddenly a black van pulled up in front. The vehicle blocked my view so I couldn't see clearly but I put down my window and heard multiple voices, both male and female. I heard the van door close and the van pulled away as quickly as it arrived. I hoped to get a glimpse of someone but there was no trace of the people I'd heard.

I had started to regret the large coffee I drank, and considered using the disposable cup as a makeshift bedpan, when the front door of the house opened. Between the flicker of the street lights and the light in the doorway, the figure of a man of medium build, and flaming red hair emerged. I didn't know why I hadn't thought of it before, but I took out my phone and recorded what was happening. The red-headed man was well dressed for the neighbourhood, and sported a sharp, dark suit. With him was a larger built gentleman, who was bald and had sunglasses on, even though there would be no need. As they walked towards the driveway, a disheveled woman sprung out of the house towards them.

Hard as I tried, I only made out what sounded like crying and possibly begging. She had fallen on her knees and tugged on the red-haired man's pant leg. The bald man stepped in and pulled her off. The woman struggled, and I noticed that the bald man had at least one gun in a shoulder holster.

"Please let me go! I will do anything!" the woman yelled.

The bald man covered her mouth with his hand and she was thrown back into the house. The main door slammed shut from the inside. I could no longer hear the screaming. The red-headed man shook his leg, as if he wanted to remove dirt from his pants without having to touch them, before the two men got into a black sports car.

They drove past me, and I crouched low in my seat and recorded as best I could. I quickly reviewed the video and I had more or less clearly captured the men's faces. I hadn't recalled seeing them before in the multitude of mug shots over the years. I had also managed to record the manufacturer's logo of the vehicle. I didn't know much, if anything, about expensive vehicles. I reverse-image searched the logo and found out the car was a Bugatti.

"What would a car worth millions be doing in this neighboured?" I asked myself out loud.

I had nothing else to go on, and was unsure how many other armed people resided in the house, so I decided to follow the car. I quickly turned my car around and found the vehicle stopped at a red light. I hadn't lost them. I stayed at least three car lengths behind while we worked our way out of the neighbourhood. We eventually entered another suburban neighbourhood, and the scenery once again became familiar, but I was so tired I could not place why. They pulled into a driveway which had a dark van parked in it. I pulled over well behind them but I couldn't see the house they had stopped at. My bladder screamed to be emptied. "Just a little while longer, come on," I told myself. I wrote down the license plate number of the sports car, which I had been repeating to myself along the drive, on the side of my coffee cup.

I waited. No one got out of the vehicle. "What are they waiting for?" I decided to pull up closer to the corner so that I could see the house. Seeing where I was had me almost forget to hit the brakes. I gripped the steering wheel. Alec Strauss' place. What were they doing here?

They hadn't emerged or moved and now my pain was increasing rapidly. The coffee cup wasn't going to cut it, so I either needed to get out of the car and find an unexposed bush or leave. I added a note of what I believed the license plate of the van was, beside the plate number of the sports car. I would head to work, after I stopped at a nearby gas station, and run a search in on the vehicles.

The men still hadn't moved and I wouldn't be able to approach them on my own. I wasn't going to disturb Joe, at 4:30 a.m., based on a hunch, for a case we were told to close. I just hoped the men either resided, or remained, in town for a while.

I slowly backed away, entered a neighbouring driveway out of the view of Strauss' house, and turned my car around. I would wait until tonight, when I had a better plan, to get a closer look at what had happened to my childhood home.

CHAPTER EIGHT

NOT SURPRISINGLY, THE LICENSE PLATE OF THE VAN TURNED out to be expired and belonged to a woman who had been deceased for five years. The plate for the Bugatti, however, came back registered to a Colin Warner and the photo matched the bald man I had seen earlier. I was frustrated to find no information on Mr. Warner. I suspected it was an alias or if Warner was his real name he was really good at covering his tracks.

"Shocking that I would find you here." I turned, and there was Joe holding two cups of coffee and a Take-Out bag from Wally's.

"What are you doing here?" I asked as I grabbed one of the cups.

"Sally took the kids to a trampoline park and I figured what better way to spend my Saturday, than making sure you don't do something stupid that would cost you your job."

"Well, the day is still young. Thanks for the coffee."

"What's all this?" Joe poured over the vehicle registrations and still images I'd printed from the video and pinned to the corkboard we were supposed to have dismantled.

"I found the house from the letter."

Joe gave me a quizzical look as if I had gone mad.

"Well, I think I did. You see the note says '*I am in THE house*.' And if Claire wrote it, there was only ever one house that we really called home. So, I figured what harm would it do to visit our old house."

"Of course, you did." Joe handed me a muffin, sat at his desk and put his feet up. I continued.

"It is completely run down and boarded up, but a van with plates belonging to a woman who has been deceased for five years pulled up. I think people were dropped off but I couldn't see anything. Then a short time later, two well-dressed men came out of the house, chased after by a very disheveled woman. She barely had any clothes on and the ones she did were torn. Her back was to me most of the time so I didn't capture her face on the video. She begged to be let go but this bald guy literally tossed her back into the house. Then, get this, they drove over to Strauss' house." Joe's feet fell off his desk.

"Strauss?"

"Yep, there is no way this is a coincidence. Whether it has to do with Claire, or Strauss' death, these men and this house have to be involved."

"Huh." Joe stood up and looked over the information pinned to the board.

"Think about it, Joe. All the inferences that Strauss was getting into the sex trade. A boarded-up house where well-dressed men visit. At least one woman seems to be trapped there. Claire was strung out and desperate for money; I think she might be in there." I sounded so confident I had even convinced myself.

"I think you might be jumping to conclusions. Trying to see something that might not be there. Frey won't have us going any further on this."

"He doesn't have to."

"Liv..."

"Joe. I am just going to go by the house tonight and see what I can see. That's it."

"That's it? And what if you see Claire? Then what, are you going to knock down the door, not knowing what's on the other side?"

"I guess we will have to see what the future holds now, won't we?"

"Frey is going to lose his shit if he ever finds out about this. Which means whatever you have found today and may find tonight is completely inadmissible should this ever go to court."

"Screw admissible. I just want my sister back."

"I do love having you as a partner. I really do. But if you get me fired over this I swear you are the one dealing with Sally's wrath. Now what else do you have?"

I wrapped him in a hug, "Thank you Joe!"

"Just start talking."

THE REST OF the morning, and early afternoon, we spent trying to identify the red-headed man and the woman from the video on my phone with no luck. We stopped by Strauss' and found no evidence the two men had been inside or around the yard. We stopped by our favourite diner and waited for the sun to go down. The cloudy night helped mask us. If I hadn't seen people leave the house last night, I would assume the house was just another boarded up and vacant home on a street of many abandoned houses.

After about an hour we had made sure there was no movement outside of the house. Joe and I snuck around the right side and stopped under the side windows. We could hear muffled voices, maybe some crying, but nothing really identifiable. We walked towards the backyard and were about to turn the corner when we heard a female voice.

"She can't stay here any longer. The women say some stupid shit on this stuff, but if what she says is true and her sister is a cop from around here, we need to move her. Tonight..." The woman appeared to be on the phone as we only heard one voice.

"No, I won't calm down. You got me workin' this shithole because you trust me. Well, trust me and move her. Otherwise we are all in trouble." Another pause. "Thank you."

A door opened and closed and then there was silence.

Joe grabbed my arm and looked at me with a 'don't you dare' stare.

"But she..."

"Could be anyone, Liv. If Claire is in there, we need to do this right. Let's go back to the car and talk this through."

I reluctantly followed Joe back towards the car. We had just crossed the street when the black van I had seen last night pulled up. We hid behind some bushes and watched as three women were taken out of the house and put into the van. With the shadows the flickering street lights created, I couldn't tell if one of them was Claire. But one was definitely blond.

"We should follow that van. The plates are expired and we can pull them over. Talk to the women."

"We are off duty, you know we can't do that."

"You heard the woman. Someone in there is the sister of a cop. Even if it isn't Claire, shouldn't we try and help out our own?" I was grasping at straws but had to try to get him on my side. "We won't go into the house, but it would be just a routine traffic stop. Everything will be fine. But if we let them go, we will probably never see those women again. Come on Joe, you know I am right."

He rolled his eyes, "I hate when you are right."

The van had left while Joe and I were debating, but we caught up to them just outside the residential area. We turned on our lights and the van sped up. We gave chase for five blocks and thought we had lost them, when I caught a glimpse of the van down an alley. Joe turned around and headed down the alley. I spotted a no exit sign at the entrance and knew we had them. Someone's face appeared in the dark back window of the van. Was it Claire? Were my eyes playing tricks on me? Even if they were, she was someone's Claire and we were going to help her...

BOOM!

CHAPTER NINE

MY HEAD IS THROBBING AND EVERYTHING AROUND ME IS spinning as I try to get my eyes to focus. Lights are flashing and I hear voices I can't make out around me. I feel something dripping down the side of my head. I try and brush whatever it is off my face. Looking at my hand, I think I see blood. I look to my left and Joe's seat is empty and his door open. A hand gently pushes my head back against the headrest. I look to the right, out my completely shattered window, and Joe comes into focus. "Don't move. Olivia. Don't move."

"What happened? You're bleeding!" I see blood trickling down the front of Joe's face and from his nose.

"I am fine. A large truck came out of the side alley. I didn't see it right away and when I did it was too late."

There was a red truck with a crushed front end a few feet away from the car. I closed my eyes as the emergency vehicle lights bounced off the truck, and the hood of our car, causing sharp pain behind my eyes.

"You were unconscious for a long time so you can't move, okay? The paramedics are going to get you out. They are going to put a neck brace on you now, okay?"

"What about the van?" I mumbled.

"It's gone. I am sorry."

"But it was a dead end, we saw the sign."

Joe pointed to where a building at the end of the alley had been torn down. "They must have driven through there."

"God damn it! We were so close." I cried.

"I know Liv. I know. We need to get you to the hospital."

As the paramedics pulled me out of the car and put me on a stretcher, there was a loud screeching of brakes behind us. A car door slammed and a booming voice rained over the crowd, "Where the hell are they?"

Superintendent Frey's face appeared over me. "Well now, how is she?" he asked the paramedic calmly, but annoyed.

"Not sure yet sir. Likely a concussion at least." The young man answered.

"Nothing life-threatening?" he asked.

"Doesn't appear so, sir."

"Good," He raised his voice about 10 decibels. "What the hell were you thinking? A completely unauthorized chase! People besides yourselves could have been hurt. I told you to close it down, not ramp it up!"

"Superintendent..." Joe interrupted.

"No. There are no explanations here. There is only 'I'm Sorry, Superintendent'. 'I was wrong, Superintendent' and 'I will gladly take a suspension, Superintendent."

"Sus..pen..sion" I tried to muffle out.

"Two weeks paid leave for you Cattaneo, as I know she dragged you into all of this."

"Sir, with all due respect, I made my own decisions here. I should take the same punishment as Beaumont."

"Are you sure about that? Beaumont may very well be out of a job by the end of the night."

Joe tried to protest further, "Sir, you can't do..." I reached out and squeezed his hand to stop him from talking.

"Joe, take your two weeks. I will deal with whatever happens."

"But..."

"It's okay."

We didn't speak as we made our way to the hospital in the back of an ambulance. Joe held my hand as I closed my eyes and brought up the image of the face I had seen in the van. I thought about the woman from yesterday, begging for her freedom. I thought of the last time I saw Claire.

TEN DAYS LATER, I unlocked my apartment door and as I turned the key, pain shot up my right arm. The doctor said I would likely be in pain for a couple of weeks as I healed. She told me I was lucky to only have a concussion, some bruises and a fractured right wrist. Thankfully, I didn't need a cast, but had been put into a wrist guard. They had kept me in the hospital for observation based on Joe's report that I have been unconscious for more then 10 minutes. After being in the hospital for a few days, I stayed with Joe and Sally until I could manage most things with one fully functional wrist.

I put my keys in the bowl on the stand by the door and made my way to the fridge. I ignored the doctor's instructions to not drink while taking my medication and opened a beer. I decided I should finally listen to the multiple voicemails Superintendent Frey had left me. I put my cell phone on speaker as I stared out the window to the busy street below.

"First message sent on May 10th at 2:33 p.m."

"Beaumont, the incident review committee is meeting next week to decide what action will result from your little adventure. I am not sure what I will be able to do for you. I will call you with an update but don't hold your breath."

"How politically correct of you sir." I said to a passing red Honda. I deleted the message.

"Next message sent on May 15th 10:46 a.m."

"Beaumont. I heard you will be home tomorrow. Take the day, and the weekend, and then report to my office for 9 a.m. Monday. The inquiry has concluded."

"I bet it has." I grimaced as I instinctively used my right hand to lock my phone and pain shot through my wrist.

I finished my beer, grabbed another one and sat on the couch. Leaning my head back, I took a deep breath. After Monday, I likely wouldn't be a detective and I doubted I would even be with the Toronto Police Service. It can be said when you join the TPS you join a family -- a family who sticks together through thick and thin. Yet my gut was telling me they might not stick with me through this.

I finished the second beer, took one of my prescription painkillers and slept the rest of the day.

I WOKE UP the next morning to the sound of someone incessantly ringing my doorbell. I dragged myself out of bed and shuffled slowly to the door as the ringing continued. "I'm coming, hold your horses," I bellowed down the hallway.

I opened the door and found Sally standing there with a bag of groceries and an exasperated look on her face.

"I have been out here for 10 minutes!" She pushed past me and headed straight for the kitchen.

"Why don't you come in?" I said to the now empty doorway.

I followed her to the kitchen, where she expertly put the food where it belonged. Once her task was complete she turned to me, leaned against the counter and crossed her arms. "We have been friends for years. And I totally get that partners are close and risk their lives for each other, but this - what you had Joe do - that was unacceptable, selfish!"

"I can explain. We..."

"I'm not done. Your sister being missing is heartbreaking but there are rules and it wasn't just your life at risk. I mean, look at what happened, hit by a truck! Joe says you may not have a job come Monday." She took a deep breath. "But if you do, you need to promise me that you will never put Joe in that position again - you understand me? He only went along to make sure you didn't do something stupid or get hurt, not that it helped. Joe's a good man Olivia. And I know you know that. But his family and his career are more important than you."

Sally paused to let the last sentence sink in before continuing. "If you do have a job on Monday I want you to request a new partner."

"What? Don't you think that's overreacting just a little?" I knew as soon as the words came out I shouldn't have said anything. Sally became even more enraged.

"NO, I AM NOT OVERREACTING! You're trying to protect your family and I am protecting mine. If you care for Joe at all you will request a new partner. And please don't contact him for a while. It will be easier for you both that way."

I felt deflated. "I am truly sorry Sally."

She came over and gave me a hug. "I know you are."

She left and I sat on my kitchen floor feeling utterly alone. Everyone I loved had been taken away from me and I was no closer to finding Claire.

CHAPTER TEN

MONDAY MORNING, I WALKED INTO THE PRECINCT AND every face turned my way. I held my head high and didn't avoid anyone's gaze as I walked to my desk. Joe was already seated at his. He looked at me with sad eyes, "I'm sorry about Sally, but you know how she is. Just worried is all."

"I get it. Don't worry." I looked over to the Superintendent's office. "I see the Staff Superintendent is here. That doesn't bode well."

"Some advice: just take whatever they give you. Don't fight it. If you do, you're done and I know how much being a cop means to you."

"Joe, you know as well as I do some of the men around here have disobeyed bigger orders and gotten away with it. What does it say if I just bend over and take it?"

"It says that a great cop is being smart and covering her own ass in order to have the opportunity to help others. Standing up to them will only make you feel good in the moment but you will regret it later."

"Bah! I hate that you're right."

"Beaumont!" called the Superintendent from his doorway.

I pushed myself out of my chair, "Well, to the firing squad I go."

The whole precinct watched as I entered Frey's office.

"You know Staff Superintendent Warwick," said Frey as he closed the door and took his place behind his desk.

Warwick stood beside the desk. She was a small but intimidating woman.

"Ma'am." I stood at attention.

Frey spoke first "Let's get to it, shall we? You disobeyed an order by continuing to investigate your sister's apparent disappearance. The evidence you brought forward that connected Claire to Strauss was far-fetched at best, and yet you continued. I understand that this was personal for you, and I take responsibility for not ensuring I had all of the details. The fact of the matter is, you endangered another officer's life when you pursued that van."

Superintendent Warwick spoke next, "There is a lot of unrest in the Toronto Police Service right now and we cannot have officers who think they are above the rules. We need to show that there is a strong leadership willing to do what is right. I am sorry that it means you have to be reprimanded for trying to help your family, but we have to do what we have to do."

"May I say something?" I asked.

"Go ahead," she said.

"I accept full responsibility for my actions and you will get no fight from me on whatever reprimand you deem fit. I acted out of order and I only ask that Cattaneo's suspension not be kept permanently on file. He was just trying to keep his partner safe. If you can, don't let my recklessness cost him."

"Very considerate of you. But as I said, we cannot bend the rules. The reprimand will stand," advised Warwick.

Frey spoke next, "Beaumont, effective immediately, your rank will be reduced to that of Sergeant and you will be on three months' paid leave. I suspect the time will do you good to reflect on your actions."

"Yes, Sir"

"Dismissed."

"Thank you, Sir."

As I packed up my few personal belongings from my desk, Frey stopped by as he walked Warwick out.

"Beaumont."

I turned around, "Yes, Sir?"

"I hope the time will also be adequate to try and find your sister?"

"Yes sir. Thank you, sir." I tried, but was unsuccessful in hiding my smile.

I left the station and found Joe leaning against my car, "Well, you look happy? What happened there?"

"Demoted to Sergeant and 3 months paid leave."

"And you are happy about this?"

I lowered my voice "Frey said to use the time to look for Claire. Pretty smart on his part. He knows I wouldn't let it go and this way whatever happens isn't on him."

"He's smarter than I give him credit for."

"You say that now, but let's see who he gives you as your new partner," I joked.

"Where are you going to start with Claire?"

"I think I will try and find Troy. As much as I loathe him, he's the best person to help me understand Claire's life."

"Listen, I know Sally told you not to talk to me, but if you get into trouble or need anything, you reach out, okay? You don't need to go it alone."

"Thanks, Joe."

I put my stuff in the trunk of my car and we hugged goodbye, holding on longer than normal. I felt a sense of relief over the suspension and invigorated at the same time. I could now devote all of my time to Claire and I wouldn't give up until I had found her.

CHAPTER ELEVEN

THE NEXT DAY I SCOURED MY BRAIN FOR EVERYTHING THAT I could recall about the case files and recorded them in multiple notebooks. I couldn't risk asking Joe for information, not this soon. With the help of a terrified Troy, I mapped out Claire's possible movements and locations, including places he told me they would get their drugs or spend time partying. Although I was sure Troy was holding something back, he was being helpful. Maybe he really did love Claire and had realized too late how their lives ended up in desolation.

Everything kept pointing back to the house. The house that seemed, whether it be past or present, full of tears and hurt. The house that I continually tried to forget but continued to haunt me.

I went to a thrift store down the street and grabbed the most run-down clothes I could find; torn jeans and a ratty grey sweater. Before putting them on, I stomped them in some mud so they didn't look so clean. Although it would have been faster to take my car, I took the bus to my old neighbourhood. After what happened with the van, I didn't want to risk anyone identifying my car and tracking me down.

I got off the bus two stops away from the house and walked the familiar streets. As I stood out front of the house I rehearsed in my head, as I had done 20 times today, what I would say when I knocked on the door. "Sorry to bother you, I grew up in this home and was hoping to see if it's how I remember it. You see my mom just passed and she loved this house. I would love to just come in for a minute and remember her." If I was going to lie I wanted to make it as close to the truth as possible.

I was mustering up the courage to walk up the steps when I was startled by a gentle voice behind me.

"Excuse me, ma'am?"

I turned around and saw an older gentleman in nicely pressed pants and a plaid shirt hunched over a cane.

"Can I help you with something ma'am"

"Oh well, do you know if anyone lives here? You see, I grew up in this house and was hoping to see if anything is how I remember it."

"I doubt that very much. This house has been in ruins for years. Vagrants squatting in it mostly, but the city won't tear it down."

"So, no one lives here?" I asked.

"People were going in and out until about a week ago. Since then I haven't seen a soul around. I am sure if you really wanted to, you could find your way in. But I warn you, it's probably not pretty in there. Why not walk away and leave your memories of the place intact."

"Well thank you very much Mr...?"

"Jones, Anthony Jones."

"Thank you, Mr. Jones. Maybe I will just check out the backyard. I spent most of my time there anyway."

"Good luck to you, ma'am."

"Take care."

Mr. Jones slowly made his way down the street and I headed around the side of the house towards the backyard. I peaked around the corner and didn't see anyone. I went up the back steps and tried to pry open the back door, but found it was heavily secured. There was a small knothole in the wood covering a window so I tried to peer inside, but all I could see was darkness. There was no sound. Complete silence. No one was here.

I stepped away from the window and fell to my knees, cursing life. God. Claire. I was so close and now nothing. As I got up from the ground I noticed a small mound of freshly disturbed earth near the raspberry bush. I went over and didn't have to dig very deep to find what I thought would have been long gone. But there it was, the faded blue shoe box. I sat down in front of the small hole and pulled out the box, placing it carefully into my lap.

I slowly opened the lid and looked down onto the vertical stack of papers now faded, dirty and yellow. But one caught my eye. There was no sign of dirt or weathering. I opened it:

O,

I don't know when or if you will get this. My friend might not even be able to get this letter into the box without being seen. I am sorry for everything. I thought I could fix it and got myself into even more trouble. I know you are going to want to find me, but don't. You are safer if you don't. These are not the type of people you go after. You've always been stubborn and I am sure you are already trying to figure out your next move but I am begging you, let your older sister take care of you one last time. Leave it alone, O. Enjoy your life, do something great with it and try and forget the last 3 years.

Love C.

I read the note four times as tears washed my face. She had been here. Here, when I was out front, and I didn't get to her. Claire was right, I was stubborn. Too stubborn to give up and let her go. It was too late now, but first thing tomorrow I was going to the Registry Office to find out everyone who has ever owned this property. From there, I will keep digging until I find the piece of the puzzle that leads me to Claire.

I stood and brushed the dirt off my clothes and made my way to the front of the house. I turned and walked towards the bus stop as I fingered the letters in the shoe box. I was so buried in thought and memory that I didn't notice the black van slowly following me. Before I could register what was happening the van screeched to a stop beside me, a man jumped out and wrapped his arms around me. I dropped the box and tried to fight but then I felt as though I had been stung by a wasp in my neck.

Then darkness.

CHAPTER TWELVE

"WAKE UP. THERE'S NO TIME FOR SLEEPING."

I struggled to open my eyes to the annoyed, yet concerned, female voice who continued to speak and shake me. "Wh... what?" I stuttered. My head was pounding and it got worse as she shook me. "Ouch, fuck." I put my hand to the back of my head and felt swelling and dried blood.

"You need to get cleaned up before The General gets here. If she sees you like this, you will be in trouble."

I glanced around a small room that looked like it used to be a pale pink. There were mattresses covering most of the floor with six other women lying on them. Each of the women looked to be in their early twenties, thin as rails and their eyes glazed over from drugs. The smell of sweat filled the air.

"Where am I?"

"You are in hell. Now get up and let me look at you."

I stood on the tiny piece of bare floor in front of the mattress I had been on. The woman turned me around in a circle before holding me at arm's length. She looked to be in her late twenties and more composed than the others. Her curly brown hair was astray and her clothes were a mess, but you could tell if she got cleaned up she would be quite beautiful.

"Straighten your sweater and take that thing off your wrist." she instructed.

"Look I got to get out of here. My sister is missing and if I don't..."

"Get out of here? Missy, you aren't going anywhere. The only people who leave are dead or moving to another house. Now give me the wrist guard. You don't want them to know you are hurt."

"Wouldn't they have already seen it?"

"Doubtful. The guys who picked you up likely just grabbed you and dropped you off without paying much attention."

I untied the wrist guard and gave it to her. She put it under a mattress.

"Wait, you mentioned another house?" I rubbed the throbbing wound on the back of my head. "What do you mean another house? Where am I really? And don't say hell." I went to the boarded-up window and tried to remove the plywood covering. It was heavily secured. I went across the room and tried the door but it was locked. The whole time the woman watched with a pitiful look on her face.

"Well you perked up quick. You are in what is called Zone 1. This is where all of the girls start and then get sorted into other Zones. Zone 2 is a bit better than this place. Zone 3, well, let's call that middle-class companionship and Zone 4 is upper-class; the upper echelon of the business. Only a select few get to work in those Zones - 3 and 4. Each Zone has multiple houses, but you don't have time to worry about that right now. If you don't get cleaned up, The General is going to be pissed and you don't want to make her mad."

"Wait, the Zones have multiple locations?"

"You pick things up quickly. That could be good or bad for you. Good if you pick up the rules. Bad if you question them. And yes, the business runs all over the world. Most cities have multiple Zones. I don't have time to explain everything. Turn around and I will try my best to fix your hair. We have very little water around here and cleaning up this blood isn't worth it right now."

She took one of the dirty pillow cases, spit on it and tried to wipe off as much of the blood as she could. Then she used an elastic band off her wrist and tied my hair into a loose bun.

"Well that's as good as it's gonna get, I'm afraid."

"I feel as though I should say thank you, but I still don't understand. Who are these women and who are you?"

"No one here has a name and people aren't here long enough for them to matter. I'm only still here because The General finds me useful in helping the girls get acquainted with their new lives."

"New lives? Seriously, where am I and how the fuck do I get out of here?" my voice was rising and the woman instinctively covered my mouth with her hand as the others stared.

"Quiet." she said firmly. "I know you're confused, but you need to calm down and follow my lead." She looked from my eyes to her hand and back again, waiting for me to nod in agreement that I would be quiet. She slowly removed her hand from my face.

I took a deep breath and spoke quietly, "How can I be calm when I am trapped in this decaying room, and I don't even know if I am even still in Toronto or how I got here. All I remember is walking down the street, a black van and a piercing feeling in my neck."

"Sounds like a lot of stories I hear."

"Shit! They were still watching the place, I knew it. They must have seen me leave the backyard, tailed me and drugged me." I realized Claire might have been brought here and switched my focus from myself. "Do you know if there is a woman named Claire here?"

"Like I said we don't use names."

"She would look like me except a lot smaller and probably high as a kite."

"Darling, so many women come through here, most of them high. I couldn't tell you if she had been here."

I wasn't giving up. If this woman had been around for so long, she had to know something. "Have you always been at this location or did you recently move?"

"You sure do ask a lot of questions."

"Look, I am a cop and I need to find my sister."

Next thing I knew, she had slapped me hard across the face. I put my hand to my cheek to try and nullify the sting.

"Don't you utter that word again. You tell anyone what you are, and you are sure as shit dead before you can say Jack Robinson."

Rubbing my burning cheek, I quickly looked around the room. It didn't seem as though any of the other women had heard me. Then I heard the click of high heels in the hallway.

"That's The General. Sit there and keep your head down. Don't speak, just listen and do whatever she says."

I sat on the mattress and stared at my feet. The woman bent down beside me, "Trust me."

I heard a key go into a lock, a click and the door creaked open.

"Good, she's awake. Bring her here," ordered The General.

The woman and I stood up and walked towards the door. I kept my head down and all I saw were The General's beige pantyhose and pointed black Mary Janes. She gripped my arm tightly and yanked me out of the room so hard, I almost lost my balance. The woman who helped me followed close behind and was given the keys to lock the door. I kept my eyes lowered from The General's face while trying to take in as much of my surroundings as I could.

After the door was secured, I was taken down a hallway of four closed doors, each with their own padlock. I wasn't sure how many doors were behind me and didn't risk looking back. The brown and yellow wallpaper was peeling, and the floors looked like they hadn't been cleaned in years. We walked downstairs and the stench of urine and sweat that had been mild upstairs was much worse on the first floor. I felt like I was going to be sick.

As we entered what would typically be the living room, I saw more mattresses covering the floor along with buckets. Without looking in them I knew the buckets were filled with excrement, urine and from the smell, vomit. From what I could see there were at least 50 women crammed together. Each looked emaciated.

We stopped in front of a closed wooden door which looked as though it had recently been replaced. There were no dents or scrape marks and the dirt that lined the door frame was not present. The other difference was this one did not have a padlock.

The General whipped me around so that our bodies faced each other. I continued to keep my head down. "Listen here. You go in there and tell the men anything they want to know. If they think you are lying, you are dead. If they think you are holding back, you are dead. If they don't like the look of you, you are dead. And no one will find you. So, the best thing for you is to tell the truth. They will know if you don't and then...?"

I replied robotically, "I am dead."

"Well you appear to have some sense about you at least. Let's hope you use it."

The General opened the door, shoved me in and quickly closed the door. The room wasn't well lit, but I could see the floor at my feet was cleaner than in the rest of the house. I felt a warm breeze coming in through a window on my right and caught a strong scent of lemon which must have been trying to mask the smell from the other side of the door.

"Who do we have here?"

I turned towards a man who was standing in the shadows across the room but kept my head down, my hair hiding my face. I could feel another person behind me but I didn't dare look. Not yet.

"I said, who do we have here!" bellowed the shadows. Then a red-headed man in a nice suit stepped into the light. It was the man from my old house. I suspected the bald man was the person behind me. I suddenly felt nauseous and my thoughts were spinning so I still didn't respond.

"I will ask one last time! What is your name?" and he stomped over to me, grabbed my hair and pulled it back so he could see my face.

"Olivia," I grimaced.

The man's face went from angry to shocked, as if he had seen a ghost, but the moment was fleeting, and he quickly transitioned back to anger.

"Was that so hard?" he pushed me to the floor and stood over me. "Olivia, what is your last name?"

I had to think quickly. If I gave my real name he would probably be able to figure out who I was, and I would be dead. I also decided I needed to act meeker than I felt. As much as I was filled with my own anger and wanted to find out about Claire, I knew I was in no position to do so. Finally, a name came to mind and I looked up at him.

"Quincy. My last name is Quincy."

I had gone to university with Sarah Olivia Quincy and hoped that she was one of the rare few who didn't showcase their entire lives on-line.

The red-headed man bent down beside me, his brown eyes burrowing into mine, "Quincy huh? We will see about that. Check it out, will you?" he said over my shoulder.

The large bald man I suspected was behind me walked towards the window, pulled out a cell phone and started talking in another language. I wasn't sure if it was Russian, German or another Scandinavian language. I made a mental note to ask the helpful woman if I saw her again.

"Well, Olivia. What were you doing poking around that run-down house?" his inquisitive brown eyes burrowed into mine as if he was trying to read my thoughts.

"I... I knew someone who used to live there years ago. I had spent time playing in the treehouse in the back yard and just wanted to see if the place had changed."

Hands on his knees, he pushed himself to full height. "There's no treehouse in that yard."

I decided not to get up and watched him walk over and lean against the front of an old green metal desk. It reminded me of the ones I had seen in 1960s movies. "Not any more, but there was." I quickly added, "My friend's father got really drunk and angrily tore it down one night."

"Well, we will verify that too." He nodded to the man still on the phone. "If everything checks out I guess we'll just chalk this up to you being in the wrong place at the wrong time. Although, from my perspective, I might consider it the wrong place at the right time." He chuckled to himself and then commanded "Stand up!"

I scrambled to my feet and got a better look at the room around me. Like the rest of the house, there wasn't much to it. The walls looked as though they might have been yellow at one point. A run-down brown floral couch was under the open, but barred, window, the metal desk was on the other side of the room and there was a rather nice high back leather chair behind it. The chair felt out of place considering the state of the rest of the room. I looked up and saw the only light source was a lone bulb in the ceiling.

The bald man was still on the phone and the red-headed man waved me over to him. I slowly walked over. I stood a foot away from him, trying to appear strong and yet submissive.

"I bet cleaned up, you are a pretty one. Take off your clothes."

Despite seeing the scarcely dressed women throughout the house, I was taken aback at his request. Seeing my hesitation, the man slammed his fist on the desk, which caused the sound to loudly reverberate off the undecorated walls. "If you prefer, I can take them off for you?"

I was repulsed at the idea of him touching me. I slowly pulled the sweater over my head, trying not to aggravate my wrist in the process. I dropped it beside my feet and tried to undo the button of my jeans. My hands were shaking and pain pierced my wrist. The red-haired man coughed loudly and got up off the desk, but stopped after I was finally able to release the button. I pushed my pants down to my ankles, stepped out of them, and nudged them beside my sweater. Next, I took off my bra as I stared at the floor. I dropped it on top of the growing pile of clothes, while I told myself I was strong. Whatever I was about to face would be incomparable to not finding Claire.

I was about to remove my underwear when the red-headed man walked over, stood in front of me. "Those can wait. For now." He ran his finger up my left arm. His finger continued along the top of my breast until he stopped at my chin, gripped it and forced me to look at him. "Just in case you haven't figured it out, you work for me now. Just like all of those women outside and upstairs. Whatever nice little life you had before is gone. Your life is now mine. I decide who stays and who goes. And you don't want me to decide that you go. Do you understand?"

"Yes," I said, staring defiantly into his fiery eyes.

"You do what I say, when I say, you got that? You eat when I tell you to eat, you smile when I tell you to smile, and you fuck who I tell you to fuck."

The blood from my face drained. He noticed and smiled. "That's right darling. You're Adam's bitch now and this," he stuck his other hand between my legs. "Is mine." He let go of my chin but squeezed hard with the other and I flinched. Adam's smile widened.

"Now let's see if you were listening. Smile."

I thought about Claire and knew I couldn't let this repulsive man get to me. If I was going to find her I would have to blend in. So, I mustered up a smile.

"Very nice."

The bald man hung up his phone and whispered something into Adam's ear, who was still staring at me. His face didn't give me any clues as to the information he was hearing. The bald man stepped behind and to the right of Adam, hands on his hips and a vacant expression.

"Is there anything you would like to tell me, Olivia?"

My heart stopped. How did they figure out who I was so quickly? My mind was racing. I needed to get out of here, but how? Well, I sure as hell was not going down without a fight and I would take at least one of these men with me if I have to. I tried to calm myself down. I was overreacting. Whoever these guys were, there was no way they knew who I was. Not yet. I feigned dumb.

"No."

"No. Really. Well, it turns out your last name isn't Quincy now, is it?"

I didn't know what to say. Admitting who I was would get me killed, but saying nothing also seemed like it might bring me to the same end.

"Quincy is my maiden name," I blurted.

"And?"

"And" *oh Lord please help* "My first name is Sarah. But I don't go by that name."

"When I asked you to tell me your name, you should have told me your full name. I don't care what you 'go' by. Had you told me the whole truth the first time I wouldn't have to teach you a lesson." He motioned for the bald man to take his place.

I looked at the bald man rolling up his sleeves. His large stature was very intimidating.

"Please, I just... I didn't know," I stuttered as I took a couple steps back.

"You didn't know. You hear that Smith? She didn't know," Adam chuckled. Smith was silent. "Well, in that case, maybe we will forgo the punishment this time - what do you say Smith?" Smith remained silent and was now directly in front of me.

Adam walked past me and my head followed his movements. Before I had time to crane it back around to Smith, the man had punched me in the side of the head. I fell to the ground in excruciating pain. Smith picked me up by the neck and punched me three times in the stomach before dropping me back onto the ground. I gasped for air and willed my tears not to flow. No matter how much pain they caused me I would not let them see me cry.

"Get up!" Adam yelled. "Or, if you have learned your lesson, stay put and apologize for making me angry. And look, Smith's shirt is now dirty. We will take that out of your earnings."

I looked up and saw blood on Smith's stark white button-up shirt. I don't know if it was my stubbornness, or maybe the years of wishing I stood up to my father, but I pulled myself onto my feet and stood up as tall as I could.

"Tough one, are you? We will see about that." Adam grabbed the back of my neck with one hand and my fractured right wrist in the other. Pain shot up my arm but I bit my lip to muffle my cry. He forced me over to the desk and let go of my arm, but still gripped my neck.

"Bend over!"

I didn't move.

"I said bend over!" and he kneed the back of my knees and I instinctively buckled. On my way down, he pushed my face hard into the desk. I used my arms to hold me up as much as possible against Adam's force.

"Smith come hold her down. She's a fighter."

Smith came around the other side of the desk, grabbed my wrists and pulled them towards him, my torso was now flat against the desk. He held my wrists tight and I couldn't stop the tears.

Behind me I heard Adam loosen his belt and unzip his pants. He pulled my underwear down around my ankles.

"I am the boss around here!" Adam forced my legs apart "I own you!" He leaned down beside my ear and whispered "You are nothing. Nothing." And he forced himself inside me.

CHAPTER THIRTEEN

MY MIND WAS DRAWN BACK TO REALITY AT THE SOUND OF Adam's belt being buckled up and Smith releasing my wrists. I don't know how long my mind locked itself down but I was thankful it did. Given Smith was the one who let go of my wrists, I was confident my body was only used by one of them. I also gathered Adam enjoyed displaying his dominance in front of others and would want Smith to witness his power.

"Get off the desk." Adam said triumphantly.

I pushed myself up and felt wet sticky semen dripping down my leg. I pulled up my underwear as I turned around. Showing no emotion, I looked Adam in the eye. I wasn't going to let him think he had broken me.

"That is your place in the world. Nothing but a body to be used as I see fit." He looked to Smith. "Go get The General."

Smith left the room, being sure to close the door behind him. I continued to watch Adam.

"You think you are tough now, but just wait." He lit a cigarette. "The

General will teach you a lesson or two and I might have to teach you a few more myself." He took a long drag and blew the smoke in my face.

I didn't react but said confidently, "Do with me what you will, but you will not win." and I spit in his face.

The rage radiated off of him with my act of defiance. He didn't wait for Smith to come back but punched me in the face himself. I didn't cower but stood my ground. "You little bitch!" With the cigarette between his lips, he continued to beat me and I continued to get up. The anger was growing more ferocious inside of him and his eyes said he was ready to kill me.

The General opened the door and quickly took in what was happening. She motioned for Smith to remove Adam, which he obediently did. She walked over to me, giving me the once over where I stood. While Adam fought to release himself from Smith's grip, I became confused about who actually ran this place; Adam or The General.

The General grabbed my clothes, thrust them at me, and dragged me out of the room. She closed the door behind her and then slapped me hard across my already battered face. "You stupid girl. You do not want to be his enemy. Doubt you are coming back from this. And look at you. You won't be able to make him money like this, which will make him angrier. You will be lucky to last a week here. Let's go." Once again, she yanked my arm and led me upstairs.

Every inch of me hurt and I could feel the bruises forming. It was hard to move anything but I held my head high as I walked. I could hear Adam yelling at someone about me, presumably Smith. The women watched me walk by, clutching my clothes to shield my nakedness, and some looked at me in astonishment, others looked at me with eyes of sadness-afraid of what would become of me.

I was locked back up in the room where I started with the same women passed out on their mattresses. The woman who cleaned me up was squatted on her mattress, her back against the wall.

"They sure did a number on you. I thought I would hear you screaming down there but not a peep. Good for you." She graciously helped me back into my clothes and invited me to sit with her. I sat down, and she laid me down in her lap.

She took out my pony tail. Running her fingers through my disheveled hair she whispered, "I hope you got your defiance out of your system. If you want to try and find your sister, you need to follow the rules. By doing that, you survive. By doing that, you might get out of here."

I stared forward, above the bodies across from us. "I know there are no names here, but what do I call you?"

She hesitated and then said "You can call me Tess."

"Okay Tess. I am Olivia."

"Well Olivia, a bit of advice. Act defeated, even if you aren't. Don't be a hero, just let him think he won. Then maybe he will leave you alone."

"The bald man, Smith. Where is he from? He spoke another language when he made a call but I couldn't place it."

"He's Swedish I think. The General regularly comments that he would be more useful building cheap furniture. Now get some rest. I suspect Adam will be back soon for another round with you."

"Why are you helping me?"

"Honestly, I don't know. I usually leave the newbies to their own devices but something told me I should help you. This may sound corny but I feel like you were meant for more."

It was corny but I didn't care. I was exhausted and I closed my eyes and thought of Claire. Her laughing at a joke no one else found funny. Her quirky smile when she solved a particularly difficult problem.

Where was she? Was she also lying on a mattress covered in bodily fluids somewhere? Or did she get out?

CHAPTER FOURTEEN

EVEN THOUGH I WAS EXHAUSTED, FEAR KEPT ME AWAKE all night. Any time I did manage to fall asleep, I dreamed of Adam. The light had been turned off for the night and was to remain off until The General either turned it on or advised otherwise. The room was pitch black and even though I could feel Tess beside me I couldn't see her. I spent the night listening to the shuffling in the hallway. It rarely stopped.

Hours went by before I heard the lock on the door click and was blinded by the hallway light entering the room. Then the ceiling light was turned on and I turned away from it as I tried to get my eyes to adjust. The women around me moaned and covered their eyes with their arms, including Tess. The General dragged me off my mattress by my arm, practically tearing it out of the socket, and started pulling me across the floor, stepping over other mattresses as needed.

"Ouch! Stop!"

She continued to pull me forward, "Let's go. Adam wants to see you."

"Please, you're hurting me." I begged. As much as I wanted to, I couldn't hide my pain.

"If he is back so soon, you are in for a world of hurt worse than this. Now get up!"

Tess scrambled off the mattress and helped me to my feet. My adrenaline was starting to kick in and I was becoming more alert. "What are you talking about?" I asked, stumbling down the hall as I tried to keep up with The General who hadn't let go of my arm. Tess followed closely behind, this time not closing the door after she left the room.

"Stop asking questions." We stopped when we got to the bottom of the stairs and she turned to look at me "I don't know you, I don't like you, but for heaven's sake, just do whatever he says." And we started maneuvering around the mattresses to get to the office when Adam stepped out.

"Thank you, General. You can leave her there. Bring down all of the girls from upstairs." I looked at The General, who looked confused, but she did not question him and headed back up the stairs.

Adam started clapping his hands and kicking women to get their attention. He addressed them sarcastically, "All of you pay attention. We have a very special person here." He came over and put his arm around my shoulder and pulled me hard into him. The women from the rooms upstairs were all crowded on the stairs.

"Olivia here is new. She thought it would be okay to talk back to me. As you can see, I punished her for that." He pushed on a couple of the bruises on my face. I couldn't help but flinch, which satisfied him, and he continued. "But then I got to thinking. Maybe I could use her as an example, to show you how it works here." He stood behind me with his hands on my shoulders.

"You see, just like Olivia, some of you are new. Some of you already know your place, but some of you might not." My knees suddenly buckled as he kicked the back of them, and I fell to the floor. "You are all worthless, no one knows any of you are here and no one cares! You belong to me and you will do what I say or you die! Understand?"

The women mumbled in agreement.

He knelt down in front of me, "Do you understand?" I didn't respond. "Smith, come over here."

As ordered, Smith now stood in front me.

"Smith here is such a hard worker and I think he deserves to be rewarded, don't you?" Adam chuckled and then looked at me.

"Undo his pants," he ordered.

I hesitated for a split second and Adam was furious. "I said undo his pants!"

I quickly got the button and zipper undone. I looked up at Smith, who was staring straight ahead, expressionless. Something told me this was not the first time he had been in this position.

"Now, do I need to spell out what I want you to do next, or do you think you are smart enough to figure it out?"

I reached to pull down Smith's pants, but then retracted my hands, sat back on my feet and stared straight ahead. The women around me started to mumble. I could hear The General say "stupid girl".

"You want to play it this way?" Adam's face was beet red with anger. Still looking at me, he yelled "General, who has she been talking to in this house?"

I looked over to The General using my eyes to plead her not to say... "Tess, Sir." My head dropped.

"Tess, come here." Adam ordered.

Tess came down the stairs looking very timid, not the strong woman I had seen her to be.

"Kneel facing our defiant new friend." She obeyed.

Adam took out a knife from his pocket, pulled Tess' head back and put the knife to her throat. "Now, do it or she dies," his voice was the most sinister I had heard so far.

Tears started down Tess' face. I didn't want to give in, but I knew he wouldn't hesitate to kill Tess. We were nothing to him. I couldn't have her blood on my hands.

He crouched down and pointed the knife at me. "Start sucking or this bitch is dead."

Smith was firmly planted in place like a statue. He didn't look like he wanted to be a part of this any more than I did. As I pulled Smith's pants down, Adam stood up with a grin of vindication. He and everyone else in the house watched as I spent the next 10 minutes with Smith in my mouth. I wanted to puke. I wanted to grab the knife from Adam, kill him, Smith and The General. But I didn't. I did what he wanted and when Smith was done Adam patted me on the head and said "Good girl". Oh, I wanted to scream!

"General. She stays down here with this riff raff, and nowhere near this one." Pointing to Tess.

The General pulled Tess up and took her, and the other girls on the stairs, back up to their rooms. Smith cleaned up the best he could and then both men left the house. I tried to sit tall, show the other women it hadn't hurt me; that they hadn't won. But the reality of everything hit me like a train and I slumped to the floor and sobbed. I hated myself for breaking down but the weight of it all was too much.

Everyone knew better then to help me. I was left alone in my puddle of tears and bruises until I cried myself to sleep in the same spot where Adam had defeated me.

CHAPTER FIFTEEN

TIME WAS RELATIVE IN THIS HOUSE. WITH THE WINDOWS boarded up, the only time we saw sun or moon light was when women were being taken outside for jobs. The stuff that was supposed to pass as food didn't appear at regular intervals, so I couldn't use meals to track the time.

Adam hadn't been back since he orchestrated the show for the house. My bruises and wrist had almost fully healed. The General came by to inspect me and said I would be ready for work soon. Having seen the faces of the other girls, I was surprised I had not been put to work already. They looked worse than I did, but I wasn't going to ask questions. I kept to myself and prayed for one more day to try and figure out where Claire was.

The other women started talking to me a couple of days after what had become known as 'the incident'. I was able to find out that Claire had been with them at the other house, but they hadn't seen her since. A woman named Gloria mentioned that Adam really seemed to like Claire and would come see her often. But he got really mad one night, and took her and two other women away. None of them had been back. The next night, everyone was put into the back of a moving truck and brought here. No one knows where "here" was, but Gloria didn't think they were in the truck for more then an hour. That meant we were either still in Toronto or at least in the area.

I asked Gloria if there was any way to get a note to someone outside the house. "The only way I can think of is if you find a john sympathetic enough, but it wouldn't be easy. They likely wouldn't want to risk jeopardizing their relationship with Adam."

I asked about the other Zones but Gloria didn't know anything. She had only been here a couple of months. I asked a few of the other women but no one knew much and I got the sense Tess hadn't shared with them what she did with me. I decided to stop asking questions as I didn't want to get Tess into further trouble and I wasn't getting anywhere.

Gloria came to me a few days later with a piece of paper and a pen one of the other women was able to smuggle out of a hotel room. I wanted to hug her but The General was nearby. That night, while The General was busy, I huddled in a corner with others acting as a wall and wrote a note to Joe.

J,

C was in our old house. The one we watched. But she was moved the night we followed the van. That was her inside. I have been taken by the same men and am now in a different house. Based on what I could find out I am still in the city. It's bad, really bad. There are so many women trapped here. I don't have time to write much more. But I am as good as can be and know I will find C. I will get you more information when/if I can.

O.

I gave the note to Gloria, who hid it in her bra. And the wall of women disbanded as a couple more women brought in pots of soup. As I was eating what might have been chicken soup, without the chicken, The General looked at me as she spoke on the phone and said "She will be ready tomorrow."

I didn't sleep and spent the night staring into the pitch-black darkness. I prayed for the strength to make it through the next day, whatever came my way.

The next morning, The General handed me a bucket of cold water and a cloth. "Wash up. Boss is coming. You are working today." She walked away.

I took the bucket and it felt as though it weighed 100 pounds. With the little food we got, I was sure I had lost 15 pounds and found it hard to carry the bucket. There was nowhere to wash up. What used to be the bathroom had been torn out and turned into a makeshift office for The General. I went into a corner and did the best I could to hide myself. However, at this point they had all seen me piss and shit in the buckets so I was not sure why I was being so modest. I hadn't washed since I had been here and although the water was cold it was nice to scrape some of the caked-on dirt and stench off of me. When I was done, The General handed me a bundle of clothes and a pair of black high heels.

"Put these on and don't ruin them. They're the only ones you get."

I unfolded the bundle and found clean black panties, a bra, and a matching black dress. As I put on the skin-tight dress I noticed it still had a tag on it. No one else had likely worn it. I tore off the tag and tossed it onto the ground. The shoes, on the other hand, were visibly worn. I wondered what had happened to their previous owner. Then I realized that the shoes were probably shared and I wouldn't be the only one wearing them.

Not long after I was dressed, Adam arrived with Smith and waited in the entryway while The General brought me to them. Adam walked around me, giving me the once-over. "Not bad. Now, you say nothing the entire time. Understand?"

I was being facetious when I didn't answer but Adam found it amusing and chuckled.

"Good. Do not tell anyone your real name. If they ask, you are Jane." He grabbed my arm with force "Now let's go." His touch made my skin crawl, and it took all I had to not recoil.

Stepping outside the house, I had to squint my eyes from the blinding sun. The warm spring breeze kissed my skin. I was put into the back of a Silver Bentley and instructed to put on a blindfold, as Adam climbed in beside me. Before I put it on, I noticed the house I left was a 1970s-style brown stucco. I didn't recognize the neighbourhood.

As we drove, I counted the seconds until my blindfold was removed. We sat outside the Lazy Traveler Inn. I had never heard of it. The drive took 19 minutes. Smith pulled a room key from his pocket and unlocked number 23. He ushered me into the room and closed the door, while he and Adam stayed outside.

I looked out the front window and saw them talking as they guarded the door and appeared to be waiting for someone. I didn't know how much time I had. I picked up the phone but there was no dial tone. I frantically went to the bathroom in hopes there would be a window. There was, but I suspected this room was regularly used by Adam and the window would be sealed. To my surprise it opened. Had no one tried to escape before? I cautiously looked out and saw the alley was empty. I squeezed my way through the window, thankful in that moment for the lack of food. My feet quietly hit the pavement and I started to run down towards the main street. As I got to the end of the alley, the Silver Bentley screeched in front of me and Smith jumped out of the driver's seat. There was no point in running,

Adam had rolled down his window and had a 9 mm pointed right at me. My shoulders slumped forward in defeat.

"Oh Jane, you didn't learn your lesson, did you? I told you she'd try and run, didn't I? Well go on, run if you want. Nothing would give me more pleasure than to put a few bullets in you."

Smith stepped between me and Adam, grabbed my arm, and put me into the backseat. I thought I saw a look of disappointment in his eyes when he closed the door.

They took me back to room 23, but this time Smith stayed in the room with me. For the next five hours I stared at the clock on the bedside table as people exchanged money for my body. Smith stood guard by the bathroom and watched me closely while I cleaned up after each person.

When it was done, Adam instructed me to get dressed, get in the car and put on the blindfold. Once we were all in the car Adam turned to me, placed his hand on my leg and said, "I am so excited for the next part of our trip here, Jane."

"Stop calling me that. At least have the balls to call me by my real name."

"YOU DON'T TELL ME WHAT TO DO!" His hand tightly gripped my leg as clenched his jaw, "You will learn your place in this world today or it will be your last day alive."

We drove for a while and when we stopped, I could hear seagulls. Smith opened my car door and, a little more gently this time, removed me from the car and took off my blindfold. We were in a shipping yard and parked in the middle of a row of towers of large metal containers. It was starting to get dark and I didn't see anyone else around.

Adam got out of the car and stretched, took a deep breath and put his hands in his pockets. "Do you know how easy it would be to put you in one of these containers and send you away? There are many men across this country, or the world even, who would love to get their hands on you."

Had Claire been shipped somewhere? If she was, how would I ever find her? Adam walked over to the water and looked across it. Smith guided me over to Adam's side. "You're such a fun toy to play with, shall we play a little game? Then I will decide your fate."

He slowly removed his jacket, gave it to Smith and rolled up his sleeves. Adam put his hands around my throat and squeezed as he pushed me back against a container. I struggled as I tried to get my fingers between his hand and my neck.

"Breath is life, and I can take yours away if I choose." He squeezed tighter and I couldn't breathe. I didn't have the strength to fight back, even though I tried. Suddenly, he let go and I fell to the ground gasping for air. He kicked me and I fell onto my back. He sat on my stomach.

"You're all the same. Whores who don't listen. It's a good thing I am such a thoughtful teacher." He punched me in the face. I turned to face him as an airplane flew overhead. I couldn't hear what he was saying, but his fists were loud enough.

When Adam was done with his lesson I could barely see or walk. Smith carried me to the car and laid me down in the backseat. I closed my eyes and passed out to the sound of rolling tires on pavement. Given the alternative, I hoped I was headed back to The General.

CHAPTER SIXTEEN

I COULD HEAR VEHICLES RUSHING PAST. I LOOKED UP AND saw stars in a dark blue sky. Smith hadn't put the blindfold on me and I could only see out of one eye. I gently touched the other one and felt it had swollen shut. I noticed Smith in the rear-view mirror looking at me. He didn't say anything. Instead, the drive continued in silence until we pulled into the driveway of the brown house. I never thought I would be so relieved to see that house.

Adam got out of the front passenger seat and personally dragged me out of the car. He threw me so hard up the steps I smashed into the door. Smith trailed behind. When we entered the house, the room was filled with gasps as the women saw my battered body. Adam tossed me aside, and I landed on top of a few of the women that were on a mattress close by.

Once again, he garnered the attention of everyone on the first floor, "This is what happens when you think your life is your own. She tried to run."

"It was a trap," I mumbled.

"What did you just say?" and he pulled my hair, dragging me up off the mattress.

"I said it was a trap. You left me in that room alone with an unlocked window, knowing full well I would use it. All so you could play your little games with me," and I spat in his face.

Adam stuck an open hand out to Smith, who pulled a gun from his shoulder holster and placed it in the open palm. Adam dropped my hair, cocked the gun and pressed it right to my forehead. I showed no fear as I glared at him defiantly.

The women around me scattered in terror. Pressing themselves up against the furthest walls possible to avoid becoming a casualty.

Somewhere behind Adam, a calm, deep male voice spoke, "Adam enough." I heard footsteps approaching from the back of the house. Everyone looked towards the voice except Adam and me. He continued to look at me, and I him.

A hand slowly pushed the gun down, and removed it from Adam's hand. My gaze followed the gun back into Smith's holster and then I turned my eyes to the stranger beside me. He was a tall, handsome man with a chiseled jaw, brown hair and pale blue eyes. His face held a stern composure. He was well-dressed in an immaculately cut suit, which snuggly fit his muscular body. He turned Adam to him and cupped his face in his hands and put their foreheads together.

"Brother, you can't keep doing this. They are what make us rich. If you destroy the merchandise - no matter how mouthy they might be - we will have no business. People will start noticing if too many women go missing."

This new man stepped away from Adam and crouched down in front of me. He gently moved my head around and examined my face. Then he held out his hand to help me up. I hesitated.

"It's okay," he said softly.

I cautiously took his hand. As I stood there, he inspected the rest of what he could see of me. He seemed kinder than Adam but I suspected he hid villainous qualities. I looked him in the eye, with the one I could still use, and swore I saw hurt. He looked away, bowed his head slightly, and rubbed his neck as if he was nervous. He regained his composure and announced. "She's coming with me. Smith, put her in my car."

"What? No! She's mine!"

"She was yours until you decided to make her your personal punching bag. When you can care for them better than this, I might actually let you keep one. Smith, if you please."

Smith slowly guided me towards the door. I tried to look for Tess but she must have been locked away upstairs. I tried to memorize all of the faces of the women in that room and vowed I would dismantle whatever organization this was.

I was put into the back seat of a Rolls Royce which already had two men up front. They didn't acknowledge me. Smith squeezed my hand and seemed to be looking at me with some sympathy. In a weird way, I wished he was coming with me. Adam's brother got into the backseat beside me and didn't say a word until we were on the highway.

"I am sorry about my brother. When he gets fixated on something, he cannot let it go. Are you in a lot of pain?"

I didn't answer. The front passenger handed him something while he opened a bottle of water. "Here, take these." He opened his palm and there sat two small pills. One white and one blue.

"What are they?" I mustered.

"They will help, and it is going to be a long night, so you will want them."

I cautiously removed the pills from his hand, looked at them, and looked at him. "Trust me," he said with kindness in his eyes, but I didn't trust him.

I hesitated, but the pain was unbearable. I put the pills in my mouth and took the bottle of water. In two gulps, they were down and I hoped I hadn't just gotten myself into worse trouble. Within five minutes there was a tingling sensation all over my body and I felt very drowsy. I could barely keep my head up.

"Just let them win," Adam's brother whispered.

I laid my head against the headrest and watched planes taking off out the window. I tried to stay awake but sleep was too hard to fight off.

"Rest now," and he took my hand as everything went black.

CHAPTER SEVENTEEN

YOU KNOW WHEN YOU ARE IN THE SPACE BETWEEN AWAKE and asleep? You feel paralyzed and it feels as though you are in danger, but you can't get your eyes open to see what is happening? I was in that space. I couldn't seem to keep my eyes open but I saw bright lights and heard voices around me. I thought I was lying down. Yes, I was lying down. Come on eyes, 'Open!'. They stay closed. Voices are becoming clearer. Is it three males? Am I hearing engines as well? I tried to move my arms but they were as heavy as cement. I laid still and tried to get my body to center itself. I slowly opened my eyes and this time they stayed open as the bright lights and small oval windows came into focus. The voices stopped.

"She awakens," a familiar voice joked.

I sat up but caught myself as everything was whirling around me. I looked across and saw Adam's brother and the two men from the car. Both of the men looked identical: short, military-style haircuts, large build, and wearing dark suits and shirts. The only things missing were sunglasses and ear pieces, otherwise I would have thought I was surrounded by the Secret Service.

I look around and find myself on a private plane. The walls are white with silver and gold art deco patterns along them. They are accented by chrome shelving. The furniture is white leather and made with crisp, clean lines. The floor was covered in a white and blue carpet. I thought Claire's condo was extravagant but this was another level.

Adam's brother sat across from me in a white leather recliner with built-in chrome accents and cup holder. The other two men sat on either side of him.

"Where are we going?"

"We will be landing in Los Angeles in about 20 minutes."

"Los...Angeles...but...no."

"Would you rather go back to my brother in Toronto?"

"I... no... it's just... never mind." I slouched back against the couch.

He stood up and made his way to a space between the cabin and the cockpit. From what I could see, the space contained grey upper and lower cupboards and a sink. I could hear the clinking of glasses, bottles and ice. When he was done he stood over me and handed me a glass of clear liquid. I took it cautiously, smelled it and figured it was water, so I drank it. I hadn't realized how thirsty I was until the water touched my tongue.

"You are going to be much happier in L.A." He went back to his seat. "Provided you follow the rules and behave better than what you displayed with Adam."

I couldn't stop myself, "Can anyone really be happy when they have no choice?"

His expression didn't change, "Happiness is relative. If one accepts the things one cannot change one can be happy with the things they have."

I had expected anger not philosophical thought. I sat in silence, unsure if I should respond further. I didn't understand what was happening. Although this man had a different temperament than his brother, I didn't know anything about him. But he hadn't overtly shown me disdain so I decided to try and see what information I could get from him.

"May I ask a question?"

"You can always ask me a question. I just may not have an answer, want to answer, or have the answer you are looking for." He smiled as he sipped his drink.

More philosophical stuff, what is with this guy? "Why did you bring me here?"

"Ahh yes. Why? Isn't that always the question?" he swirled his cup and took another sip before continuing, "If I am honest, I don't really know. Was it to teach my brother a lesson about the dangers of pride? Maybe. But the likelihood he would put two and two together is minimal. Was I just showing him I am in control and at any moment can step in? Did some part of me see you fighting back and wish to see you win over him? Or did I just happen to be in a giving mood and decide that, rather than my brother killing you, which was inevitable given his apparent hatred of you, I would give you another shot at life?" He finished his drink then continued. "Sure, it may not be the life you would choose but it is life. I guess this may relate to happiness after all. I mean you could be dead and not be able to experience anything, or you could embrace this new life I have gifted you and be happy. But then again, maybe I just like to piss my brother off."

Really? This guy is odd. "Um. Okay. Clearly you and your brother have issues."

He chuckled and went and made himself another drink.

"Who are you?" I asked towards the alcove.

"William. I run the family business. Adam freely demonstrates the family trait of anger and although I prefer not to, I am not opposed to expressing it when it is beneficial. Rule #1 - you listen to me and my appointed men. You do that and you will be adequately taken care of. You will be in a modest, but more comfortable place than the shithole my brother had you in. Rule #2 - you will make me money or you don't stay. You can use your imagination as to what that means. There are eight other women that you will be working with. It is not expected that you will get along with everyone but you will tolerate them. There are house rules, but the ladies will fill you in on them when we get there."

He came and sat beside me as the plane started to descend. I tried not to show how upset or confused I was that I was thousands of kilometers from where I last saw Claire. I was also scared to do anything that would give William reason to show if his anger was different from Adam's. I must not have hidden my emotions well.

"You are scared, understandable." He gently turned my face towards him, "I take care of those who take care of me. You will see this soon. You may not think so now, but you are very lucky. It takes a lot to get to work at my house. Many would give anything to be sitting where you are right now."

As I looked into his blue eyes I saw tenderness, but I also thought I saw a tinge of wickedness lurking in the background. His next comment proved it was there. "When we get off this plane if you make one move to signal to anyone, or try and run, the pain Jack and Kevin will inflict on you will make you wish you were back with Adam."

He let me go when the wheels of the plane touched down. As we were not fastened I collided into him as the plane rapidly decreased speed. William stood up, buttoned up his suit jacket and walked to the cabin door. He looked back at me with a small smile before walking down the steps.

I pushed myself off the couch and made my way to the door. One of William's men in front of me and one behind. William stood by a limousine talking to whom I assumed was the driver, given the driving cap. I slowly made my way down the stairs and noticed even if I wanted to, there was no one around to signal for help and I was in no condition to run. It appeared William made sure the private runway was just that, private. My only hope was that William had taken pity on Claire and I was being taken to her.

CHAPTER EIGHTEEN

IN THE CAR, I HAD HALF EXPECTED TO BE BLINDFOLDED to prevent me from knowing where we were going. But then, William was quickly becoming someone I didn't expect. He poured me a drink from a small bar in the side of the limousine. This time it wasn't water. I don't know what it was but I somehow trusted it hadn't been laced. We sat in complete silence as I watched the nighttime landscape of L.A. pass by.

I lost track of time, but as we started up the drive towards the new house I started to question what William's definition of modest was. On top of a winding hill sat a large, three-storey, grey stone Georgian mansion the size of two football fields; and that was only what I could see. I felt like I was approaching a castle. We pulled up to a covered entry loggia of white stone. I got out of the car and noticed there was a chandelier resembling a Victorian street lamp above the car.

I looked around me and saw an immaculate yard with tall hedges beside the house that appeared to get shorter as they went down the drive.

The gardens were filled with brightly coloured flowers and I couldn't believe the stark contrast to the house I just came from.

William looked over the car at me, "Nice, isn't it? Well, come on in and see the rest of it."

I followed William through the large wooden double doors and stepped into a very chic and modern grand foyer, a sharp contrast to the historical exterior. The large entryway had black and white checkered marble floors with a large crystal chandelier lighting up the room. There were additional gold wall sconces on either side of the white pillars we stepped through. On my right was a large staircase with a mahogany banister, sitting on top of beautifully designed black wrought iron, which led up to the second and third floors. The railing led all the way around each floor and I pictured the Von Trapp children from The Sound of Music singing from above me.

William and I moved to an open doorway on our left, which opened to a large dining room. It had hardwood floors and a table set for 30 filled the middle of the room. We didn't stay long but it appeared there was antique furniture pieces and art decorating the room.

"We don't eat much there. It's mostly for show. You have free reign of most of the house. Feel free to use anything. The only places off-limits are my office which is through that door," he pointed to a hallway tucked under the staircase. "My room and those of Jack and Kevin. No one is ever to go in there. Understood?"

I nodded my head in agreement as William ushered me through the foyer, the two men following behind, and through an archway which opened to the largest living room I had ever seen. There were three couches positioned in a U-shape around a large rectangular coffee table. The couches were beige with blue and grey accent pillows, and could easily fit five people on each. On the left side of the room were built-in floor-to-ceiling bookshelves filled with an array of antique and modern works. There were three sets of double doors out onto a stone terrace, past which was a large back yard, pool and pool houses. On the right wall there was a large fireplace with two red Wingback chairs positioned cozily in front. On either side of the fireplace there were doorways into a ballroom. As we left through the door we'd entered by, I noticed a large wood cabinet hanging on the wall. I suspected a television was tucked away inside.

We walked down a hallway, which continued the pattern of the black and white marble floors, and passed an elevator I was told was only for William, his men, guests or special people. I was too caught up in the glamour of my surroundings to ask who was considered special.

We entered the kitchen. Except it wasn't just a kitchen. There was a regular-size living area with couches, as well as a breakfast room, which was encircled by windows on three sides and looked out to the backyard. There was a whitewashed table big enough for 15 people. The kitchen itself had white wood cupboards on the walls, and dark wood under the large marble-topped island in the middle of the room. Two Victorian chandeliers similar to the one in the loggia hung over the island. The detail in the crown molding was like nothing I had ever seen. I was in complete amazement.

"As I said, the women will fill you in on the rules, however, you should know every night at 6 p.m. we have a house meeting here in the kitchen. Don't be late." he said sternly as he looked through the double paned doors into the backyard. "It looks like everyone is out by the pool."

One of his men opened the door, and William led me out onto the cream-coloured stone terrace which overlooked a lush green yard. It was a warm evening and I could see why people would want to spend it outside. The tall trees that fenced in the front yard continued around the back and had white lights embedded in them, which gave the feeling the trees were full of lightning bugs. From where we stood, I could see the landscape of

L.A. It was a magnificent view, without a neighbouring house in sight. We walked down the stairs, which were lined on either side with a lighted dark-grey stone walled waterfall. I looked back over my shoulder and saw the design of the back of the house matched the front. The only difference was there were two balconies on the third floor that were supported by large cream pillars.

As we walked along the grass, my heels kept getting stuck, so I quickly took them off and carried them, as we passed pool houses on either side of the lawn. There were six in all. Two on either side, and two at the far end of the yard, behind a large pool which reflected the moon.

As we approached, the eyes of the women strewn across the patio furniture turned to me. I looked around and they were all beautiful, appeared to be between 20 to 35, and all had very different looks. They looked nothing like the women I had been staying with. I was slightly confused why William thought I would fit in here. Especially as he had only seen me battered and bruised.

William addressed the group, "Ladies, this is Olivia. Make her feel welcome and help get her settled. As you can see, she won't be working until she heals, but I expect you will educate her on how things are done here."

A caramel-haired woman, who appeared to be in her 30s, responded with "We sure will." The way she said it ran chills down my spine. The house may be nice, but I had a feeling the people inside it may not be.

CHAPTER NINETEEN

AS WILLIAM AND HIS MEN WALKED AWAY, THE CARMAMEL-haired woman uncrossed her long legs, stood up and walked towards me holding a martini. She stood so close I could smell the alcohol on her breath. She took the olive out of her glass, ate it and then spoke.

"The first thing you need to know is, I'm in charge. You listen to me or the ladies will make you look worse than you do now. Got that?"

I looked around to a number of unimpressed or uninterested faces. I wasn't in the mood for a fight, so I agreed, "Got it."

She walked behind me, "Second thing - Stay away from Will. He is mine. If you so much as put a finger on him, I will have you out of this house so fast your head will spin. We will all be watching you. Any questions?"

I didn't know if that was an actual or rhetorical question, so I didn't respond.

"Good," then her voice changed from domineering to what I

perceived as 'fake' friendly, "I am Jenna, by the way. So, where are you from, Olivia?" She took her seat again and one of the other women, who had smooth chocolate skin, curly brown hair and stunning green eyes, brought me a chair.

I thanked her before responding, "Toronto."

"Long way from home. What did you do there?"

I looked at her quizzically, "None of us started out wanting to sell ourselves for sex so that someone else can make money. I was a waitress at an upscale restaurant here in L.A. I partied with so many celebrities." she bragged, "Then I met William and, well, here I am." Her face was beaming. "So, what about you?"

My mind raced as I tried to come up with something. There was no way I was going to tell them I was a cop. "I used to be an executive of a property management firm, but that didn't work out."

"Wow!" said a woman with long blond hair, who had one green eye and one blue. "What happened? I am Reyna, by the way." She sounded and looked young.

"Well, short story is, I fucked it up. Met a guy that wasn't good for me and lost it all. One of his contacts said I could make some easy money. The next thing I knew, money and I were exchanged." The woman who had brought me the chair looked skeptical. I hoped my lie would hold up.

"How the mighty have fallen," Jenna said condescendingly. "I am going to get another drink and check in on Will. Ladies, why don't you introduce yourselves while I'm gone so that I don't have to hear your boring stories again." She strolled across the yard and into the house.

There was Whitney, the woman who brought me the chair. She had run away from an abusive husband and came to L.A. for the sunshine and dreamed of being an actress. She quickly ran out of money and started working at a gentlemen's club. She got into a relationship with a regular customer of hers, and after a year was coerced into performing sexual acts for his friends. Eventually, she tried to get away, however, he caught up with her. Figuring her to be more hassle than she was worth, he sold her to the Hammonds. She worked in other houses before she was moved to this house four years ago. I would be sharing a room with her, as her roommate had departed.

Jessica was an only child from Iowa and had lived on the streets on and off, after running away from, what she called, a very strict household. Given she was mostly homeless, no one would hire her. As a result, she entered into prostitution. After a long night of working, she went home with a man who said she could stay with him. She remembered falling to sleep in an immaculately made bed, but woke up on a soiled mattress in a run-down house. She worked in three houses before she ended up here seven months ago.

Jessica roomed with Reyna, who was from Delaware and the youngest in the house, at the age of 20. A year after her mother got re-married, her stepfather had started to come into her room at night. Disbelieved about what was happening to her, she left and hopped on a bus to Philadelphia. She was alone, desperate and vulnerable. A woman, who she thought she could trust, took her in. It wasn't long until the woman put her to work for the Hammonds. A couple of months later she was flown here by William.

Saria was from Japan and had the most amazing alabaster skin I had ever seen. Unlike the other women, she did not travel here by plane, but in a shipping container, after being kidnapped off the streets of Kagoshima. When the container was opened upon arrival, some men separated her from a group of young girls. She didn't know where the other girls were taken but she had been here for three years.

She roomed with Fay, an Egyptian with dark eyes who had aspirations of making her own American Dream. She replied to a job posting to be a nanny in New York City, but when she arrived at John F. Kennedy International Airport, it was not to the American Dream. A man and a woman, claiming to be her employers, took her passport and Work Visa paperwork. They told her that there was a problem at immigration before her flight landed. They had taken care of it; however, it had cost them a lot of money so she would need to work extra hard to work it off. Not understanding American immigration policies, Fay trusted the people until she was taken to a rickety motel and locked inside a room with nothing but the clothes she had on. They starved her and forced her to work 18 hours a day. A year ago, the man and woman got wind their operation was under investigation and sold all the women to others in the business. Fay ended up somewhere in Colorado, before being brought to L.A. six months ago.

Eloisa was the oldest at 33, with black hair and pale blue eyes. She was married to a porn director and had been in the adult film business in Texas. She had met a couple of William's men at a premiere of one of her films and, at her husband's urging, went out with them a couple of times. One night, she was brought to a derelict house and never let out. That was six years ago. About three years ago she was brought to William's. Eloisa wondered if she could claim to be married, as her husband probably thought she ran off with one of the men.

Eloisa roomed with Lily, who was a makeup artist. She didn't want to share about her past and only said she was brought here at the same time as Jenna.

I got the sense that none of the women actually wanted to be here, but I also felt they were not too worried about ever leaving. Life here appeared to be better than the other places they had been. Maybe it was the fact I had been here less then an hour, but all I could think about was getting enough information to find Claire and getting out of here. If I could get these women out too, so be it, but I was not going to be staying here any longer than I needed to.

It started to rain so we headed into the house. Whitney put her arm through mine and jokingly said "My lady, may I show you to your room?" then whispered, "I'll fill you in on everything you need to know to survive here. Trust me, it isn't easy. Especially with Jenna around."

CHAPTER TWENTY

RATHER THAN GOING UP THE GRAND STAIRCASE AT THE front of the house, Whitney took me up a set of hardwood stairs I hadn't noticed tucked away, like a secret passage, in the corner of the kitchen. The rest of the women went ahead of us, knowing we weren't going to be moving very fast. Walking up to the second floor was slow and painful but Whitney was patient with me. We had to stop a couple of times so I could catch my breath and let my bruised muscles take a break.

Whitney leaned against the railing, "I am sure Mr. Hammond will have the doctor come see you. He likes to make sure we are all healthy and fit for work."

"Well that's nice of him," I grunted, out of breath. "Are we supposed to address him as Mr. Hammond? That's not how he introduced himself."

"Mr. Hammond or William is fine, but never Will. Even though Jenna used it earlier, he hates it and she would never say it in front of him." I was confused and Whitney could tell. "It's one of her little power trips. You'll get used to it and then start to ignore it like the rest of us."

I laughed but it hurt, so we waited a few more moments for the sharp pain to subside before we continued up the stairs. We stopped at an unmarked doorway and I stared up the continuing stairs.

Whitney noticed, "They will take you up to the third floor, however the only time you will be up there is if you are with a guest. There are three guest rooms up there and rooms for Mr. Hammond, Jack, Kevin and Jenna."

"Why is Jenna on the third floor?"

"She is Mr. Hammond's *favourite*," to which Whitney rolled her eyes, "So she gets her own room, which is much nicer than the rest of ours. It has a separate bathroom and a small balcony. Since I have been here, Mr. Hammond has had three 'favourites,' so if you have any interest in ousting Jenna it probably wouldn't take too much," she joked. "In all seriousness, I don't much recommend messing with her. She once beat a girl because Mr. Hammond was starting to take more notice of her. He spends most of his time in his office or out of the house, so you won't see him much outside our nightly meetings."

"Well, I have no interest in favourites. At least not right now," I winked at her with my one good eye.

We stepped out of the stairwell, through a small alcove and onto a lush cream carpet which covered the hallway. I walked over to the railing, looked down and saw the crystal chandelier and marbled floor of the foyer. Large windows across from me, at the top of the 2nd floor landing, let in the bright moonlight. I still couldn't believe the extravagance. Along the U-shaped floor there were seven rooms. Some of them were labeled with the women's names and on others, the door front was empty.

"As you can see, our rooms are labeled. The unmarked rooms are for visitors who aren't necessarily guests here to see us. These could be out-of-town business partners, or Mr. Hammond's brother, Adam, comes by every so often. Watch out for him."

Hearing the name Adam drained the blood from my face and I felt faint. I grabbed the banister and eased myself down to the carpet.

"You look like you just saw a ghost. Are you okay? Do you want me to get you some water?"

"I'm okay. I... Adam is why I look like this. I was really hoping I wouldn't see him again."

"Shit! Well, Adam isn't here often and Mr. Hammond tries to keep him on a short leash. Mr. Hammond is quite protective of us. It seems odd I know, especially based on where you probably just came from. Now let's get you cleaned up and in bed." Whitney helped me up and we walked arm in arm as she filled me in on some of the inner workings of the house.

I learned Saturday nights were the main work night in which a large party was held for prominent customers. However, any of the women could be requested to work outside the house. But only when the customer had established a trustworthy relationship with William and an armed man accompanied her. These outings would likely start after I had been here for a minimum of six months as I, too, would be required to earn William's trust. Additionally, there were security cameras throughout the property and the gate surrounding the entirety of the grounds was electrified. Lastly, Whitney advised there was to be no communication with anyone outside the house, unless I was in the presence of William or his men. No one had phones, the only computer was William's laptop which was usually locked in his office and mail did not come or go from the house.

"Well, this is us."

Whitney opened a door that had already had my name added to it under hers. As I stepped in, Whitney switched on the light and I was presented with a stark white room with minimalist design. There were two double beds along opposite walls, each with a plain night stand with a small lamp and alarm clock. Under the window sat a wood vanity with a slim oval mirror and accompanying bench. Beside the closet was a four-drawer dresser the same colour as the vanity. There was a small en suite with a nice but modest shower. Whitney opened the bottom drawer of the dresser and pulled out a pair of pink striped pajamas. "You get the bottom two drawers. I'm not sure if the clothes will fit you, as you're smaller than Tiffany was. But they will do, for now."

I took the clothes and hugged them to my chest. They smelled of spring air and they were softer than I ever remembered clothes being. "Where is Tiffany now?"

Whitney sat on her bed and started to play with the hem of her shirt. "I don't know for sure, but this place is at the top. You can't get better than here. So, she was either sent down, which is unheard of, or..."

"Or what?"

"Or she is dead."

Sadness covered Whitney's face but she didn't cry. I desperately wanted to hug her, but refrained. Having just met, I wasn't sure if it would be accepted. Whitney quickly pulled herself together. "Why don't I show you how the shower works, it can be finicky sometimes. Then I will find you some food, you look famished."

"Thank you," was all I could muster.

The hot water felt like heaven against my sore body, even with the stinging of some of the cuts. From what I gathered, I had been taken three or four weeks ago, and hadn't had a shower since. I only got out of the shower once my legs started to lose their strength to keep me upright.

I was focused on getting clean and hadn't looked in the mirror. But when I wiped the steam off, I finally saw the damage Adam had done. Purple and black welts covered my body. Some overlapped old yellow bruises. My lip was split and swollen. My hair, although now clean, had thinned out and I had some small bald patches I was thankfully able to hide if I positioned my hair the right way. I barely recognized myself.

CHAPTER TWENTY-ONE

I SAT ON MY NEW BED AND DEVOURED THE CHICKEN sandwich Whitney had made me, sore jaw and all. After I finished the milk, I asked for the date.

"June 21." Whitney had changed into her pajamas, which were the same pant and long sleeve shirt design as mine, however hers were blue plaid. She sat across from me, on her bed, with her arms crossed around her knees.

"So, I have been gone almost a month. I wonder if anyone has noticed?" I said with a small ounce of hope.

"You can't think about that. It only makes staying here even more depressing and it won't help your situation. You won't last long if you sulk about and don't get with the program. I am sure you understand what I mean by that. The quicker you pretend to be happy, the quicker life around here will be a little more bearable."

"You seem to have been here the longest. Is fake happiness how you have survived?"

"That and I keep to myself, mostly. I don't let Jenna get to me and I stay as far away from Mr. Hammond as possible. I make sure that I do my job well so that I 'earn my keep,' so to speak. Otherwise, I keep my head down and recommend you do the same. Mr. Hammond brought you here looking as you do, which is surprising given he can't tell if what you normally look like will make him any money. This can be a good and a bad thing for you. Good, that something about you made Mr. Hammond bring you here. That could mean your safety for a little while. Bad, because Jenna is smart and has probably already picked up on that and she can become very jealous very quickly. She likely won't wait until you've healed to make your life here a living hell."

"Great, more torment. Just what I was hoping for."

"Let her win, grit your teeth and take what she gives - she may eventually back off. However, it will take her a while to get to that point. Also, think positively - would you rather be tormented here with your own bed, good food, and a friend than where you were before? Just remember, it could be worse. A lot worse."

There was something about Whitney that made me feel I might be able to trust her. I was confident she knew everything that went on in this house and perhaps beyond it. I wanted desperately to ask about Claire, but knew I would need Whitney to trust me as well. I did, however, want to know more about William.

I slowly climbed under the covers and looked over at Whitney. "Tell me about William. How did he set up the business?"

"I suppose you'll likely find out eventually. But some advice, don't go asking questions outside of this room. They will get you killed."

I didn't doubt her. To keep an operation like this running there were bound to be actual skeletons.

Whitney continued "From what I have gathered from some of Mr. Hammond's 'favourites,' he and Adam were born here in the USA, however his father, Douglas, came from Great Britain sometime in his adulthood. I am not sure why. His father ran the business until he got sick. When their father was sick, a power struggle ensued between Mr. Hammond and Adam, as both had opposing views on how to run the business. No one officially knows how it came to be Mr. Hammond, the younger of the two, as head of the family. I suspect the decision was made before Douglas passed away."

"When did he die?"

"Sometime before I got here. All I know is, I am glad Adam is not the one running things."

"He was the one who thought I looked good in purple. Did most of this himself."

"Girl, you are lucky you are alive. I know it doesn't take much, but what did you do to him?"

"I may have not been as much of a pushover as he would have liked."

"Wow. You are either crazy or courageous. I'm shocked you're even here. Adam only gives up a grudge when the other person isn't breathing."

"Adam did have a gun to my head in front of everyone at the house I was in. But William stepped in, and here I am."

"Really? I bet Adam didn't like that very much."

"He was furious."

"Did Mr. Hammond tell you why he brought you here?"

"Not really. He rambled on about upsetting Adam and his own general good nature. I didn't have the courage to push for more on a plane where three of the four passengers probably had guns."

"Good call. But it is interesting that Mr. Hammond took such an interest in you."

"Why do you say that?"

"He is very particular about who he has brought here. And he rarely brings them personally. Reyna is the only other one I know of. Plus, in my time here, there have only been two women who hadn't been up to the high standards of this house upon arrival. And you are one of them."

"Who was the other?"

"It's not important. She didn't last long." Whitney said curtly.

I wanted to ask more questions but her tone told me to not push it. So, I went another direction. Self preservation.

"How often does Adam come here?"

"We usually only see him when Mr. Hammond is away for long periods of time and needs help running the household. Thankfully, it isn't very often, as Adam does tend to bruise the merchandise. Which means a loss of profits, so Mr. Hammond will only have Adam step in when he is desperate."

"Why do you call William 'Mr. Hammond' and Adam, 'Adam'?"

"Well, Mr. Hammond treats us all quite well, even if we are trapped here. So, I sorta respect him for it. Adam, on the other hand. Well, you know. He doesn't deserve anyone's respect."

I was growing tired but didn't want the conversation to end. I was learning a lot and I had only been here a few hours. I couldn't stop now.

"Do the guests ever hurt you?"

"Not really. Mr. Hammond is very strict about that. We had a weirdo in here a couple years back that turned out to have a fetish around cutting the women. He tried to cover it up and blamed the women when Mr. Hammond found out, but Mr. Hammond was furious. He said it was unacceptable and made us promise to immediately tell him, or his men, if anyone ever wanted to do anything like that. The guy came back the next week and Mr. Hammond himself gave him a beating in front of us. I heard he intensified background checks on guests after that."

"Who are the guests?"

"Mostly well-off people, or those who hold influential positions that would benefit Mr. Hammond. They want to be entertained and relieve some stress. You will get to know the regulars and what they want. Some like it a little rougher than others, but you don't have anything to worry about. Mr. Hammond makes sure the guests know what happens to them if they get out of hand."

They way Whitney talked so nonchalantly about being forced to have sex with people sent a chill down my spine. I didn't think I could ever get used to that. I also hoped I wouldn't be here long enough to know.

"What is this whole thing between Jenna and Mr. Hammond?"

Whitney chuckled and laid down on her bed. "Jenna and Lily were at a popular dance club one night when Mr. Hammond was entertaining potential investors. I don't know what happened, but a few weeks later, both women are here and Jenna is immediately residing in the 'favourites' room. Jenna likes to lord over us the fact that she just waltzed right in here, the queen of the castle. She won't tell us how she did it, but she doesn't let us forget it."

"What happened to the woman that was in there?"

"Moved to one of the other high-end houses. You can't have a current and past favourite in the same house. Mr. Hammond tried that once and they nearly killed each other during dinner with their steak knives."

"I'm confused. Are William and Jenna in a relationship? How does that work, given the nature of her 'job'?"

"It's not your typical relationship that's for sure. Pretty much, she is his to be with whenever he wants. He doesn't share anything personal or about the business with her, or she would lord that over us too. But he does buy her presents every once in a while. She gets to accompany him outside the house to different events, if he doesn't have another date."

"She gets out of the house? I may have to rethink this whole favourite thing." I was revolted at the thought of being with a man who may be involved in Claire's disappearance, however, having contact with the outside world would be beneficial. I felt like I had a better chance at that than waiting to be allowed to see guests off the property.

"I wouldn't, if I were you. Favourites end up under more scrutiny and heavily guarded when off the property. In my opinion, the only good thing Jenna has going for her is that Mr. Hammond doesn't like to share. Guests only get to be with her if they bid enough money that Mr. Hammond can't refuse."

"What do you mean by bid. You're auctioned off?"

"Pretty much. During the party, we mingle with all of the guests. After an hour or two, usually once they are a few drinks in, they place their bids on their top 3 choices. Mr. Hammond reviews the bids and either approves or declines them. If there are any guests without a girl by the end of the bidding, another round commences for those remaining. Repeat clients get a small discount, which is taken into consideration after the bids are approved. There is a camaraderie amongst the guests so you can sometimes hear negotiations about who is going to bid for who. Mr. Hammond tracks the bids from every party and determines the earning trends for each of us. I think it's so he can see when someone may need to be replaced."

"Wow. I must say, I am a little impressed with the organization of it all."

"You should be, Mr. Hammond runs this place like a legitimate business and takes it very seriously."

"Am I right to guess the clientele includes cops and politicians? There is no way they don't know what is going on here."

"He has some in his pocket, but they don't necessarily attend the parties. Some do, and they are aware if they were to ever turn on him, he could ruin their careers and even their lives with the dirt he has on them. Provided he doesn't decide to kill them."

"Has he killed a guest before?" The more the conversation progressed, the more I grew concerned about William's true nature.

"A few guests have suddenly stopped attending parties and a week or so later their body is found under mysterious circumstances. At the next party, Mr. Hammond will make an announcement offering condolences and thanking the guests present for their loyalty and commitment. Everyone knows what he really means."

"Even with cops in his pocket, people have to be connecting the missing people, are they not? I know it's hard to shut places like this down, but there is no way no one has noticed."

"It wouldn't surprise me, but I would also bet Mr. Hammond has covered up his tracks well, or knows the right people in the right places. When I first got here, one of the girls told me that the entire house had been rapidly relocated from Michigan. Something tells me someone gave Mr. Hammond a heads-up just in time."

"Huh," I made a note to try to find out what happened in Michigan. "You mentioned, and I noticed, all of the cameras. Do they only record video or do they record sound? I am getting the sense Mr. Hammond wants to know every little thing that goes on around the house."

"I have gotten so used to the cameras in all of the rooms, except our sleeping quarters, that I never think about it. But I suspect if there was sound recorded, there wouldn't be a guard outside each of our rooms when we are with guests."

I wasn't sure if my hands were starting to shake with the thought of being recorded with the guests, or if my body was so tired it was shutting down. I hid my hands under the covers, as I wanted to ask one more question now that I knew I might be able to have conversations about Claire without Mr. Hammond knowing.

"Has anyone tried to leave?"

"Attempts have been made, but none were successful. One didn't realize the fence was electric and was electrocuted. Another tried to sneak out with a guest but Jack caught her."

I opened my mouth to ask which of the two men that accompanied William was Jack, but Whitney answered as if she knew what I was going to ask, "He's the taller one. Well, the girl was taken out of the house the next day by Jack and when he returned he had blood on his shirt. At our dinner meeting that night, Mr. Hammond mentioned she wouldn't be coming back and if anyone else decided to try and 'spend more time' with a guest they would join her. You seem like you might be one to try and leave. Don't. It hasn't worked before and it won't work now. Take the next few weeks to heal, get used to the place and the rules. No matter how smart you think you are, Mr. Hammond is smarter. Now let's get some sleep."

She turned off the light and I heard her roll over. I stared at the moonlight that flickered on the ceiling. I didn't doubt William was smart. What I doubted was that he had ever met someone like me.

CHAPTER TWENTY-TWO

I SLEPT BETTER THAN I HAD IN YEARS. I DON'T KNOW IF Whitney put something in the milk, or if it was pure exhaustion, but for the first time my sleep wasn't disturbed by nightmares or worry. I rolled over and saw Whitney was still asleep. I looked at the clock and saw that it was 7:30 a.m. I wasn't sure if anyone would be up this early, but I wasn't told I had to stay in the room until a specific time, so I quietly got out of bed. Trying not to wince too loudly from the pain, I got myself dressed.

As I walked towards the stairs to the kitchen, I noticed a regular wooden door with elevator buttons beside it. The climb down the stairs was going to be hard and I was tempted to use the elevator. I could feign forgetfulness if I got caught, but I decided better of it. I had been here less then 24 hours, I should at least try to not be a nuisance quite yet. I was also really hoping to have time to myself to try and get acquainted with the place and think about my next steps. I didn't want the sound of the elevator waking anyone up, or drawing attention to the fact I was awake. I played it safe and slowly made my way down to the kitchen.

I fumbled around the kitchen as I made myself a tea. Leaning against the counter I watched some birds dancing on the stone railing of the terrace. I wondered what Joe was doing at this moment. Then I realized it was 10:30 a.m. back home and he would be cursing the mountain of paperwork he kept putting off. The thought made me chuckle.

"There's something you don't hear much around here."

The voice startled me and I quickly turned around to find William standing in the doorway.

"Ouch! Fuck!" I grabbed my side, as I had moved too quickly.

"Now, that I hear a lot," William laughed and walked over to the freezer then handed me a bag of peas. "Here, this will help."

"Thank you." I sat at the table and strained to get myself comfortable while positioning the peas on my side.

"You're up early?" William started making himself a coffee.

"Surprisingly I had a good sleep and once I'm awake I can't just lie around. I got restless and I didn't want to disturb Whitney, so I thought I would come down. Should I not be here?" I winced as I started to get up from the chair.

"Sit, sit. It's fine. I am just not used to seeing anyone else this early. Have you eaten?"

"No."

"I will make us some omelets."

"Oh, you don't have to, I can make something."

"You probably shouldn't be on your feet at all and I promise I make a pretty mean omelet."

He wasn't lying, the ham and cheese omelet was delicious. It wasn't until we were both done eating that William spoke again.

"I am truly sorry about my brother. I haven't seen him take out so much anger on anyone since his fiancé canceled the wedding. Awful thing really, poor woman can no longer walk."

I couldn't believe what I was hearing and how nonchalantly William said it.

"The doctor will be here at 11:00 a.m. to look you over and see what we can do to get you healthy. Did the ladies go over the rules?"

"I believe so, but if they missed anything I wouldn't know."

"Touché. For right now the main things you have to worry about are making meeting and meal times, and getting yourself better."

As he cleared my dishes I noticed the start of a scar on the inside of his arm under his shirt.

"The ladies can be pretty mean to newbies but they will come around. I have a good feeling about you."

"You do?"

"Yes, and my gut is rarely wrong. More tea?"

As he was pouring my tea, Jenna walked in and I could feel the calm get sucked out of the room. "I thought I heard someone down here." She walked over to the sink and found the dirty dishes. "What's this? You made breakfast without me?" she whined.

"I make breakfast every morning at 8 o'clock. You know this and if you aren't down here, you don't get any."

Jenna glared at me as she poured some coffee.

"I best get back to work, this place doesn't run itself. Olivia, you should get back to bed and rest. I will have one of the men bring up the doctor once he is here." He walked towards the front of the house before turning around and adding "use the elevator. The stairs are probably making it worse. Once you are healed, however, back to using the stairs. Understood?"

"Yes. Thank you."

I stood up and took a sip of my tea to help hide my smile at the fact Jenna was furious. I took my tea, and the peas, and followed William out of the kitchen. I didn't want to hang around to receive Jenna's wrath. I could hear Jenna mumbling behind me. William helped me into the elevator and as he closed the door I made a mental note to be downstairs for breakfast every morning by 8 a.m.

CHAPTER TWENTY-THREE

DR. BOYDEN WAS EVERYTHING I EXPECTED TO HIM TO BE: middle-aged, balding, wearing glasses, and acting nervous. He was the one doing all the poking and prodding, so I wasn't sure why he was so nervous. Although, the fact that the man I now knew to be Jack was standing inside the doorway, which he barely fit into, watching every move the doctor made, could have been a factor.

When Dr. Boyden's examination reached my vagina, he seemed to take a little extra care. "It's rather swollen and there might be an infection. I'm supposed to put in an IUD, but if you are infected it could end up causing more issues. I will have to wait."

"It's okay. I'm on the shot and just had one," I lied. I did not trust the doctor enough to insert anything that would permanently reside inside of me. Claire had enough complications with her IUD I didn't want to have to deal with that on top of everything else.

"Mr. Hammond has a mandatory condom policy so you should be

safe. Just make sure they wear them. IUDs or your shot do not protect against sexually transmitted infections."

After Dr. Boyden was done he packed up his bag and told me "it doesn't appear anything is broken however the pain from when I touch your ribs is concerning. Without an x-ray, I can't be sure. I also cannot be sure there is no internal bleeding, and, with all of the bruises, I fear the possibility of it."

He looked to Jack, "Tell Mr. Hammond we should get her to the hospital to be sure. I can get her in tonight without anyone noticing, if someone can bring her for 10 p.m. at the Pediatric entrance." He looked back at me. "Here, take these twice a day with food. It is going to be a few weeks until the pain subsides, and these will help." He handed me an unlabeled bottle of white pills.

"What are they?"

"Oxycontin. They are strong, so be careful." He leaned over to whisper in my ear, "Don't let the other girls know you have them, otherwise they may go missing."

Jack coughed, and Dr. Boyden straightened up. "Alright. Well, hopefully I will see you tonight. If not, hopefully you will still be alive in a couple months when I am due back to see everyone."

Jack moved to let Dr. Boyden out of my room and motioned for me to stay where I was. The door remained open, but I could hear the men making their way down the hall. I looked at the pills and thought about flushing them. I could heal without them, plus the more pain I was in, maybe the more pity William and the others would have on me. Whitney walked in as I was rolling the bottle in my hands.

"You better hide those. Lily will be on you like a snake on a mouse."

"Dr. Boyden said the same thing. Well not about Lily. I was going to flush them. I can't take them with my history of addiction, now, can I?" My lie wasn't noticed.

"Are you serious? In your state, I would recommend taking them, but if not, keep them. Drugs are a hot commodity around here and you may need something to get the ladies on your side. Jenna is already talking about how she is getting you out of here as quick as she can." Whitney pulled up a loose floorboard, "we can put them in here." I gave her the pills. "Anything else you see in there doesn't exist, okay." I nodded as I glimpsed letters and other pill bottles.

Whitney continued, "Now what did you do to Jenna to get her on your tail already?"

"Nothing. Well, nothing intentional. I was awake early and William made me breakfast."

"Well, you're fucked. Jenna surely took that as a sign you are trying to weasel yourself close to Mr. Hammond. Stay far away from her and Lily if you can."

Jack came back to the doorway, "Boss says you are going to the hospital tonight. Be at the front door by 9 p.m. Kevin will be the one taking you." Then he was gone again.

"That's crazy, you don't look like you are dying and you get to leave the house on your second day. What did you do, blow Mr. Hammond during breakfast?" Whitney laughed at her own joke, while I sat silent. "God dammit you are one lucky woman, even if you can't see it yet. I give it two weeks after you've healed and you will have Jenna's room to yourself."

I didn't know if I was naive, or if Whitney was, but I wasn't joking when I replied, "You're right, I don't see it. Dr. Boyden was seriously concerned about internal bleeding. I could be dying right now or need surgery. I doubt William is going to pay for me to have surgery, no matter how you think he is treating me. And what about this Kevin guy? What if Jenna has him rough me up or have his way with me? I am definitely not strong enough to fight someone off me right now, and it wouldn't surprise me if Jenna had power over a couple of the guys. She seems manipulative enough." I silently cursed myself for letting my stress and anger get the better of me.

"Kevin wouldn't do that." She started to nervously play with her fingers. "Trust me," she whispered.

"Why would you think that? Have you had to be alone with him?"

"Had to...no. He is a really nice guy, most of them around here are, unless Mr. Hammond tells them otherwise. They just act tough."

"Whitney, I know I am new here, but men in this line of work aren't typically nice guys."

"Kevin is, I promise." She started to blush.

"Are you and Kevin, you know?"

"You can't tell anyone or I swear all of that Oxy will end up in your food." She wasn't joking.

"Okay."

"Swear it." she said sternly.

"I swear."

"Never. No matter what happens." Whitney looked scared and intimidating at the same time.

"No matter what happens," and crossed my heart like I used to when I was a child.

"Good. Now I will go get you some lunch, and likely bring you dinner later. Mr. Hammond said you are exempt from meals and tonight's meeting. Plus, with Jenna on the warpath you are safer up here."

We spent the rest of the day in our room, and I told her Claire's life story as if it was my own. I learned all about Whitney, her family and her dreams of being the next Viola Davis. Her roommate, Tiffany, had been gone for six months and that was when she and Kevin started seeing each other.

"It was innocent enough. He checks on us at the end of the night to make sure we are all in our rooms. We got to talking, and that was all it was for a while. It evolved and he would stay longer and eventually we fell in love."

"Shit, Whitney. Does William know?"

"No, or at least I don't think so, otherwise I don't think Kevin or I would be here. Most nights Kevin does his checks when Mr. Hammond is out or has gone to bed.

"But, there are cameras everywhere. Isn't it possible someone could notice Kevin going into your room and staying there for a while?"

"We are discrete and Mr. Hammond trusts his men to report anything that happens. He doesn't re-watch the nightly video."

"I hope you are right."

Whitney noticed it was getting close to nine o'clock. "We should get you downstairs. It's going to take a while with how slow you are."

"We can take the elevator."

"Bullshit. No one is allowed to take the elevator unless they are with a guest."

"Would I lie to you?"

"Ha! This day keeps getting better. I bet Jenna is on fire. She sprained her ankle once and Mr. Hammond still made her take the stairs. Oh, I wish I saw her face when she found out."

"It was pretty great." I smiled at the recollection of Jenna's expression.

Whitney went to the closet and pulled out a long, sleek black jacket with a hood and helped me into it.

Kevin was waiting in the entryway. Now aware of their relationship, I caught the subtle glances between him and Whitney. To their credit they hid them well and I felt confident no one else would pick up on them. He took me down the hallway towards Mr. Hammond's office and through to the garage where he opened the back door of a simple black Cadillac. He helped me ease into the backseat.

Silence filled the drive to the hospital and Dr. Boyden barely said anything when we got there. He quickly ushered us down hallways, stairways - which required Kevin to carry me - and into the X-ray and MRI rooms. I got shuffled around so much over the hours I was there, I was so disoriented that I didn't know which way was out.

Once the results were ready, Dr. Boyden handed Kevin a folder, patted me on the back which made me wince, "So sorry. Habit of mine. Looks like you are all clear. No bleeding or fractures, just some good ol' bruises. You will be back to work in a few weeks, which I am sure will make Mr. Hammond very happy."

Kevin handed the doctor a white envelope which looked like it was stuffed with cash. Based on my experience back home, I would guess there was at least ten grand, if not more, in it.

The same silence accompanied the ride back to the house. Once inside, Kevin ensured I got to my room with no troubles and without anyone seeing me. Whitney must have been downstairs as our room was empty.

I got into bed and remembered to set an alarm for 7:30 a.m. I didn't think Whitney would mind the minor morning disruption given her dislike for Jenna.

CHAPTER TWENTY-FOUR

OVER THE NEXT THREE WEEKS, I MADE SURE TO BE IN THE kitchen either before or just after William arrived. We ate together and I got to learn more about the business and him. Although he didn't talk much about his father, I found he had a lot of respect for the man and wanted to grow the empire he'd started.

Douglas Hammond started with nothing and through strategic manipulation, blackmail and street smarts he grew a common street brothel into an upscale institution in Michigan. Over the years, the business evolved from guests walking in and having a woman who was available, to pre-booking appointments with the girl of their choice. William transitioned to hosting parties where the guests have the experience of an event. William also created the bidding program which allowed him to decide which woman a guest 'wins'. Usually the decision was based on the bid amount, but, on occasion, he recognized when there was a need to keep the guests coming back. Although customer satisfaction was important, having the same guest keep 'winning' a particular woman others were interested in would alienate customers. I had to hand it to William, he seemed to have thought about everything.

I don't know if William had a little something extra in his morning coffees, or was happy to talk to someone new, but he wasn't shy speaking about the business. He even told me his only real concern was if Adam would fuck everything up, and get the whole thing shut down. Apparently, Adam was reckless with information, and tended to reveal too much if he was drunk or angry. According to William, Adam always felt he knew better, but ended up costing the business more money with his tactics. It was Adam's fault Michigan got shut down. He had said too much to a couple of cops who were not on the payroll, and it turned out they had enough clout that the information wouldn't disappear. William showed his ruthlessness when he told me if Adam hadn't been his brother, he would have been dealt with a long time ago. I knew what that meant.

With William being so open, I tried to test my luck and inquired as to how it came to be that he was chosen to run the business over Adam. "Wouldn't the eldest son be the heir to the empire?"

It turned out Adam was the result of a drunken tryst with one of Douglas' workers when he was starting up the business. Douglas had always suspected the woman had planned everything in order to get pregnant. Even though he admired her tenacity to try and better herself, he also resented that he had to support a child he hadn't wanted. Right up to his death, Douglas didn't take responsibility for his actions that had led to Adam being born, let alone the man he had become.

William was born four years later out of a loving marriage with Margaret, the heiress of a family who owned a large hotel chain. Margaret had an idea about the nature of the business Douglas was running, but hadn't known the women weren't there by choice. After 13 years of marriage she found out the truth, and instantly filed for divorce. She was packing William's things and was about to leave when Douglas walked in. He refused to let her leave and kept her locked in the house. After a year, Margaret smashed the mirror in her bathroom and, before anyone got to her, had slashed her wrists. William rubbed his own scar as he recounted the events.

William was at school when one of her guards found her in the bathtub. Douglas vowed to put all of his energy into the business and William, likely to spite her. William knew something was wrong when his father showed up at his high school. His father had never stepped foot in the school since William had attended it. From that day forward, Douglas focused a lot of his energy on teaching William the business. He sent him to Harvard business and law school where he not only got an education but met valuable contacts. One of William's highest paying guests was a fellow student, who was now a judge in California.

Adam had been sent to a local university and left to find his own way in the business. William recognized that their father's favourtism created a rift between the two brothers and tried to mend it. He included Adam in the business as much as his father would allow. He even brought him along on trips around the world when their father wouldn't be there. Nothing worked, Adam was bitter and resentful to the point that William gave up trying.

Whenever it came up, which thankfully wasn't often, I stuck with making Claire's story my own. William didn't seem very interested and I didn't mind, as I was less likely to reveal too much.

For the most part, I managed to avoid Jenna. She found out I was having breakfast with William every morning, and tried to make a point of getting up. However, one morning she was very irritable after staying up late the night before and William asked her to go back to bed. She hadn't been down since.

A few days later, Jenna made a comment to the women that once I started working I wouldn't be able to keep up the breakfasts so I shouldn't get too comfortable with my time with William. I believed she was saying this out of fear of losing her position. Whitney and I had both noticed William wasn't paying much attention to Jenna and she hadn't been bragging about any nights with him, as she had done when I first arrived. Lily followed Jenna's lead on how I was treated but the other ladies didn't pay me much attention. It didn't look like I would need to trade my Oxy for friendship. At least not right now.

My original goal with attending breakfast was to gain information on the business, which would lead me to Claire, and get me out of here. With Jenna's comment, I was now motivated to create some sort of connection with William. Show her she would be one person who would not win against me. Even though I despised William and everything he stood for I was going to show Jenna that I would be able to maintain the early mornings. I had to, if I was ever going to find Claire. Keep your enemies closer, as they say.

On party nights, I was confined to my room once the guests started arriving. William didn't want anyone to know I was there until I was ready to be revealed. I felt like I was a prized pig waiting for the country fair. I gleaned a lot about how the parties worked from Whitney, and from watching and listening to the activity below through the bedroom window. I saw how the women worked at the party and the guests. The guests were putty in their hands and the women knew it. Any guests who tried to get handsy were quickly put in their place by the many guards around. I counted 10 at the last party in addition to Jack and Kevin.

A typical party started at 10 p.m. However, women started getting ready right after dinner when they wanted to have a bath in the large, pale pink, 5-piece bathroom rather than a shower in their own room. Everyone was expected to be in the yard by 9:30 p.m., where William or one of his men would go over the guest list for the evening. The women would take their place at their respective starting tables. The guests arrived and randomly drew a starting table number. For the first 20 minutes, the woman and guest remained at the table. This is where William encourages the women to build their list of interested guests for the future. After the 20 minutes, William would announce that the bar was open, which was a signal to both the guests and the women that they could leave the tables and mingle with everyone. At 11:45 p.m., William then gives a 15-minute warning that the bar would be closing. The women gathered in a display line on the steps of the terrace, as the guests submitted their bids. Just after midnight, William announced the 'winners' and their room location for the night. The women with the highest bids used the pool houses, and the rest used the guest rooms on the 3rd floor.

After the bids were submitted and final payments made, the women escorted their guest to the appropriate room and one of William's men stood guard for as long as the guest remained. Some guests didn't stay long, and others stayed all night.

The measures William took to protect the women, or as I saw it, keep them captive, made me fear that even if I found out where Claire was, I wouldn't be able to get to her.

CHAPTER TWENTY-FIVE

I KNEW MY RECOVERY TIME WAS COMING TO AN END WHEN, one afternoon, William stopped by the pool where we were all lounging around and announced Karey would be coming by to fit me for some dresses. Reyna's gentle voice informed me Karey was a small Italian woman who had worked for Douglas and was kept on when William took over. She found, or created, all of the outfits the women wore and would stop in every few months to make any alterations or bring new pieces.

"It's about time she was put to work" Jenna mumbled. William gave her a harsh stare and she pretended not to notice as she emptied her wine glass.

"I have also calculated that our numbers are lower, and guest reviews are saying some are getting bored."

Jenna lost her head. "Bored! We do whatever those horny assholes want and they are bored! What do they think this is?"

William gripped the back of the chair he was standing behind and raised his voice ever so slightly. Enough to have an impact, but not enough to be yelling. "They think this is a customer service industry in which they are paying for a service and believe they should be 100% satisfied. Which they are right to expect. It is my job to run the business in a manner which results in their satisfaction, whether any of you like it or not. Don't forget you're here because I say you are and I can make other arrangements for you if you feel the desire to complain. These evening meetings are a courtesy to keep you all informed on what is happening, and allow all of us to contribute to the success of the business. I can easily end them and start treating you like caged animals; locking you in your rooms until you are needed. Is that what you prefer?"

There was a resounding mumble of "No, Mr. Hammond".

"I didn't think so. Now I am feeling generous, so I am going to give the cleaners a paid day off. I expect this whole place to be cleaned. Every inch and no breaks until it is. Equal work will be done by the group and I will be watching to make sure that it is." He looked at Jenna who slumped down in her pool chair. "You too, Olivia. Your only exemption is when Karey is here, but you will get right back to work once she is done."

I nodded in agreement. Like everyone else I was not looking forward to a day of cleaning, but I was satisfied it didn't appear Jenna would be able to use her status to get out of the punishment.

Once William had left, Jenna tried to re-establish her authority. "Alright ladies, here is how we are going to do this. Olivia, you get all of the bathrooms, including the one in my room. Plus, the living room. Don't forget to dust under and behind every book, he will check. Reyna, Saria and Fay you get the guest rooms. Jessica and Eloisa, you get the kitchen and guest houses. Lily and I will take the yard, foyer and Mr. Hammond's room."

None of us looked impressed but we knew better than to say anything.

Jenna looked like she was itching for a fight.

"Well, don't just stand around!"

As the women dispersed I walked past Jenna and desperately wanted to slap her, but kept my hands in my pockets. I knew, even with everything they had drunk so far today, she and Lily would be done within the hour. The terrace would only need to be swept and the tables wiped down. The foyer needed a light dusting and I suspected, based on how orderly Mr. Hammond kept himself and the business, his room was likely immaculate.

We all grabbed some cleaning supplies, and I made my way to the third floor. I figured I should get Jenna's bathroom done first. I would likely feel her wrath if it wasn't done before Karey arrived. I also didn't want to give her the opportunity to stand over me and criticize my work.

I stood outside the door to Jenna's room, staring at it. I suddenly wondered if this was a trap. I wouldn't put it past Jenna, after she told me on my first day to never go into her room. Was Jenna waiting to pounce when I stepped inside? I looked over the balcony railing and saw Jenna in the foyer lazily dusting a painting, and she didn't appear to be paying any attention to me. I figured I was safe but would clean as quickly as I could.

I opened the door and stepped into a very large, pink room which looked like a Disney princess should reside in it. There was a white four poster bed with a canopy top and matching nightstands on either side. A larger vanity than Whitney and I shared was on one wall, and by the balcony doors sat a desk. There was a puffy pink lounge chair in the corner.

The bathroom was enormous with white marble floors and countertops. The pink walls from the bedroom had not seeped into the bathroom, however, the curtains hanging from the arch window over the jacuzzi tub were pink and so were all of the towels. A crystal chandelier hung in the middle of the room that I did not look forward to dusting it. There was also a steam shower big enough to fit four people.

Both the bedroom and the bathroom were a disaster. Jenna had magazines, clothes, towels and make-up strewn everywhere. I suspected Jenna did not entertain guests in her room. I put on some rubber gloves and got to work. I made my way from left to right around the room, which took me over an hour. I scrubbed every surface and removed Jenna's hair from all of the drains. I suspected she would meticulously inspect every inch so I got down and cleaned behind the toilet bowl. It made me laugh to think about Jenna crouched down beside the toilet with a white glove to look over my work.

When I finished, I took one last look around Jenna's room and wondered if Claire had ever seen it. I quietly closed the door behind me, and started on the guest room bathrooms. When I got to the second one, my body started to tell me I wasn't 100% healed. I was thankful there weren't any cameras in the bathrooms, as I was able to rest a bit. As I leaned against the counter, I overheard Saria and Fay talking about how they were tired of Jenna's attitude.

"I wish she would just put a sock in it sometimes." Saria complained, "She keeps getting us into trouble, and I am worried we will be the ones to go and not her." I peeked my head out the bathroom door, and saw Saria hand Reyna the soiled bedding to be added to the pile to be washed in the hallway.

"She needs to spend some time with Mr. W. - he sure loves to gag a girl." Fay replied and they both laughed.

I figured they knew I was there, as I hadn't exactly been quiet, so I stepped out of the en suite to move on to the next.

"Hey Olivia, sorry you got bathroom duty AND the living room." said Reyna.

"Thanks. It's no big deal. No cameras in the bathrooms, so who knows what I am really doing in there." I winked. I suddenly realized what I said and hoped they wouldn't repeat it back to Jenna.

"Huh, I never thought of it that way. Man, I am volunteering for bathroom duty next time," Saria said and all four of us laughed. I was confident my slip-up would be safe.

Karey arrived just as I was finishing up the bathrooms in the guest houses. Jack came out to get me, and, as we walked through the kitchen, I could feel invisible knives being thrown at me by Jenna and Lily. Even though William had said no breaks, Jenna appeared to think that rule did not apply to her as they were taking a wine break as Jessica and Eloisa cleaned around them. Jack took me to a room I hadn't seen before off the hallway to the garage. I placed my cleaning supplies outside the door. The room looked like a very nice locker room with dark wood stalls each filled with dresses organized by colour. In the middle there was an island with drawers that I guessed were filled with the accessories I saw the women wear. I felt like I was in a private department store.

Karey was waiting when we arrived. She was small in stature, as Reyna had said, but her personality and outfit were big. She had on a bright yellow pant suit with large white polka dots. She could see I was impressed. "You think this is nice, come look at the shoe closet."

I was never one for owning more than 3 pairs of shoes but I could not believe the number and beauty of the shoes in this large closet within a closet.

"I will say one thing about Mr. Hammond, he sure does get the best stuff for you ladies. Now, take off all of your clothes and step up over here." She pointed to the platform with the three-piece mirror.

"Are there cameras in here?"

"Yes, dear, there are. There are a lot of valuable pieces in here."

I hadn't felt as though I was being watched since I entered the house but I started to tremble at the thought of William and his guards watching this moment. I tried to keep it together, but Karey noticed my hands shaking, "Let me help with that shall I?" She gently helped remove my t-shirt.

"You better get used to people seeing you naked. With your face and those hips, I predict you are going to be one hot commodity around here. You look to be a good investment if I do say so myself. Now, let's measure you up and see if there is anything in here that will fit."

I spent the next hour trying on dresses and being poked with pins. By the time we were done, she had a handful of clothes to alter. I thanked her for her help and grabbed my cleaning supplies as she closed and locked the door. She saw me watch her.

"Only Mr. Hammond and I have a key." She swiftly walked down the hallway to the foyer and out the front door.

I made my way to the main floor bathrooms. After being in a room naked in front of cameras, I longed for the imagined safety of the bathroom. I stopped in front of William's office door. I wasn't sure if he had a bathroom connected to it, although I would presume he did. I also wasn't sure if I was supposed to clean it. I was weighing the options of knocking on the door and the wrath that could come with it, or not cleaning it and the wrath that could come with that, when Kevin came up the hall from the garage and saw me pacing.

"You know he can see anyone out front of the office, right?" he pointed to a camera on the ceiling pointed directly at the door.

"What, oh crap. Well, I...um...I am on bathroom duty and I wasn't sure if there was one in there."

"And you thought pacing out here would get it cleaned?" he joked, which made me smile. "I will check with him, wait here."

He went into the office and opened the door a moment later, "Come on in, but be quick about it."

The office was very spacious and housed a large wooden desk facing the door, which William sat at, with his nose buried in his computer. He took very little notice of me. There was a blue couch, a couple of chairs and a gold roll-away bar. Behind the desk, where one would expect a window, was floor-to-ceiling double wooden doors. Although they matched the desk, they didn't fit the room, and I couldn't figure out why they were there. I walked quickly into the bathroom and saw there wasn't much for me to clean. I quickly wiped down all of the surfaces and gave the toilet a clean, the floor a sweep and stepped back into the office.

Kevin was on the couch reading a newspaper. I noticed the date said July 18, 2018. Mr. Hammond was still working on his computer. "How is the cleaning going?"

"I can only speak for myself, but I am getting there." I didn't want to tell him that the work put me at a seven out of ten on the pain scale.

"Good. If you learn anything from Jenna, I hope it is to never question me. You ladies got off light today, but if another toe is put out of line I am not going to be so nice."

I opened my mouth to say something but thought better of it. William noticed, "What is it?"

I looked at the floor. William stopped typing and came around to the front of the desk and leaned against it.

"You obviously wanted to say something, so what is it?"

"I believe it would be questioning you, and you just said not to do that."

William looked at me curiously and smiled.

"I will give you a free pass this time, no repercussions. What is it you wanted to say?"

"If Jenna questions you, and seems to be disliked by most of the women, why is she here? Does the money she brings in outweigh the happiness of your employees?" I could feel my stubbornness taking over and for some reason couldn't stop myself from continuing. "I mean if guests aren't returning, is it relational to the ladies' happiness and willingness to perform? Or is there a common denominator among who the guests spend time with?"

William held up his hand for me to stop. "I give you a free pass, and you sure use it."

He looked to Kevin who smirked, and raised the newspaper to hide his face.

"I'm sorry."

"Don't be. You took advantage of an opportunity provided to you. If you do that working for me, you will be quite successful. Now, to answer your questions. I have noticed the tension and unease Jenna creates among all of you, and should she deserve a comeuppance she will get it, however, say she was to leave, would someone else not try to fill her shoes and thus land us in the same boat?"

From the weeks of breakfast conversations, I'd learned that when William ended on a question he was inviting an opinion, so I responded, "Possibly, but isn't it also possible, if you made it clear to everyone they were all equal and any attempt to exercise power over another would not be tolerated, there could be harmony? Provided you haven't tried that already, of course."

William was silent for a moment "I have learned most people will try and find power even when there doesn't appear to be any readily available."

"You seem to have built an empire on your ability to manipulate people's behaviour. How would this be any different? It could increase your bottom line."

William stood up, and the look on his face signaled I had crossed a line. Even Kevin peered over his newspaper.

"You seem to think you know a lot about my business."

"No... not really," I stuttered, but quickly recovered my conviction. "I just know business in general and I know people." My business knowledge was limited to what Claire told me about how she handled her deals, or got the board to give her what she wanted. I was flying by the seat of my pants and realized I needed to get out of here before I gave myself away. "I'm sorry. I overstepped. I should really get back to the cleaning. The living room still needs to be done and I expect that will take me a couple of hours."

"Yes, you should." He said sharply and walked back around the desk. As I opened the door he addressed me sternly, "tell no one of our conversation." Then his voice became softer, "See you at breakfast tomorrow," and he went back to whatever he had been doing on his computer.

I closed the door, unsure what just happened. I seemed to have upset William and yet he wanted to see me at breakfast tomorrow. I stood there trying to put the pieces together when I heard Jenna yell, "No breaks!" Startled, I looked up and saw her leaning on her broom in the foyer. I walked quickly towards the living room and Jenna followed me.

"Were you just in Will's office?"

"I had to clean the bathroom." I stepped around her and started to clean the end tables.

"What did you two talk about?"

"Nothing. I just cleaned."

"You're lying to me. I can tell."

I stopped and looked at her, "I am not lying. Now please leave me alone as I have a lot of work to do in here." I started to puff up the couch pillows.

"I am not leaving until you tell me what you talked about." She started pulling books off the bookshelf and tossing them on the floor.

I was starting to get more frustrated with every book that hit the ground. I was going to have to pick them all up and knew she was acting out of spite. I tossed a pillow onto the couch, "Okay, fine, I will tell you what we talked about." Jenna looked satisfied.

"Sunshine, pixies and unicorns. Oh, and our big evil plan to take over the world."

The look of satisfaction quickly evaporated and she lunged at me. I stepped out of the way causing her to land on the floor. She quickly got up and came at me again. I climbed over the couch and headed toward the foyer, but she caught my foot and I landed face-first on the marble floor. Jenna kicked my side, right where a bruise had been, and I screamed loudly. I was now at a nine on the pain scale. She turned me over and sat on my stomach. I punched her sides as hard as I could and tried to roll her off of me like I had been taught in the academy but even the adrenaline was not giving me the strength I needed. Jenna could tell I was struggling and raised her fist. I could see her eyes telling me she wanted me dead and wasn't afraid to do it herself.

A booming voice filled the house, "STOP!"

We froze. Jenna's fist still in the air.

William stood over both of us.

Jack came over and pulled Jenna off me, holding her arms tightly behind her back. Kevin helped me up slowly but held my hands loosely behind my back and whispered "Say nothing."

Lily was in the archway to the kitchen, while the rest of the women were now standing at the railings of the second and third floors with terrified faces.

William's voice bellowed again "WHAT IS GOING ON HERE?"

Jenna answered with an air of superiority. "She started it, she provoked me. I told you she was bad news."

"IS THAT RIGHT? YET YOU WERE ON TOP OF HER?" William walked towards Jenna and Jack until the space between them disappeared. He lowered his voice slightly but the fear it instilled got worse. "And how did she provoke you?"

"Well...She...uh..."

"GET IT OUT, GIRL!"

"I know she is trying to get rid of me," she started to sob. "And when I saw her coming out of your office... well I knew she had to have been talking about me. Please, I love you."

The women gasped. I doubted many, if any, said 'I love you' in this house. Especially with William.

"Did she tell you that we were talking about you?"

Jenna looked at me and must have hedged her bets when she confidently replied "Yes," tears streaming down her face.

William looked over at me and started in my direction. Kevin tightened his grip just as Jenna smiled at me as if she had won. William walked over and stopped in front of me, locked his eyes on mine and didn't speak. I wanted to plead my case, but heeded Kevin's words, kept my mouth shut and maintained eye contact. Something told me if I looked away he would take that as a signal of guilt. The atmosphere was so tense it was as though everyone had stopped breathing.

Finally, William spoke while keeping his eyes locked on mine "And what did Olivia tell you?"

"Uh, something about how I treat the other woman." My stomach dropped but my gaze did not. I had to hand it to her, she chose something which had a high probability of being true.

"What EXACTLY did she tell you? Her exact words now, Jenna?"

"I can't remember her exact words. I lost my cool after she

mentioned..."

"ENOUGH!" he finally released his gaze and turned his back to me. "Jack, release Jenna and stand over there." I suddenly felt as though I was going to be sick. "Jenna, don't move." As he turned to face me I saw another look of triumph cover her face as she massaged her wrists. Jack went and stood by Lily.

William once again locked his stern eyes to mine, and I could see the same evil that had resided in Adam's. He pulled out a gun from somewhere inside his jacket and cocked it. "I believe her exact words were '*Sunshine, pixies and unicorns. Oh, and our big evil plan to take over the world.*'" Then a gunshot rang out, the noise ricocheting off the tall walls of the foyer.

I was frozen and in shock. I couldn't even feel the wound from the bullet. Kevin released my wrists and I realized William's back was to me. I could see an arm on the floor past William. He stepped towards the middle of the room and that is when I saw Jenna, a bullet hole in her head and blood slowly spreading around her.

CHAPTER TWENTY-SIX

I RAN TO THE CLOSEST BATHROOM AND MADE IT TO THE toilet just in time. I could hear the same sound throughout the house. In the seven years as a police officer I had developed a tough skin when it came to the sight of a dead body. However, today was different. Today, I was almost the body.

I was leaning against the sink when Lily rushed in and flung herself over the toilet. I reached over and held her hair back as she went for round two. She fell back against the wall and started to cry. I went over to console her but her glare told me to stay away. I pulled myself together as best I could and went back to finish cleaning the living room. I knew we wouldn't be given much time to compose ourselves. I now also knew that William could hear our conversations. At least in the common areas. I doubted our rooms were bugged otherwise Whitney and Kevin would have been in trouble by now.

When I walked back to the living room, Jenna was still lying on the marble floor, completely surrounded by a pool of blood, with her eyes staring at the chandelier. I stopped, bent down and closed her eyes. I looked over and saw everyone but Lily was cleaning their way around the living room. I could have cried, and I felt a sense of togetherness I had so far only felt with Whitney.

We worked in silence for the next hour. No expressions on our faces. Our bodies moved like zombies around the room. As I put the books back onto the bookshelf, a couple of men I hadn't seen before came and took Jenna's body, while a couple more cleaned up the blood.

After we were done with the living room, we went to the kitchen and found Lily sitting at the table with a half-empty bottle of whiskey. We each took a swig in honour of Jenna and went upstairs to get ready for the evening. None of us had an appetite. Lily stayed in the kitchen, clinging to the bottle.

There was no fighting over who got the bathtub first or who was taking too long. Everything went smoothly and in silence. My nerves had already been heightened, with it being my first night working, but were now even more so, as like everyone else, I was terrified about what else could happen.

William had zero hesitation when it came to killing Jenna. Zero. And she was supposed to be his 'favourite'. If that was how he treated the favourite, what were the rest of us in for? I decided I was going to keep my head down tonight and try to get through it without William taking much notice. I then remembered what 'getting through it' would mean. I shuddered and told myself I would just have to push through and pretend I enjoyed what I was doing. If I didn't, I could end up like Jenna and never find Claire.

I gripped the door frame to my room, as I felt the blood drain from my face. I thought I might faint.

"You don't look so good," Whitney said, and she helped me to my bed.

"I don't know how I am going to do this?" My hands had started to shake. I wished I had some undercover work under my belt to help me through this.

She calmly, but sternly, replied, "You are going to go out there, pretend you actually care about these rich perverts, close your mind off, and get through what is hopefully only a couple of hours." Whitney went back to her bed and slipped into a silver dress that had been laid out for her. It fell perfectly against her curves. I was amazed how one piece of clothing could transform a person.

"How are you so calm after what happened?" My training from the academy, and the adrenaline, had gotten me through the rest of the cleaning, but I started to feel like my plan wasn't going to work. My chest tightened.

"It's called acting, and it's what you have to do tonight. If I let myself break down over what happened to Jenna, or any of the horrible things that have happened since I was taken, I would be dead. To stay alive, I bury the anger, the hurt, and the fear. They won't help me here." Whitney went into the bathroom and started to put on her makeup.

"I don't know Whitney, to have these people touching me . . ." A shiver went down my spine.

"Don't think about it. They will sense you are nervous and they will prey on that. They are already going to be excited that there is new blood. When it comes to actually having sex with a guest, I don't know what will work for you to get through, but whatever you do, don't just lie there. You need to be actively involved if you don't want to get in trouble."

"But how? My skin is already crawling at the thought."

"I pretend it is someone I actually want to be with. Then I try to get them off as quickly as possible." Whitney walked back out of the bathroom and turned her back to me. I zipped up her dress.

I grabbed the basic black, strapless dress that had been laid out on my bed. After I silently cursed myself for my display of weakness, I prayed I would not draw too much attention to myself. Whitney was right, I was going to be a new fish in a tank of sharks. That would bring with it enough attention. I was thankful the dress wasn't flashy, as I wanted to look as commonplace as possible.

Whitney was gracious enough to do my makeup. I had been practicing, however, I had never been one to wear makeup and I still could not figure out how to get the eyeliner to go on straight. I was baffled by how much blush was too much, or too little for that matter. As I stood in front of the mirror I told myself to "be strong" and "survive one more day." At least I still had a day to make it through.

CHAPTER TWENTY-SEVEN

AS WE GATHERED AROUND THE KITCHEN TABLE FOR THE pre-party meeting, it was evident Lily had only moved to get another bottle of whiskey. She was holding a 3/4 full bottle, and an empty one sat beside her. Reyna tried to talk to her, but nearly received a black eye for her efforts. I looked at the women and each one had a somber look painted on their faces. Although Lily was the only one who liked Jenna, we wouldn't wish her dead. It was going to be a tough night for everyone.

William walked in, wearing a dark suit with a red tie and a smile on his face. It was a little unnerving, given the events of the day. But, then I reminded myself, I am surrounded by the inappropriate, so why would William's mood be any different?

He stood at the head of the table, "Ladies, I understand tonight may be a little more tense than usual, but you all have a job to do and the incident today will not hinder your performances. My expectations have not changed and I expect you to show the guests an exceptional night.

If anyone asks where Jenna is, you simply state that she has moved on. Nothing more. Understand?"

We all nodded; everyone but Lily. She staggered up out of her seat, leaning on the table to keep herself steady. "Mmmoved on is one way to ppput it" she stammered and took another swig of whiskey. "She was nothing but loyal to you and...and you killed her! What does that mean for the rest of us?" She motioned to us with the hand holding the bottle of whiskey, some of the contents spilled over the table and down her arm.

William's smile faded as he stared down Lily. He motioned for Jack to bring her to him. She wrestled the whole way while still holding onto the whiskey bottle. William pulled the bottle from her grip and threw it against the wall. "You forget," he whispered just loud enough for us to hear. "Your loyalty is a requirement to stay in this house, not a privilege that I get to receive. You have 20 minutes to pull yourself together, or you will be moving on just as your friend did."

Lily stared defiantly at William. I looked around the room and everyone was stone- faced. Some were gripping the arms of their chairs, others the table. We all held our breath until Lily pulled her arm out of Jack's grasp and stomped loudly up the stairs.

William waited until Lily had slammed the door when she got to the second-floor doorway of the stairwell and then continued, "Anyone else have anything they would like to say? No. Good. Now, Olivia, as this is your first night why don't you stick with Reyna until I tell you which guest you will be with. She can show you the ropes. But, I expect you to be on your own for the next party. Okay let's go make some money."

The smile returned to William's face and I wondered if it was real, or if, like the rest of us, he was trying to just make it through the night.

CHAPTER TWENTY-EIGHT

THE GUESTS STARTED ARRIVING IN THE BACKYARD, THROUGH the arched gateway beside the house, promptly at 10 o'clock. By then, the alcohol I had been drinking rapidly had started to numb my nerves. I stood at a table with Reyna gripping my wine glass tightly. I looked around the yard and all of the women had replaced their grim faces with expressions of excitement and joy. I tried to mimic them but was confident I wasn't doing it well.

Reyna familiarized me with every guest who entered the gate, their profession and the name they used. The guests were Mr. or Mrs. A through Z. The letter didn't necessarily correlate to the first letter of their actual last name. They weren't supposed to tell you their real names, but after a few drinks people can slip up. Other times, the guests were famous enough that everyone knew who they were, so there was no need to try and hide it.

Tonight, we had a Senator, a city councilor, a couple actors, but most were influential businessmen. As each one entered the party, it was as if they could sense there was someone new. They all paused and looked around the tables with a curious smile while they were being welcomed by William. Each one stopped and stared when they got to me. The first couple of times, I took a large gulp of my wine, before I realized I was signaling weakness. After that, I mustered up a small smile and turned to Reyna to ask questions about the guests. The only good that was going to come out of this night would be the knowledge, and I was going to get as much of it as I could.

With drinks in hand, the guests made their way around to their assigned tables, each stopping quickly to say hi to Reyna and I as they passed. I took my cues from Reyna and tried to flirt as best I could, but I knew I was rubbish. A couple of the men appeared to find that endearing and put a hand on my arm, told me not to try so hard and gave a small chuckle as they went to the next table. I felt I was participating in a round of speed dating, however, unlike the real thing, I would not have a choice in what happened in the end.

Reyna seemed to be a natural. She could turn the switch from the real her to the working her with a blink of an eye. As I watched her, I told myself to never flip the switch. The day I started to do that, was the day I would forget who I was and why I was here - Claire.

"Ouch!" a hard jab in my ribs brought me back to the present. Reyna and two tall, well-built men with dark hair were looking at me. There was an age difference in the men and their appearance made me wonder if they were related.

"Were you visiting anywhere good?" the older one asked.

"I uh, not really. I'm sorry."

"Don't be sorry, dreaming is an activity the mind has no control over. I believe it is God's way of speaking to you. What was he saying?"

"Father, I am sure she doesn't want to talk about it," the younger and taller man seemed annoyed. "You are new here, aren't you? I haven't seen you before." He brought his glass to his lips and I thought I heard him mumble "I like new". Something about him made me feel uneasy.

I quickly answered "Yes, I am new," and turned to his father. "I'm Olivia." I held out my hand. He took it and kissed the top of it.

"Mr. Z. Pleasure to meet you."

"If it was God speaking, I believe He was telling me not to give up. Keep searching and I will find what I am looking for."

Mr. Z. Smiled, "Very insightful, and what are you looking for?"

"Father enough with the theological bullshit. No one cares. I am Mr. Y," and he grabbed my hand from his father, squeezing it aggressively.

The next 20 minutes were spent listening to Mr. Y talk about himself. His luxury car relocation business and his love of spending time at the gun range. Finally, William advised the bar was open. Mr. Y swallowed the last of his drink, put the glass on the table and as he walked behind me whispered, "I will show you what you are looking for."

Reyna and I decided it would be easiest to stay at our table. Over the next hour and 45 minutes, I flirted with every guest as best I could. All were eager to meet the new girl.

Promptly at 11:45 p.m., William announced the bar would be closing in 15 minutes. I hadn't noticed it when I had watched the parties from the window, but everyone pulled out their phone and were using an app to submit their bids. That meant there was a data trail somewhere. If William used an app for this part of his business, there was a data source somewhere for other aspects of the business. But how was I going to get access to it without a computer or phone of my own? I needed to try to get a letter to Joe and soon.

Reyna and I went to the terrace steps and she took my hand with a look of worry. "If Mr. Y wins you, I am sorry." A waiter came by and gave us all a glass of champagne. I drank it quickly and gave the glass back to the waiter.

William gained the crowd's attention and started to announce the winning bids.

"Lily - Mr. C and you are in pool house four.

Eloisa - Mr. And Mrs. J. and you are in pool house one.

Whitney - Mr. O and you will enjoy room seven."

William continued to announce the winning clients, who came up and joyfully claimed their prize. Although the women had smiles painted on their faces, their eyes made me feel as though they were being led to the slaughter. Even if life in this place was better than the decrepit places they came from, unwanted hands were going to be touching them.

When Reyna and I remained, she took my hand, as William called out my name.

"Olivia - Mr. Y and you are in pool house six." My heart dropped into my stomach. Of course, he won. Why wouldn't I have been so 'lucky' to be forced to be with someone who made the hair on my arms stand on end?

Reyna squeezed my hand "Just do what he wants, don't fight him; otherwise it will be worse."

By that point, Mr. Y was standing in front of me with a vile smirk across his face. He held out his hand. As I put my hand in his, I willed myself to stop shaking. He pulled me aggressively forward, so much so I almost fell into him.

"This is going to be fun. Well at least for one of us."

After I was in the pool house, Mr. Y turned to close the door and stretched his arm out to the guard out front. I couldn't see what they were doing but the guard nodded and then turned his back to the door. Mr. Y closed the door, turned back around to me and I don't know if it's possible for someone's eyes to actually turn red, but I swear I saw the devil lurking.

CHAPTER TWENTY-NINE

ON THE GRAND TOUR WITH WHITNEY I SAW THE POOL houses were specially designed to be luxurious bedrooms rather than guest houses per se. Designed to accommodate almost any fantasy, each had a king size bed with silk linens. There was a bedside table full of different sex toys. A leather couch and recliner were set up at the front of the rooms.

Where I was, in pool house six, the walls were a deep red and there were silver curtains covering the entire windowed front of the house. There was a fully-stocked bar and I was able to down a glass of whiskey while Mr. Y was in the four-piece bathroom.

Mr. Y came out and stood beside the bed. "Come here!" he commanded.

I tried to confidently walk over to him but all the alcohol was impacting my ability to walk straight. He gripped my wrist and pulled me close to him while his other hand tightly took hold of my throat. "I like to break in the new ones."

We stayed like that for a moment and then he let go of my throat. "Undress me."

I fumbled with his tie until he got frustrated and removed it himself. "Useless!" He slapped me so hard his ring split open my lip.

"Do you think you can remove your dress or do I need to tear it off of you?"

I slowly unzipped my dress as he quickly removed his own clothes. He was in front of me when my dress hit the floor. He pushed me onto my knees. I hadn't expected it so I grabbed his legs for support. He pulled my hair back, "open your mouth". I did what I was told and the rest of the night was a blur. It felt like I had just woken up from a dream where some parts could be recalled vividly while others were faint or not there at all.

Once Mr. Y was satisfied orally he sat in the chair staring at me while I was hunched on the floor. I didn't move. The next thing I remember is the sound of a condom wrapper and being lifted off the floor by a strong grip on my arms and being tossed onto the bed. Mr. Y climbed on top of me with an evil look in his eye that matched the grin on his face. I wanted to fight back but I kept hearing Reyna say it would be worse if I didn't let him have his way with me. I saw a vision of Adam sitting on the couch watching with gratification at what was being done to me.

Mr. Y must have noticed I zoned out and flung me onto my stomach and then punched my head. I couldn't help but yell loudly and reach for the back of my head. He yanked my hand away and pinned it down at an angle that made my shoulder scream in pain. I resisted reacting. I slipped up the first time but I wasn't going to show him how much he was hurting me. He pulled my hair and I arched backwards so that my head practically touched the middle of my back. He thrust into me so hard that it felt as though I had been punched. This is where my mind blocked out the rest. I laid there and felt the odd punch or thrust otherwise my mind was closed off. I heard and saw very little.

When I came to, I was on the bed on my stomach with my legs spread apart and my hands tied tightly behind my back. I was surprised Mr. Y hadn't opened the curtains to put his work on display. Then I realized the guests want to keep what they do within these walls as secret as possible. It's just between them and William.

As my mind started to piece together the evening, the sound of whistling from the bathroom alerted me to the fact I wasn't alone. I didn't move and willed Mr. Y to ignore me and leave me as I was. He sat in front of me, fully dressed and smiling. As he fixed his tie he said "I can't wait until next time. The things I have in store for you." He laughed maniacally and I watched him leave. I didn't move. I was afraid any noise would bring him back.

There was no clock in the room but specks of sunlight peered through the cracks in the curtains. I had been with Mr. Y for at least five and half hours and yet I barely recalled any of it. Eventually, I rolled over onto my back and got my arms under my ass and over my legs so that my arms were in front of me. I was sore everywhere and I mean everywhere. My hands, my scalp, I could barely feel my cheeks not to mention the burning sensation from what I surmised was very rigorous penetration.

I slowly made my way to the bathroom, but before I went through the door I looked into the camera on the wall. How was it that no one stopped Mr. Y? I thought William was supposed to be protecting us at all times? Or was that just something he wanted us to think? Was he mad at me about Jenna so he decided to have me punished in another way?

Mr. Y had left the bathroom a mess but I couldn't have cared less. I looked in the mirror and started to cry. My face was already starting to bruise, my hair looked as though I had gone through a wind storm. Looking at my neck I could see Mr. Y's hand firmly imprinted. I looked down and saw small scrapes all over my thighs. I sat down on the side of the tub and turned on the water, "How am I going to do this?" I cried to myself. "I am not strong enough for this." I tried to wipe away my tears, but my cheekbones hurt when I touched them, so I just let the tears fall down my face. "Is my new reality to constantly look like a punching bag?"

I climbed into the hot water and immersed myself and my face until I needed to breathe.

"Claire, how did you do this? I am so sorry, but I am not going to be able to find you if this is what I have to go through."

I don't know how long I was in the water, but my fingers and toes were shriveled and looked like prunes by the time I scrubbed off as much of Mr. Y as possible. I sat in the tub until the last drop of water went down the drain. I was unsure what I was going to do next. Was it time to ask the ladies about Claire? If the other guests were like Mr. Y it wouldn't be long until I fought back. When that happened, William would undoubtedly make an example of me, just like Jenna. Claire has been gone for three months now and I need to act quickly to find her.

Standing, once again, in front of the mirror with a soft towel wrapped around me I looked into my eyes. I looked past the bruises and envisioned the woman I was a couple of months ago. The woman who stood her ground. Stood up for herself and for Claire. I *can* do this. I *will* do this.

I put my dress back on and carried my shoes through the sunlit yard. I used the stairs in the kitchen to get to the second floor. I was thankful I didn't see or hear anyone. I put my ear to the door of my room and heard nothing, so I slowly turned the handle and entered. Whitney was asleep in her bed. I quietly put my shoes at the end of my bed and I climbed into bed without taking off the dress.

I laid awake for a while, listening to the sounds of the house. Floorboards creaked, doors opened and closed and whispers trickled under the bedroom door as the ladies said goodbye to their guests. After an hour, I decided, with the events of yesterday, I wasn't going to get any sleep. I put on my bathrobe and decided I would go to the kitchen and find something hard to drink.

I needed something to help me forget, but I didn't want the Oxy. I needed to forget Jenna. Forget Mr. Y. Forget my failures as a sister.

CHAPTER THIRTY

I MADE MY WAY DOWN THE BACK STAIRS TO THE KITCHEN and noticed there was a light on. I stopped just before entering the room. What if there is a guest in there? I don't want them to see me like this. I was about to turn around and head back upstairs when I heard the fridge close. It was unlikely a guest would be courageous enough to eat William's food - or at least get it themselves. I decided whoever was in the kitchen would either not pay much attention to me, or would see me eventually. I took the last remaining steps and was confronted by William seated in the living area on the other side of the room. He hadn't seen me yet.

I walked over to the liquor cabinet and grabbed the first bottle I saw, found a glass and poured a large drink.

"Mr. Y was very impressed with you. I think you established your first repeat guest. Good job."

I downed my drink as I continued to hide behind the door of the liquor cabinet and filled my glass.

"I know he can be a bit rough but you'll get used to it."

All of my anger boiled over, "Used to it! That man is a monster and you want me to get used to it! You said you would protect us and yet look at me. What kind of protection did I get last night?" I slammed the cabinet door shut.

William's face was covered with concern. He jumped out of his chair and briskly walked over to me. He reached for my face and I flinched before he took my chin in his hand. As he moved my face around in the light I could smell he had also partaken in quite a few of his own glasses of whiskey. He released my chin and stepped back.

"I told him to be gentle with you and to stay away from your face. You are already starting to bruise." He punched the door of the liquor cabinet and walked to the island and took a seat. I looked and saw a fist-sized hole beside where my head had been. I didn't move.

"What does the rest of you look like?"

"About the same."

"For fuck sakes!" William threw his chair across the room. "If he thinks he can get away with this..." he trailed off. I was not sure I was allowed to leave, and I didn't want to remain standing, so I joined William and sat on one of the island stools.

"I don't understand. He knows it's $10,000 a bruise and by the looks of you, this is going to cost him a lot."

I couldn't help but laugh. William was not impressed.

"What's so funny?"

"$10,000 a bruise. #1 - How did you come up with that value? #2 - How do you enforce that? And #3 - Aren't most of the clientele filthy rich? What is $10,000 compared to feeling powerful beating the shit out of one of us?" I knew as soon as the last words left my mouth I shouldn't have said anything.

"Are you once again questioning how I run my business? I have been doing this for seven years and have rarely had any problems. I had Mr. Y under control. He hasn't hurt anyone like this before. And I do protect my girls. You should have had a guard with you."

"There was one outside the door. Or at least there was when I entered the room, but Mr. Y gave him something. I don't know what it was, but not once did he come to help me. There was enough noise to at least warrant a check-in. So, who was he protecting? And what about the camera - does no one monitor them? Or are they just for show?"

"Are you insinuating Mr. Y paid my men off?"

"You tell me. If you have all of these measures in place to protect us, why didn't they work?" I finished my second drink. "From what I saw of Mr. Y last night, and from what I've heard, all he wants is power. With his wealth, he obviously doesn't care about your rules and deliberately defies them. I just wonder..." I trailed off as William's breath was becoming rapid, and I thought he might toss me and my chair across the room.

"Spit it out. You obviously have more to say!"

"Well, why is he still a guest? All of the girls seem to be afraid of him. Is there no one else that has the money he has, that could take his place and not hurt your product?"

William looked at me and I could no longer read his expression. I decided not to back down. "Or does he have power over you, too?"

William glared at me and stood up. "No one has power over me!" and he stormed out of the kitchen towards his office. I sat at the counter until I heard his office door slam shut. I poured one more drink and finished it in one mouthful. I got up and headed back towards the kitchen stairs. Before I went up, I turned around and looked directly into the ceiling camera over the island. I could feel the swelling in my face becoming worse, and wanted William to see what he let happen to me.

CHAPTER THIRTY-ONE

THE WHISKEY KNOCKED ME OUT LONG ENOUGH TO GET A few hours' sleep, but when I woke up, I felt as though I had been dropped from the roof of the house. I was not liking how common this feeling was becoming. Rolling over to try and get out of bed caused a searing pain to shoot up my back. When I was upright, Whitney looked up from a book and leapt out of bed when she saw the state I was in.

"Holy shit, girl! What the fuck did he do to you?"

"Whatever he wanted." My words came out a little muffled as my lips were swollen.

"Good God. I don't think I have seen anyone look this bad after a visit with Mr. Y."

"Well, that makes me feel extra special."

"Don't move, let me help you."

Whitney put my arm around her and slowly helped me up off the bed. "Can you walk?"

"Yeah, I will be fine. Slow but fine. I just need to get dressed."

"Ooh I wouldn't do that. They are going to want to document this for the fines so, unless you want to put in all the effort to get dressed and undressed, I would just stay in the dress and robe. At least for now."

"Document how exactly?"

"Photos darling, what else? Let's go get some breakfast, and then I will take you to Mr. Hammond. He is going to freak the fuck out."

"He already did."

Whitney stopped in her tracks. "He saw you?"

"This morning. I couldn't sleep and so I went to the kitchen and he was there."

"Shit. What did he say?"

"Not much. I think I actually pissed him off as, after he admitted he knew Mr. Y played rough, I called him out."

"Damn girl, you are gutsy. Either way, I would recommend you keep your mouth shut for the next few days. Mr. Hammond's already on edge with the whole Jenna thing and then this on top of it. Don't piss him off if you want to live, is all I am sayin'."

"I'll try, but no guarantees."

We slowly made our way down to the kitchen and were met with gasps from all of the ladies. Fay had been working on a puzzle at the end of the table, and was so stunned she dropped the puzzle piece from her hand. Even Lily got me an ice pack and made me a tea.

"There's no way Mr. Y stays a guest! What precedent would that set for the other guests?" exclaimed Fay.

Saria put down the fashion magazine she was reading, "I don't know, he is, by far, the largest benefactor. That would be a lot of money lost."

I tuned out most of the conversation as the women debated what would happen next. I could barely chew, but was able to get a banana down before Kevin requested I go with him. I pushed myself off the chair as if I was pregnant, unable to move with ease. As we left the kitchen, Kevin's vacant expression turned to concern and he shook his head. I followed him down the hall to William's office.

William was at his desk but he wasn't facing the door. Instead his back was to us and the wooden doors I had seen before had been opened to reveal a large screen on the wall. The screen displayed all of the cameras on the property. One of the cameras in the kitchen had been zoomed in. I didn't understand why the screen would be behind the desk until I noticed a smaller desk to the side and slightly in front of Williams. Jack resided there and had a full view of all of the cameras. He was busy on his phone.

The door closed behind me and William's chair turned around.

I presumed William had seen me on the camera, and therefore wasn't as shocked upon seeing how my state had evolved as the women were. He got up and walked to the front of his desk. He looked to Jack, who promptly finished his call and stood beside his own desk.

"Come forward," William instructed.

I walked over and stopped a few feet in front of the men. Jack raised his phone and moved in closer to me.

"We are going to take pictures of everything to capture what happened to you. We will make this as quick as possible but it has to be done properly otherwise we won't receive proper compensation. Please remove the robe and dress then stand with your legs shoulder-width apart and your arms raised at your sides."

I obeyed and stood naked in front of all three men as I stared blankly at the large screen of windowed images. The events of the last month and a half made it so that I barely felt uncomfortable. In fact, I barely felt anything. I watched the ladies finish breakfast and make their way to the living room. Some read, others picked at their fingernails while the rest watched television.

Pictures were taken of my arms and sides first so that I could rest them. William's hands were soft and tender as he positioned me to ensure the photos had the best light. When they were done he wrapped the robe back around me. As he tied the belt he leaned in and whispered "I'm sorry." He handed me the dress and Kevin led me out of the room.

I stood outside the closed door for a moment staring out the hallway window. It was raining outside, which was fitting for my mood and that of the house. Kevin didn't move but stared at his feet. I wondered how many times he had brought women into the office in the state I was in.

Without registering what my body was doing, I made my way to the living room, sat in one of the chairs by the fire and stared at the dancing flames. No one said anything. I got lost in the hues of red, orange and yellow kissing each other as they moved around the logs of wood. William's "I'm sorry" replayed in my head. Did I hear him properly? Was he actually sorry? It had been less then 24 hours since he coldly killed Jenna. How could a person like that feel remorse?

CHAPTER THIRTY-TWO

THE FIRE HAD DIED DOWN TO FLICKERING EMBERS WHEN the ladies took me up to my room. Their faces had returned to the sullen and scared looks from the night before. They helped me find a large navy sweatshirt and grey sweatpants that were a size too big, so they didn't put pressure on the bruises. I almost opted to just stay in the robe, but I was cold and needed something more. Whitney and Reyna stayed behind after the others had all hugged me gently, before they left me to rest.

Reyna fussed about my pillows and made sure I had water and books to read. Whitney told me I was to stay in bed until Doctor Boyden could see me. A bed had become a place I loathed and yet where I felt safe.

Whitney and Reyna looked worried as they sat and watched me from Whitney's bed. I felt now was the time that I needed to ask about Claire.

"I have to ask you both a question, and you cannot mention it to anyone else. Promise?"

"Promise," Whitney replied.

"You both have seen a few people come and go, right?"

They looked at each other. "Well, yes," Reyna answered.

"Has there ever been a woman named Claire? Around 30 years old. Blond hair, green eyes?"

"Why are you asking?" Reyna asked.

Wiping the hair from my eyes, I continued, "She probably looked a little bit like me, but not enough for anyone to make the connection we are sisters unless we stood beside each other."

Reyna and Whitney both looked at each other, shocked and confused. Reyna elbowed Whitney, nudging her to be the one to speak. Whitney got up and sat beside me.

"We had one girl recently named Claire, not bad looking, but you could tell drugs had taken away much of her beauty. I am not sure how she made it past Adam and got here, given she obviously had an addiction. Right away, she didn't fit in and Jenna took to pushing her around. All Claire could talk about was finding her next fix. We got her cleaned up as best we could, but one of the guests must have slipped her something. Within a few weeks she was a mess." Whitney stopped and tried to halt the tears that were building up, so Reyna continued. "William got fed up and had her removed from the house a couple of weeks before you got here."

Reyna's sweet voice couldn't soften the blow of her words. I couldn't believe what I was hearing. "She was here just before me. Oh, I was so close!" I couldn't hold the tears back, I was heartbroken. Once again, I had almost found her.

Reyna continued, "My dear, if she was still here, you wouldn't be. There are only nine women here at a time. I am sorry, but you likely would have never been here together."

Whitney had already told me the likely outcome of women who left the house, but I couldn't believe that is what happened to Claire. "Where would they have taken her?"

Reyna and Whitney exchanged worried glances again. Whitney spoke up.

"If you didn't see her where you came from then... well...honey, she was more work for William then he usually puts in. To be honest..." she trailed off, not wanting to tell me the truth I refused to accept.

"What?"

"They may have moved her on."

"You mean killed! No. You guys told me they have a whole network of houses. Maybe she is in one of those? I mean, I saw Claire with two other women, being taken from a house back in Toronto a few nights before I was taken. Where did those two go? Maybe she's back with them."

Reyna added, "It's possible. None of us really know where we were before here. Olivia, I know it hurts, but you gotta think about it. It's possible, given how strung out she was, she might have been a risk to keep alive?"

"No! No, no, no. I won't believe it. She can't be." I had gone full-on hysterical.

"Shhh. Quiet now, you don't want the guards to hear you."

"Fuck the guards!" I yelled "Let them come in here. I have some questions for them!" I tried to pull myself off the bed, but Whitney pushed me back down.

"Girl, don't make me muzzle you. You will get us all in trouble if you cause a scene. Not just yourself."

I took a deep breath and tried to calm myself down. No matter how upset and angry I was, Whitney and Reyna had only been kind to me. I didn't want anyone to get hurt. They didn't deserve to be punished because I was too late in getting to Claire.

"I didn't come this far, and go through all of this shit, to not find answers." My face was drenched in tears which were now making their way down my neck.

"You're not going to get any answers. None of us know anything," Reyna said with a soothing voice.

"Somebody knows something. Who would know what happened to her? Without them speculating?"

"Mr. Hammond, of course, but you can't go asking him. Jack, and maybe Kevin. But they usually use people outside the house for that type of work. Limits the risk of people talking." Whitney replied.

I looked to Whitney, "You could ask Kevin."

"Are you crazy? If I ask Kevin, we risk three lives. You, me and him."

"Whitney, please," I begged. Reyna hadn't reacted so I suspected she was aware of Whitney's relationship with Kevin.

Whitney rolled her eyes, "Only if the moment presents itself, but I am not going out of my way to jeopardize everything for someone who, and I am sorry, is likely dead."

I knew it would hurt but I hugged her and softly said, "Thank you."

I didn't have high hopes Whitney would be successful, or that I would be patient enough to wait.

"But, be warned, I can't wait forever. If Claire is out there, the longer I am here the more likely I won't find her. I will do whatever it takes, even if it means asking William directly."

"Oh, no, you won't. Are you crazy? Do you want to end up like Jenna?"

"Of course not, but I am finding out what happened to my sister one way or another. Claire has been gone for three months. I cannot continue to take these beatings in hopes I will stumble across what happened to her. Every day counts, and if I end up dead finding out the truth, then so be it."

Whitney shook her head, "Man, you got some balls. I will give you that. Let's think this out before you go blowing the place up, shall we? First, we need to get you to a point where you can at least walk unassisted. You aren't going to be able to protect yourself in your current state. Second, I am sure there is a better way to get the information you need with a less likelihood of you, or us, getting shot. Now, will you listen to us and give us time to come up with a plan, or are you going to go all cowboy on us and blow the roof off this place?"

"I will try to give you time, but not much. I am not putting up with this," I said, motioning to my battered body. "If William thinks..." Just then there was a knock on the door.

All three of us stared at it until Reyna got up and opened it.

William looked in at us.

CHAPTER THIRTY-THREE

"HELLO REYNA," WILLIAM SAID FIRMLY, "HOW IS OUR patient?"

"Um, fine. I guess."

William walked into the room and surveyed each of us and then spoke to Reyna, "Gather all of her stuff."

"What is happening?" asked Whitney desperately. "Where are you taking her?"

"Don't sound so worried, she's going somewhere where she will be more comfortable. Hopefully, there she can heal faster."

I could hear both girls exhale their fears and, although I didn't breathe a sigh of relief, my heart rate slowed down a little. I was worried William had been outside the door for a while prior to knocking. If he heard what I said... I shook the thought from my head, I didn't want to think about that right now.

William led us to the elevator and held its door open as Whitney and

Reyna helped me and my few belongings in. I gripped the railing to keep myself upright.

"I can take her from here," William announced.

Reyna and Whitney stepped out of the elevator and William stepped in. I stood as far from him as possible, in a space which felt like a closet. The look of fear had returned to my friends' faces. William reached over me and pressed '3'. At least I wasn't going down.

The elevator engine began to hum and we slowly started to rise. The thirty seconds it took to go up one floor felt endless. Once the door clicked, to signal it was safe to exit, William grabbed my things and opened the door, holding it open for me. As I stepped out, my foot got caught on the gap between the elevator and the landing. I fell forward and landed hard on my knees. "Fuck!" the pain seared up and down my legs.

William reached out his hand. I looked at it, but I tried to get up without his help, wincing at the pain as my legs refused to hold me up.

"Don't be stubborn. Let me help you, I won't bite."

"Bite no, but shoot..." I mumbled.

William chucked, "Well, that can be true, but not today." He grabbed me under my arm and helped me to my feet.

"I presume Whitney went over the rooms on this floor with you on your tour, however, to make sure you are up to speed, the two middle rooms belong to Jack and Kevin respectively. The room at the end of the hall is mine. You are not to enter these rooms. Understood?"

I nodded.

William led me to the door which used to have Jenna's name on it, but now had mine. He guided me into the room, placing his hand on my back. I didn't have time to react as he quickly removed it.

"What do you think?" he asked.

Nothing had changed since I'd cleaned the bathroom yesterday. "I think my grandmother puked doilies and Pepto Bismol everywhere," I said bluntly. It was a nice room but nauseatingly pink. "And what is with the creepy figurines?"

"Ha. Yes, well all of that can easily be changed. What colour would you prefer?"

"Um well, I always liked yellow - but not bright canary yellow, more mellow."

"I will get Jack to bring you some paint and furniture samples. We will get this room to your liking, in the meantime, I will have the doilies and figurines removed when we are at dinner." He winked at me. "Is there anything else you need?"

My confusion must have been painted on my face as he clarified, "As I said, I'm sorry. That never should have happened, and I am handling it."

He helped me to the bed and sat down beside me. "If your first night was any indication, you are going to make me a lot of money once you are healed. Almost every guest placed a substantial bid. And, as a rule, the person who routinely brings in the most money stays in this room."

"You don't know I am going to do that. It's highly likely everyone was interested in the 'new girl'."

"I have been getting calls about you since the party. You are not a novelty. You are going to be very successful here. Now, rest up. We need you back to work as soon as possible. I will have Dr. Boyden come by as soon as he can."

William left and closed the door behind him. I looked around the room and pictured Jenna lounging in the chair or yelling at the ladies in the backyard from her balcony.

I wasn't sure if I was moving up in the hierarchy, or if William just felt bad for the beatings I had taken. Then I reminded myself that William probably didn't understand any emotion outside of anger and was only concerned with making himself money.

As I laid on the bed, I realized what else came with being 'the favourite' and my skin crawled.

CHAPTER THIRTY-FOUR

THE SLAM OF A DOOR WOKE ME OUT OF A DEEP SLEEP. THE kind of sleep where you don't dream, which I was thankful for. I had just stopped having recurring nightmares about Adam, but I knew it was a matter of time before nightmares about Mr. Y would start. I checked the clock on the bedside table, and saw that I had an hour until dinner and the accompanying meeting.

I made my way to the bathroom, and managed to hold myself up in the shower long enough to get fairly clean. Washing my hair was too difficult with the scrapes on my head, and how hard it was to raise my arms. I just let the hot water rush over my head and down my body.

I put back on the track pants and sweater I had been wearing, and slowly made my way to the stairs. I wasn't better than anyone else in this house and I didn't want them to think I believed otherwise. I tried to take the stairs, but only made it down a handful before I had to go back and take the elevator. The pain was too much and climbing down three storeys wasn't worth it. At least not today.

Whitney must have heard the elevator, as she was waiting for me when I opened the door on the main floor. She helped me into the kitchen. Saria got out some wine and poured everyone a glass. "One last toast to Jenna, and then we move on." She looked to Lily, who huffed but raised her glass.

"To Jenna" we all said in unison, and took a sip.

Jessica and Eloisa put their glasses down and, as the established cooks in the house, finished putting dinner together. I could smell the aroma of chicken and garlic alfredo sauce from my chair. It was only then that I realized I hadn't eaten anything in 24 hours. They placed the pots on the table and everyone served themselves. Whitney helped with mine.

William came in and took his seat at the head of the table. Jessica passed him a plate of the chicken alfredo. A glass of wine had already been poured for him. He raised his glass of wine and we all mimicked him.

"Ladies, to a successful night. Cheers."

"Cheers," we all repeated with an air of compliance. I drank half the glass.

We all stared at our plates as we ate in silence. Halfway through the meal William spoke, "I know it wasn't all successful. What happened to Olivia was unacceptable. Never has anything as outrageous as this happened under my roof. Mr. Y will no longer be visiting us, I have seen to that."

Everyone stopped eating and looked between me and William. Somehow, I couldn't believe what I was hearing. Yes, William had killed Jenna and, maybe I was naive, but would he have killed another so soon?

He continued, "None of you deserve to be treated like that. I am raising the fines, should you be injured on the job. Please keep eating." Nothing else was said until we had all finished. By the time I was done with my dinner I had also finished two glasses of wine.

William got up and topped all of the wine glasses. "You also may have noticed I have moved Olivia into the third-floor bedroom." The women started murmuring. "Even if Mr. Y hadn't placed the top bid of $100,000, Olivia pretty much tripled everyone else's bids."

Everyone's jaw dropped, including mine.

"That's impossible!" Lily said.

As the whispers increased in volume I heard the words "new", "unfair" and something along the lines of "William's favourite".

"Not impossible, Lily - improbable, yes - but why would I lie? As I told Olivia, I don't think it has anything to do with her being new." He paused and stared at those who had related my 'success' to it being my first night. "She is in high demand and, as long as that continues, we shall be very profitable. Now, as with all our debriefs, what items do you want to talk about?" He sat back down in his chair.

Everyone was silent for a few moments before they started bringing up concerns about their guests. How late they stayed, how Mr. L kept professing his love for Saria and talked about sneaking her out of the house. Mr. L. was 80 years old and no one took him seriously, but he did need to be watched cautiously. He got attached to women and then got aggressive when they didn't form the same attachment. Then everyone looked to me, William included.

By now, I was on my fourth glass of wine and my filter was gone. "Oh, I don't think I need to say much. My body is evidence enough that money reigns in this house." All of the women were wide-eyed and looked to William.

William sipped his wine, leaned back in his chair and said calmly, "Go on."

I had already voiced my concerns about guards earlier this morning, and although I was sure some of the other women may have shared my concern, I didn't think bringing it up would help my situation. However, I wasn't going to let the matter go entirely, "As we seem to have to be able to take care of ourselves, maybe we need an emergency button somewhere in each room. Provided we can get to it."

William sat expressionless but didn't say anything. Lily was smirking as she watched me unravel and Whitney squeezed my hand to try and get me to stop talking, but I couldn't.

"I would say teach us self-defense, but that would be counterproductive when we are being held captive."

William sat up and slammed his hands on the table, causing the dishes to clatter against the wood. "ENOUGH! Not that it is any of your business, but I have handled the issues with the guards. They are no longer employable." He let that sink in for a few moments before his voice went back to calm and he continued, "You all will have better protection going forward. I will look into your suggestion about the button. Now Dr. Boyden is out of town, and although you look horrible, I suspect you will live. As such, we will wait for his return to get you any medical help.

He stood up and finished his wine, "I will be out of town on business for a while. Adam will be here to watch over everything."

Everyone groaned and tried to object, saying Jack or Kevin could do it.

"I know, I know. But there is no sense in complaining. Unfortunately, that does mean he will oversee the next party." He looked right at me, "Try not to do anything to piss him off. Goodnight Ladies." He walked out of the room and everyone started to talk about their hatred for Adam.

Jessica started to cry and Whitney explained that Adam had taken a particular liking to her the last time he was here and left her with a couple broken ribs. I painstakingly got up from the table. "All this talk about protecting us and William won't even bat an eye about letting his monster of a brother in here! He can't be blind to what happens can he?"

Reyna advised, "He's not blind, just more complacent, to a point.

He doesn't trust anyone else with the business, even Jack or Kevin. Even though I don't think they would ever cross him. With Adam, William knows what he is getting and can keep him relatively reigned in."

I was furious. Even after the battered wives and dead bodies I had seen at work, I couldn't understand how someone could just sit by and let others, without the means to defend themselves, be hurt. "Reigned in! You call Jessica's broken ribs reigned in. You call the state I was in when I arrived reigned in! If this man thinks..."

"OLIVIA SHUT UP!" Whitney yelled and then lowered her voice. "You know he can hear you, and before you tell me you don't care, think about the rest of us. You are still new here and have been very lucky with respect to how you have been treated by William. Yes, you got the short end of the stick when it comes to Adam and Mr. Y. But, the faster you realize that in this house, to these people, you are not seen as a person but a product, the safer you and the rest of us will be. YES, we appreciate that you want to protect us, but you are doing more damage than good. As your friends, we beg you. Stop."

I looked around the room, "Is this what you all want? As my friends, you want me to just sit back and take whatever beatings are handed to me?"

The women looked solemn but no one spoke up. "I see. Well then, I guess I better get with the program. Resign myself to the fact I am nothing more than a punching bag."

Whitney reached for my hand but I pulled away, "It won't always be this bad."

"Ha. And how do you know that? It's been one beating after another since I was taken. Jenna is dead. I am pretty sure things can get worse." By now I had exerted most of my energy and took a seat on a stool at the island.

Reyna came over, "It will only get worse if you let it. Unfortunately, in this world, that means not being as strong or opinionated as we want to be. If you want to survive here you need to back down. Let them win."

Everything in me wanted to continue to protest. Tell them that their lives were worth more than this place and what they had been made to become. But I knew they were right. If I kept angering William it would only be a matter of time before he lost all sympathy and where would I, or the others, be then? I would never find out what happened to Claire. I hugged Reyna.

"You're right. I will try."

I vowed to at least keep my head down as long as it took to find out what happened to Claire. After that, I made no promises.

CHAPTER THIRTY-FIVE

ADAM'S ARRIVAL WAS NOTHING LESS THAN A SPECTACLE. Smith made sure we were all lined up in the lobby before Adam would even enter the house. Adam inspected us all as if he was a First Sergeant. He found something to criticize about everyone, whether it was Fay's hair, Eloisa's clothes, Lily's stance. "You think men are going to approach you if you are hunched over like that?" he yelled. Lily straightened up quickly, but I could feel her glare as he made his way down the line.

When he got to me at the end of the line, he didn't hide his pleasure in seeing the bruises. He reached out and ran his hand down my face. It took everything I had not to react. He turned my head side-to-side. "Heard what happened, and I must say purple does seem to be your colour." Then he leaned in and whispered in my ear, "Seems my brother has taken a liking to you. He's told me hands off, but then again, if it turns out we end up having a Jenna problem that I have to take care of..." he trailed off and stepped back smiling.

I had to resist the urge to tackle Adam as he walked away. It would only take 20 seconds for me to break his neck, and none of us would ever have to deal with him again. As tempting as it was, I knew it would only take another 20 seconds for me to end up like Jenna.

After Adam and Smith went into William's office, the atmosphere in the house remained on edge. We all headed to the backyard, in hopes of being as far away from Adam as possible. By this point, I could manage to walk with relative normalcy. It was still hard to sit down or get up from furniture, but I could do it on my own. Nevertheless, I made a mental note to exaggerate my difficulties while Adam was here. No sense in him suddenly deciding I was fit enough to work.

We spent the afternoon by the pool drinking and talking about the best ways to get through the coming weeks. Whitney and Reyna were still the only ones who knew about Claire. After the conversation at dinner, I didn't want to expose any more of my friends to the risk of that knowledge. As I watched the mist trails of clouds pass by overhead, I tried to figure out how I was going to get more information on Claire. When William said the guards were "no longer employable," we all knew what he meant. The rest of the guards would too. This meant I wouldn't be able to befriend one to transport information in or out. They would have no sympathy towards me. Once again, I felt as though I was alone in my fight to find Claire. I would never be able to get word to Joe. I was trapped and could do little about it. My thoughts were interrupted by a figure casting a shadow over me. I put a hand above my eyes, shielding the sun, looked up and saw Smith standing over me. My stomach dropped.

"Adam wants to see you," he said firmly.

No one spoke. I slowly maneuvered myself up off the pool chair. Smith moved his arm slightly, as if he wanted to help, but refrained himself.

As I walked towards the house, I looked back and saw fear in the ladies' eyes. I turned back to the house, and kept repeating my promise to the women to not get into any more trouble. I didn't know if this was a promise I would be able to keep.

CHAPTER THIRTY-SIX

ADAM STOOD IN THE KITCHEN CUTTING VEGATABLES WITH a large knife. He pointed the knife at a spot beside him for me to stand. I made my way over and kept my eyes on the knife.

"I find it curious that you have only been in my brother's house for a month and already seemed to have weaseled your way onto the third floor." He continued to chop as he spoke. "I am not as easily fooled by you, Ms. Olivia. You are hiding secrets from my brother. Secrets that could destroy his business." He stopped chopping, moved right up to me and placed the knife against my cheek, "I don't know what game you are playing, but be sure, I will win it."

I looked him in the eye, showing no fear, "I don't know what you are talking about." He stood there for a few more seconds and then went back to his food.

"I thought you might say that. Well it makes it more fun for me, I guess. Smith, put her in my office. We are going to have a nice long chat, and maybe a few other things." He winked at me.

I found it interesting Adam referred to William's office as his own. He was clinging to any power he could.

Smith took me gently by the arm. Once inside the office, Smith sat me on the couch and stood by the closed door. After a couple of minutes, he mumbled, "Just tell him something. Anything."

"What can I tell him? And why would I tell him anything?"

"He obviously has it out for you, and he will make his stay here hell for you if you don't tell him something, anything that he could use."

"I don't have anything to tell him. And besides, he likely won't believe anything I say. Even if I did make something up, wouldn't he just use it to hurt me?"

"Yes. But he will think he has won, so he might take it a little easier on you."

I couldn't tell if Smith was trying to help me and actually believed what he was saying.

He continued, "I am not sure if Adam actually thinks you have anything to tell him, but he is bound and determined to make you less desirable to his brother." Smith stopped, opened the door slightly and looked out. Seeing nothing he closed it again. "Adam is still upset William brought you here. He wanted you as his own little pet. The only way to make that happen is for William to dismiss you from this house."

"Why are you helping me?"

Smith looked bothered and said, "I have seen Adam be particularly gruesome to women and, outside of his fiancé, I have not seen him be as cruel as he has been to you. When I gave him that gun, I thought he would actually pull the trigger. Not surprisingly, he has killed before. Sometimes out of spite, but mostly at William's orders. I'm not making excuses, but Adam is a broken man; both of them are. But I can't change that. What I can do is protect you as best as I can, without drawing attention to myself. But to do that you have to give him something."

I chuckled and it caught us both off guard. "Protect me, ha. If you were protecting me, I wouldn't be in this place."

"I protected you by making sure you got into this place."

I quizzically looked at Smith and thought back to the day I first met William. I realized Smith had left the room when Adam first had the gun, but was back before it was against my head. It was after that when William's voice bellowed from behind me. I was speechless. Why would this man help me? Then my thoughts turned to Claire. If Smith was willing to help me get away from Adam, maybe he had helped Claire find a way out. Maybe he would help me find her. We heard shoes on the marble floor in the foyer and we both stayed quiet. I wracked my brain to try and come up with something to tell Adam. What would be good enough to make him happy but not result in William giving me back to his brother?

Smith opened the door and Adam walked in and sat in William's desk chair. He leaned back and put his shined shoes on the desk. He motioned for Smith to leave the room, who dutifully did so. I noticed the shadow of his boots under the door. He would be able to hear whatever was said.

"What do you have for me?" Adam asked, as he cracked his knuckles.

From interviewing suspects, I knew giving anything up too soon meant there was more information to gain. Plus, I still didn't know what I was going to tell him. I stayed silent.

"Do you intentionally try to piss me off? You know what happens when I get mad, and right now a few more bruises would just blend in." Adam got up and stood over me.

I still said nothing.

Adam grabbed my hair and pushed my face into the couch "You are going to tell me what you are up to, otherwise your face goes through this table!"

I knew he wasn't making an empty threat. "Fine. Fine." He let go of my hair and sat in front of me on the table.

"I asked Mr. Y to beat me in hopes that your brother would take pity on me and not have me work." Adam looked at me waiting for more. "I have seen the way Mr. Hammond looks at me when no one else is watching. Now, Mr. Y took it too far, but it got me to the third floor. And soon it will get me into your brothers' bed."

I risked Adam's wrath, mentioning sex with William, but the satisfaction of getting under Adam's skin was worth it. He was right - what were a few more bruises at this point?

Adam stood, but rather than hurting me, he paced the room. He paced for a few minutes and then asked, "And what was your plan once you got into my brother's bed? Jenna would frequent his bed and, well, he shot her."

"Well..." I wasn't expecting this, I needed to think quick and yet sound confident "Well. I would slowly gain his trust, infiltrate the running of the business by providing ways for him to make more money, in exchange for me not working at all."

"And then?"

"No 'and then', that's it."

"You expect me to believe that all you want is to be my brother's whore of a girlfriend? I know you are smarter than that." He sat on the edge of the desk "Isn't your end goal to get out of here?"

I didn't know what he was getting at, but I knew not to take the bait.

"I know the only way I am getting out of here is if I am dead. So why focus on the impossible and instead focus on the probable." I held my breath as Adam sat thinking.

"If that is true, how do you plan to have this place make enough money that you won't have to work? You made $100,000 on your first night, so you would need to have some impressive plans for my brother, to keep turning down that kind of money."

"Umm. I haven't gotten it all worked out yet, but... well people have fetishes do they not? School girls, bondage, nurses etc. And the clientele seems to be a rather small pool. Sure, they are rich, but rich people get bored."

Adam looked quite interested in what I had to say, and his face didn't look as terrifying as it usually was. He motioned for me to continue.

"So, you have themed parties and not only invite the "regular" clientele, but start introducing new people with these specific fetishes."

Adam went and sat behind the desk. "You seem to have given this quite a bit of thought."

Not wanting to tip him off that I had just come up with the idea, I added, "You could charge a premium for the themed nights, while still hosting the traditional parties for those who may not want to partake. But that's all I have come up with."

Adam laughed, "And you think my brother is going to let you help run his business and not work these parties?" He leaned over the desk, "You know nothing about my brother. But thank you for these ideas, I might just have to use them myself." He winked at me. "You can leave now."

Relief overflowed my body as I quickly left before he could change his mind. As I opened the door Smith turned to face me, and backed up to give me room to leave. Before I stepped out, Adam spoke again.

"Oh, and you will be working this week, even if it's just your mouth. Smith and I will make sure you're ready before the party."

Even without looking at Adam, I could hear the grin on his face. Smith didn't react. I mouthed 'help me' to him, before I walked past and made my way down the hallway.

CHAPTER THIRTY-SEVEN

AS I SAT OUT ON MY BALCONY, SIPPING A TEA, I STARED AT the stars and tried to work out what I was going to do next. All I told the ladies was that Adam was going to make me work. Adam appeared interested in my ideas for themed parties but I didn't want to tell the women just yet what I may have gotten them into. They would likely think I overstepped again and be upset. Would Adam use the ideas and try and push William out of the business? Would he tell William where the ideas originated? Given Adam's propensity to hurt me emotionally and physically I suspected he would. I needed to get to William first. But how?

Could I go through Smith? Possibly. He genuinely seemed to care. Although I was not by any means attracted to him, I could see how Whitney would fall for someone working for the Hammonds. Like Kevin, Smith was starting to look like a caring human being, and that was hard to find around here. I refocused. Could I get rid of Adam? The only way he never came back was for him to die. But how could I do it so that William wouldn't then kill me? I wondered if it would be so bad if William did kill me?

I felt so lost and alone. The women, with the exception of Lily, were becoming my friends, but I still felt like a lone wolf within a larger, cohesive pack. My only hope was that Adam either stayed away from me or kept me around as his little toy long enough that I could find my way out of the mess I had created. I suddenly heard the elevator door open and people disembark. I closed my eyes and clenched my mug, praying there would not be a knock on the door.

My prayer was not answered.

I slowly opened the door, and there stood Smith. I was sure he could read the relief that I felt upon seeing him. He silently motioned for me to let him in, so I stepped aside and quietly closed the door. He didn't move far from the door and I went and sat on the bench at the end of the bed.

We both sat in silence for what felt like forever, but I am sure it was only seconds.

"I heard what you told Adam. And shockingly, you would make a good Madam, but you are going to have to follow through on your plan."

"Wait, what? I would have thought Adam would have used the ideas himself? Or at least told William about them to get me out of here and moved back to being under his control."

"I guess not. It looks like he wants to see if you have the guts to follow through on your plan. No doubt, Adam will continue to plant seeds of mistrust of you in William. Although I suspect William will continue to dismiss them. Adam has been telling William since the beginning not to trust you, so I doubt they will be taken seriously."

"Wait. Just so I am clear, when William comes back, Adam is not going to tell him anything?"

"I suspect he will mention something about keeping an eye on you, but he has been saying that all along. I should go, if I am seen in here."

"One more thing," I looked at him pleadingly. "Please."

"Fine but make it quick."

"Have you ever met a Claire while working for Adam? Claire Beaumont."

CHAPTER THIRTY-EIGHT

SMITH CLOSED THE DOOR BEHIND HIM AS I SLIPPED OFF THE bench onto the floor. A waterfall of tears streamed down my face. Images of Claire's last moments ran through my mind.

Smith told me Claire was becoming too disruptive, as Whitney and Reyna said, and William had ordered her removed from the house. Adam had been around at the time and told William he would handle it. Smith recalled Adam and William had gone into the office and, by the time they had come out, he and Jack had restrained Claire and got her into a van. As Smith drove the van, Adam injected Claire with a concoction of drugs and raped her for two hours. When they reached Rice Canyon, Claire was a mess. Adam took off Claire's restraints, opened the back of the van and told her to get out. She slowly stumbled out of the van and Adam yelled at her to "Run!"

Smith watched in the rear-view mirror as she slowly backed away; she seemed unsure what was happening. Adam kept yelling at her to run, so

Claire turned and started to walk faster. Tripping over her feet as she went. Adam shot her in the arm, and she fell. Adam laughed and told her to get back up or he would shoot her again. Claire got to her feet and looked around for help, but there was no one in the desert but the three of them.

She refused to move and begged Adam to just kill her, as she knew he would anyway, "So just get it over with!" Claire cried.

"What would be the fun in that?" Adam asked with a maniacal laugh as he jumped out of the van.

Claire was in tears and continued to beg, so Adam shot her in the other arm. Claire laid in the dirt, covered in her own blood. Crying and screaming for it to end.

"Get up!" Adam yelled as he walked over to her. She didn't move, but stared at the stars. He pulled her up by her hair. He stood back and pointed the gun at her "RUN!"

Claire looked around again but instead of running away she ran towards Adam, bent over like a bull, and pushed him towards the cliff. He stopped them as they got to the edge.

"You little Bitch!" He shot her in the shoulder. "You don't get it, do you? If you run, it ends faster. Either way, I have fun."

Claire stood up, "Fine." She looked Adam in the eye, said something Smith couldn't hear, and jumped backwards off the cliff.

Smith got out of the van and saw a glimpse of Claire's limp body at the bottom of the cliff. Adam was furious and unloaded his clip of bullets down the cliff face. Smith took Adam back to the house and then returned, and, by camp light, buried Claire. He told me he built a small cross out of nearby stones and prayed that she now had peace.

It wasn't until after my first meeting with Adam that Smith found out what Claire had whispered;

"Olivia is going to get you for this."

CHAPTER THIRTY-NINE

I PACED AROUND MY ROOM ALL NIGHT TRYING TO FIGURE out my next move. Adam had put together that I knew Claire, which explained why he had it out for me. But now, knowing this gave me an advantage. He seemed to want to keep me alive. Whether it was so he could continue to torture me, or for another reason, I wasn't sure. I just prayed he wouldn't expose me before I had time to find out if William was the one who ordered Adam to kill Claire, or if it was Adam being the monster he is. Reyna had mentioned women would be sent back down to lower status houses, but William didn't keep tabs on the women who left. I would kill Adam, that was a fact. Given William had killed Jenna, and appeared to have ordered the deaths of others, he too would die. I just needed closure on what happened to Claire first.

Smith's life was hanging by a thread. He willingly told me what happened to Claire and, in his own way, tried to protect me. But even then, he didn't try and prevent Claire's death or my beatings. Could I fault him for wanting to protect himself? I needed more time to consider his fate.

By the time the sun rose, I had gone through numerous plans in my head and I decided subtlety was the best move. There was no need to rush into anything and I wanted to speak with Whitney and Reyna before I did anything. I needed to protect the women and make sure whatever plan I ended up using didn't put them in danger.

CHAPTER FORTY

ALTHOUGH I HADN'T SLEPT, I ARRIVED AT BREAKFAST feeling a little lighter and with half a smile on my face. Whitney noticed.

"What has gotten into you?" she whispered, as she poured me a coffee.

I know what happened to Claire," I whispered back.

"What? How?" she tried to keep her voice down but a couple women looked over, so we turned towards the coffee machine.

"It doesn't matter, but I have a plan, or part of a plan. I will tell you later. I don't trust all the ears in this room." We sat, with our coffees, at the table with the rest of the women just as Adam and Smith walked in.

He stood behind the chair at the end of the table, placed his hands-on top of it and puffed out his chest. "This week, we are going to do something different. New clientele and new outfits."

I looked to Smith, who was stone-faced. I had thought I was going to be left to pitch this plan to William. I wasn't going to complain. This could end up working in my favour, if Adam messed up badly enough. Even if William was told it was my idea, Adam was the one who implemented it.

"Karey will be by this afternoon to take your measurements for your nurse outfits."

"Wait, what? Are we shooting fucking porn now?" exclaimed Fay.

Adam walked over to Fay and slammed her head into the table. She screamed in pain as blood poured out of her mouth and all over herself and the table. "Anyone else have anything they would like to say?"

We all stared at Fay but were too afraid to help her.

"Great. This week we are going to be making some serious money!" He walked out with an air of gravitas.

I grabbed a wet cloth, towel and some frozen vegetables, as the others went over to Fay.

"What does he think he is doing?" commented Jessica.

"Mr. Hammond would never go for this. Would he?" asked Eloisa.

"No way. He has built his reputation on classy parties. I doubt he would risk losing what he's built by putting us all in cheap uniforms and changing up who the guests are. He would have done so by now if he was interested," replied Saria.

I tried to give what little encouragement I could, "We have been through a lot lately, but we can get through this ridiculous dress-up party. William will be back soon enough and hopefully we can forget this all happened."

"Easy for you to say, you don't even have to work," protested Jessica.

"Actually, I do. Partially. Adam has made it clear that as my mouth still works, it will."

"What a prick!" said Saria.

I advised, "We will put on his stupid costumes, pretend we like them and then talk to William when he gets back."

"Ha. You saw how Mr. Hammond brushed us off, when he told us Adam would run this place while he was gone," said Whitney.

"Okay, maybe we all don't gang up on him at dinner. Maybe I could speak with him for all of us."

The ladies looked from one another. "Why would you do that? Do you think that, because you are the new favourite, you have some extra pull or something?" asked Lily

"No. I was more thinking that I am already purple and blue, so if William wants to add a few more bruises it doesn't make much difference." I was hesitant, but I decided to move my plan forward, I needed their support. The last thing I needed was for them to try to undermine my efforts, if they thought I was just trying to get in William's good graces. I walked over to the kitchen entryway and made sure no one was around. "Let's head outside."

After we got comfortable, I told them I had a plan to deal with Adam but I needed to know that I could trust them. Everyone turned to Lily. "If it means getting rid of that son of a bitch, you can trust me," Lily said.

I told them about Claire, who she was to me and what happened to her. I said I couldn't tell them who told me, but that I trusted them. I advised them of what I told Adam when I was pulled into the office and apologized that they now had to wear costumes. I told them my plan was to kill Adam, but I needed it to look like an accident, and I also needed to get close to William in hopes he wouldn't suspect me. To make sure they benefited from the plan, I added that I wanted to make sure they were treated better after Adam was gone. What I didn't tell them was that I was going to kill William. I knew they would think it was too risky. Once again, I didn't tell them I had been a cop. No one asked if I had lied about being an executive, so I didn't tell. That piece of information was still too valuable, and would be tempting to trade if anyone ever thought my plan wasn't working or they were not benefiting enough.

Everyone was silent. Then Whitney spoke up, "Damn girl, that is a lot to take in but I am with you. Whatever you need."

Fay wiped tears from her eyes, "I can't believe Claire went out like that. We knew he was a monster, but that is pure evil." Her head fell into her hands.

"Are you really confident you can get close to Mr. Hammond?" Jessica asked. "Jenna tried, and look where that got her."

"If I'm completely honest, my plan could fail. William is not someone you can easily get close to. But I'm not Jenna. I have a feeling she used less subtle tactics than what I am going to use. My vagina isn't going to be doing the talking. At least not if I can help it." That comment seemed to loosen the mood a little. "I cannot guarantee that my plan is going to work. But I can guarantee one thing: Adam is going to die, and none of you will be held accountable."

"So how are you going to do it?"

"That part I haven't completely figured out yet. What I do know is that, if we do it while William's away, he will surely suspect us. Specifically, me, given my history with Adam and my recent outbursts. For your own safety, I think the less you know the better. But I will tell you once I have a plan. Do I have everyone's support?"

Everyone agreed, and then started proposing wild ideas of how they would love to see Adam die. None of which were actually feasible, however cathartic they may have been.

CHAPTER FORTY-ONE

THE PARTY WAS A DISASTER. THE GUESTS WERE RUDE AND inappropriate during the party, trying to fondle and take "free samples" as they called it. We knew Karey had tried her best on such short notice, but the costumes were scratchy and gave Eloisa a rash. We looked cheap, and that is exactly how the bids ended up. Not a single one of us brought in more than $5000, which is a fraction of what we would make under William. For myself, the guests were very interested in my bruises, and asked if receiving them was part of the service I provided. Thankfully, Adam wasn't around when they asked, as I am sure he would have loved to extend that 'benefit'. I lucked out and ended up with a nicer gentleman who took pity on me and was satisfied with a hand job. The rest of the woman came out unharmed but were not happy as to how they were treated.

Adam was equally unhappy with the results of the party. "You girls are shit! I barely broke even on the night, after paying Karey for your costumes and plus I bought new decorations. What the fuck did you do all night?" He tossed anything he found across the kitchen from the sugar bowl to hand towels.

"Maybe it was the clientele?"

"Who said that?" Adam's face was almost as red as his hair.

"I did," and I stood up.

"YOU!"

I knew he wanted to blame me for last night but he wouldn't want to tell anyone where he got the idea from. Not only would it show that he could not come up with business ideas on his own, but it would be an example of how he could not weed out the bad ones.

"You little bitch. Get in my office!"

"You mean William's office." I said obstinately.

I was egging him on and knew what was coming next, but that was my 'in' with William. Adam was told not to touch me, and not to make me work. He hadn't listened to one of the orders and now it was time for him to disobey the other. Adam didn't wait until I was in the office to attack me. As I walked past him, he punched me hard in the gut. Perfect, witnesses that will support my story when William asks what happened.

Smith picked me up off the floor and helped me towards the office as Adam kept yelling at the rest of the women for not making him any money. I heard a few more dishes break as we made our way.

"What are you doing?" Smith asked. "You are in for one serious beating and I am not going to be able to stop it."

"I know. But William will be pissed if he comes back and I am as bad, or worse than he left me."

"I hope you know what you are doing."

"Not really, but I have to do something."

Adam walked into the office, yelled at Smith to leave and slammed the door.

"You think just because you have moved up to the third floor I can't hurt you?" He pulled me by my hair across the room to the desk.

"Did you know the little finger isn't as useful as the others? People who lose it barely notice it's missing."

I tried to resist, but he bent my fingers so that only my left pinky was exposed on the desk. Holding my hand down he made a fist and smashed my finger so hard the desk vibrated.

I screamed and fell to my knees, my hand still pressed by Adam's against the desk.

"Get up!" and he pulled me up by the hand he was still holding.

"I told you, when I met you, that you were mine. Just because you're in this house doesn't make that any less true. In fact, when my brother gets back, I will see to it that you leave with me." He let go of my hand and I fell back on my knees.

Adam kneed me hard in the head and I fell over. Blood poured from my eyebrow and started to blur my vision as I tried to crawl to the door. I kept telling myself I just needed to get through a few more days. Adam wouldn't be defiant enough to kill me. Not yet. He didn't stop me from making my way across the room, but instead continued to kick me like a soccer ball until I was at the door. A trail of blood was left in my wake. I reached the door and pulled myself to a seated position by the handle, which didn't turn. Adam crouched down beside me.

"Your sister didn't win against me, and you won't either, you bitch." He spit in my face and laughed, "Who knew when Mr. Strauss brought your little old Claire to me that I would end up having fun with two people for the price of one."

Hearing Adam say Claire's name invigorated me and the adrenaline made me forget about my plan to play weak. I got to my feet and punched him hard in the nose. We both screamed as blood poured from his nose and now both of my hands throbbed. I desperately wanted to grab the bronze deer statue from the table beside the door and beat his skull in. The temptation was growing within, but instead I wiped the spit off my face and braced for what was next.

Adam body checked me against the door, the doorknob digging into my lower back. Then he smashed my head against the doorframe and dropped me to the floor. "I swear if I didn't want you alive right now, I would take you to visit your sister."

He kicked me away from the door, opened it, and shouted "Out!"

Adam was standing behind the door, so he didn't notice that it wasn't Smith on the other side.

CHAPTER FORTY-TWO

I NEVER THOUGHT WILLIAM'S PRESENCE WOULD BRING ME joy. But in this moment, not only was there joy, there was relief. My plan couldn't have worked out better, I now wouldn't have to prove Adam had hurt me, he could see that for himself. From the doorway, William took in the scene of my broken finger, the blood dripping down my face and the bloody trail across the floor. I could see his jaw clench slightly but he did a good job of hiding any other reaction.

Adam started towards me with the back of his hand raised, ready to hit me again, but he stopped dead in his tracks when he saw William.

William stepped past us, staring at Adam as he walked and calmly spoke, "Smith, take Olivia to her room and call Dr. Boyden. He should be back in town. If he hasn't returned, tell him I will pay triple his usual fee if he gets back tonight. Then tell the ladies to meet me in the kitchen at 8 p.m. Olivia, I would make it a priority to join."

I looked from one brother to the other. William was still emotionless but I sensed an aura of anger enveloping him. Adam tried to hide his fear and replace it with defiance, however, was not doing a very good job. Smith gently took my arm and slowly led me to the elevator in the foyer. Nothing was said behind us. The only sound was the closing of the office door.

All of the women had heard my screams and were waiting to see how bad I had been hurt this time. Smith pressed the elevator up button and told everyone to be in the kitchen at 8 p.m. He recommended everyone go to their rooms until then. Smith didn't say it, but I knew he was trying to protect us all from the inevitable wrath of either Adam or William. As the elevator doors started to shut I smiled and mouthed "I'm okay". A couple of them winked or smiled back and headed up the stairs.

The elevator jerked as it started to move and Smith spoke, "What were you thinking? You could have gotten yourself killed if William hadn't come back early."

"He wasn't going to kill me. Not yet. Actually, this worked out better than I could have planned. William unexpectedly returning is perfect." I couldn't contain the smile and hoped no one was watching the elevator camera.

"What are you talking about?" The elevator stopped and I stepped out first.

I said quietly over my shoulder, "The less you know the better."

"I don't like this," he said as he walked me to my room.

"You don't have to like it. You will probably be out of here tonight and have nothing to worry about. Now, shouldn't you be calling the Doctor?" I was thankful for the broken finger and very thankful it was only a finger that was broken.

I paced around the room as we waited for Dr. Boyden, trying to make myself comfortable on different pieces of furniture, but the pain was too distracting. I was tempted to ask Smith to retrieve my Oxy from Whitney's room, but decided better of it. Neither he nor Dr. Boyden would pay much attention to the fact I hadn't finished my prescription when I first received it. However, I suspected if William joined the doctor for the examination, he would not be very forgiving. I could try to pretend I didn't want to fall back into an addiction, but I had been in worse pain than the broken finger. William would see through my story and everything about me could come into question. Instead, I decided I would once again push through the pain. At least until after Dr. Boyden was done.

Smith helped clean the clotted blood out of my hair and eased me into clean clothes. The whole time he asked more questions about my plan, but I kept refusing to answer so eventually he gave up. I turned away from the grey L.A. skyline and went over to Smith, who was now seated in the chair in the corner, and kissed the top of his head. "Thank you for telling me what happened to my sister."

He squeezed my good hand and I thought he was about to say something when Dr. Boyden opened the door. Smith immediately dropped my hand.

Dr. Boyden was particularly chipper, "What have we this time Ms. Olivia? You seem to be becoming a regular client of mine. I apologize for not being able to see you last week. I was in Jamaica with the family. Have you been? You should really..." He trailed off as he realized I would likely never leave the country. At least not for a vacation.

William followed closely behind the doctor and motioned for Smith to leave. My door remained open so I could see him wait by the elevator. It gave me some comfort to know that he was there. I sat down on the chair Smith had vacated and held out my left hand.

"Ah well now, I am going to have to reset this, otherwise this finger isn't going to look so pretty now, is it?" He laughed, but quickly quieted when neither I nor William joined in. "I warn you, this is going to hurt.

William, grab her a pillow to squeeze with her other hand."

Rather than give me a pillow, William held out his hand. I looked from it to him and for a fleeting moment saw concern in his eyes.

"Ready?" asked Dr. Boyden

I took William's hand, closed my eyes and, before I could take a deep breath, Dr. Boyden had snapped my finger back in place. I squeezed William's hand so hard that we both let out groans from the pain. Dr. Boyden put my finger in a splint and then wrapped my hand to prevent me from trying to move any of my fingers. My head didn't need stitches and after a full examination of my body, Dr. Boyden stated he didn't have any other concerns.

After talking to Smith and Dr. Boyden in the hall, all but William headed down the stairs. William stood at my door staring at me. I felt uncomfortable but didn't want to move. Once we heard the front door close, William turned and held out his arm for me. I got up from the chair, took his arm and we made our way to the kitchen.

CHAPTER FORTY-THREE

EVERYONE LOOKED UP AS WILLIAM AND I WALKED INTO the kitchen. William led me to my seat, then went and made himself a drink, drank it and made another before he sat down. The fear in the room was palpable. Even Jack and Kevin, standing on either side of the entryway, appeared to not know what was going to happen next.

Finally, William cleared his throat, "It seems I sit here once again and have to condemn the actions that have been taken against Olivia. I had provided strict instruction that she was to be left to heal. I take full responsibility for my brother's actions and promise you this." He took a sip of his drink. "Adam will never set foot in this house again."

We were too shocked to say anything. I was ecstatic! But how would I kill Adam if he wasn't going to be coming back? I suddenly realized everyone was staring at me. "Sorry. I dazed out for a minute." I looked at William, who continued without a concern about my distracted thoughts, "Other than Olivia's broken finger and head injury, what else happened while I was away?"

Fay talked about the party, the nurse uniforms and the new clientele, to which William looked annoyed but he sat in silence.

Eloisa informed William that Adam had spent nights with her, Jessica and Reyna.

There was general chatter about how the guests treated us. We didn't want to sound like a bunch of whining children so we kept our comments to items being thrown at us and the guests physically tossing us around.

"Well that sounds like a very unpleasant week. I am sorry my brother's incompetence created another mess." He finished the dregs of his third drink "Is there anything else?"

"One more thing," said Whitney, as she looked at me with sad eyes.

"Yes?" William followed up.

Whitney looked back to William, "Adam made Olivia work the party."

William's anger exploded through his hand as he squeezed his glass so hard it shattered. Lily jumped in her seat, as the rest of us watched William, not moving a muscle. I looked at Whitney who motioned her head towards William. I didn't understand what she was getting at until she pointed to a towel and then William. He had blood pouring from his hand. I finally got the hint. If I was going to get close to William, now was the time to take some initiative.

I grabbed a couple towels, gave one to Fay, who was beside William, and she started to clean up the broken glass. I took William's hand, and without any hesitation on his part, led him to the sink. As I moved his hand under the running water, I tried to stand as close to him as possible. I could feel his breath on the side of my neck. I looked at him and gave a slight smile but quickly looked back at his hand. I needed to play this slow. William didn't flinch as I removed a couple of small pieces of glass from his hand. It was as if he didn't notice the pieces were there. I rinsed the hand again and then wrapped the towel around it.

"I have some gauze in my room that Dr. Boyden left. I can get that for you if you want?"

"Bring it to my office," he said softly. "On second thought, I will come to your room in a while. I need to make a couple calls." He turned and left the kitchen. Jack and Kevin followed him.

I turned to Whitney, who was smiling. She had heard what he'd said.

After the glass and blood had been cleaned up, we moved into the living room and spread ourselves across the couches. We all had the same blank faces we wore just over a week ago, when we worked together to clean the room after Jenna's death. It felt like no one wanted to speak first. Then Fay, fiddling with the seam of a pillow, spoke, "Do you really think Mr. Hammond is going to keep Adam away from here? He could just be placating us?"

"Why would Mr. Hammond lie to us about this? We couldn't do anything, no matter what he decided, so I don't think he's just pacifying us," Saria answered.

Eloisa added, "I hope Adam stays away, I can't stand another night with that man. The things he makes me do." She shuddered and Jessica wrapped her arm around Eloisa as tears started down her cheeks.

Whitney added, "Adam has caused issues in the past and Mr. Hammond brushed it off. But something is different this time. Mr. Hammond seems different." She looked at me, "I haven't seen him this protective before."

"I, for one," said Reyna. "Am going to believe Mr. Hammond. I have to. It's the only good news we have received in awhile. I want to enjoy it." She got up, turned on the satellite radio, sitting on the gold and mirrored cabinet along the wall in between two of the entryways. She changed stations until she found an upbeat song I didn't recognize and started to dance.

Reyna's mood was contagious, and others started to dance with her. Whitney looked at me, came over and held out her hand. I could barely move, let alone dance, but I let her pull me off the couch and we joined the others. Reyna put her hands on my shoulders and slowly swayed me back forth, as if mocking my inability to dance in my current state. For the first time, there was a smile on everyone's face. I was still unsure how I would follow through on my plan for Adam, but I wasn't discouraged. I was going to find a way to take him down, one way or another. For now, I was going to enjoy this time of joy with my friends. I would worry about Adam later.

A new song came on and Lily squealed, "My favourite!" she ran over to the radio and cranked up the volume. The ladies were dancing on couches and singing into candlesticks. I remained swaying slowly on the floor. Adding the element of furniture would only increase my probability of falling over.

I danced to a couple more songs and then made my way to the doorway. I didn't know how long William would be with his calls, and I didn't want to anger him if I wasn't in my room when he arrived. I surveyed the room one last time as I left. Everyone was laughing, dancing and hugging each other. If I had walked by this room, not knowing where I was, I would have no idea the pain that resided in each of these women. They looked like a happy group of friends enjoying an evening of music. I slowly backed out of the room as I took it all in. I hoped one day soon we all could find some form of permanent happiness.

CHAPTER FORTY-FOUR

AT FIRST, I PUT THE BANDAGES AND OINTMENT ON THE bedside table, but thought that might be suggesting an action I didn't want to take. At least not unless I absolutely had to, and it definitely was too soon for that. I moved them to the desk and kept repositioning the chair for him to sit on. I was very nervous about moving forward with my plan to get close to William. It was dangerous and I was starting to lose confidence that I could pull it off. Even if I could get this hard shell of a man to open up to me, how was I going to influence his thoughts enough to give me the opportunity to kill Adam? Was there a way I could get William to do it himself? His tolerance for Adam was waning, but I doubted I could break that bond. I know I wouldn't have been able to take Claire's life, no matter what she did. I had to figure out a way to get William to bring Adam and I together, one last time.

I stood out on the balcony and watched as the sun painted the sky hues of purple, pink and red. I recalled the adage my father used to say, "Red sky at night, sailor's delight. Red sky in morning, sailor's take warning." Hopefully, the sky was a sign that good things were coming. As I watched the colours of the sky change, I pondered how I was going to get William to open up about Claire. I knew very little about William, and yet had to find a way to get him to talk about a murder he may have been involved with. He had no reason to speak to me about anything. Claire was always the persuasive one, not me. I would always do what was expected of me, not impose my expectations on others. This was going to be hard. I desperately wanted Claire's advice.

What would Claire say? She would probably tell me I had bitten off more than I could chew. Or that I was going too far - I knew what happened to her, why did I need revenge? Lastly, I figured she would give up trying to change my mind, and tell me to be careful, and to never underestimate my opponent.

I stayed outside as the sun disappeared behind the California mountains. When I walked back into the room, I pulled out a bottle of vodka I had hidden in my bedside table. I would need as much courage as possible to help me convince a man I loathed that I wanted to be closer to him.

I jumped as William opened the door without knocking. "Sorry to startle you."

I smiled and I pointed to the desk and put down the bottle. William looked around the room and then sat at the desk. "We really do need to change this colour," he chuckled. "Did Jack get you the samples?"

"Yes, I am trying to decide between two colours." I went over to the small table in front of the couch and brought William my selections. "What do you think?"

"Is there any difference?" he joked. "They both look yellow to me."

"Yeah. Well, one is a matted colour and the other has a little more sheen to it."

"I see." He closed his eyes and randomly pointed in the direction of the samples, "This one."

I looked at the sample closet to the air he was pointing at, "Lightning Bug, it is!"

William took the sample and placed it in his inner suit jacket pocket, "I will have someone come by tomorrow."

I smiled, put the other sample on the desk and then unwrapped the towel from William's hand. The bleeding had stopped, but there was some blood caked around the wound. I went to my bathroom, grabbed a wet cloth and sat on the floor by William's feet as I gently cleaned off the blood.

William filled the silence first, "How is it that, after everything you have been through, you are so gentle? I can barely feel your touch."

I willed myself to blush and looked up at him. "I guess I try to not let my past influence my present." Where I came up with that, I don't know. Was William's tendency to speak theoretically at breakfast rubbing off on me?

"I should heed that wisdom sometimes. But, I fear my past may always influence my present."

"Why is that?" I asked, as I started to apply the ointment to the cuts.

"Without my past I would not be where I am today. I fought through turmoil and judgment to build what you see here. This place wouldn't be the same without my past."

I wanted to scream - 'Turmoil, you don't know turmoil' but I held my tongue and instead said, "Maybe not. I guess the bigger question is what pain do you need to let go of in order to make you and this place better?"

William didn't respond. I finished wrapping his hand in the gauze and wondered if I had pushed too far too quickly? I could feel my heartbeat start to quicken. I got up when I was done with William's hand and fiddled nervously, as I tried to get the remaining gauze back into its box. William leaned over, elbows on his knees, and ran his fingers through his hair. He looked up at me, "I'm sorry."

He held out his left hand. I instinctively took it. He stood up and he was now looking down at me. "I'm sorry," he bent down and kissed my forehead, his lips lingering. I didn't know what to do, so I did nothing. As much as I needed to get close to him, I needed him to be the one to seemingly be making that decision. If I pushed it, he might see right through me. As he removed his lips he brushed my hair behind my ear and held my head in his hands. He looked at me with intrigue, as if he was searching my soul.

I hoped I was looking back at him with eyes of love and not eyes of revenge.

CHAPTER FORTY-FIVE

OVER THE NEXT FEW WEEKS, WE BARELY SAW WILLIAM. We only caught glimpses of him around the house, and he rarely joined us for dinner. He no longer came to breakfast, and barely looked at, or acknowledged, me during the rare dinner conversations. Was he ashamed of the ounce of vulnerability he had shown me? How would I get close to him if he left any room I entered? Time was moving forward but my plan was not.

Parties had been cancelled for the moment. William wanted to repair the reputational damage caused by Adam and his inferior party and clientele. The little William shared with us included the fact that existing guests feared having to socialize with "riff raff", as they called them. He doubted many guests would attend, or feared lower bids, if a party was hosted right away. Once bids fell, it would be hard to get them back up again, so William wanted to visit each guest and make sure they understood their importance to him. William wanted to ensure guests understood he offered a unique experience, and only the elite were invited.

Although we didn't work parties, when William went to visit guests, he would bring one of the women along. Everyone who left the house brought back the same story. They were taken to a guest's home, where William flattered their egos over a drink or two. The woman remained silent, all while flirting with their eyes and body. Once the guest had committed to returning to the parties, the woman was handed over as a thank you. No one knew what William did while the guests' loyalty was being repaid, but Kevin or Jack remained outside the door to ensure no one was hurt.

I tried to see if there was a way to get a letter to Joe, but those who left couldn't see a way it would be feasible. They were never alone and the guests they were meeting were not sympathetic to anyone's needs but their own. I was not requested to attend any of the meetings. This didn't surprise me. I was still healing and William likely didn't want the guests to know just how little control William had over his brother.

The time off allowed my 'new' room to be redecorated without the hassle of working around it. I moved back in with Whitney for three nights as the Pepto Bismol pink walls turned a calming yellow. The princess-like white and pink furniture was replaced with natural wood. I picked out a red classic love seat which popped in front of the yellow walls. When the room was done, everyone came up to inspect it and were happy with the changes. Lily's only complaint was that the wall sconces on either side of the bed looked like cheerleader batons with large lights on each end. Given the hostility that still lingered between us, I took the minor complaint as a sign she was slowly letting Jenna go.

ONE EVENING, AFTER a particularly cold and silent dinner with William, I sat on my balcony with Reyna and Whitney. This high up, we could see the whole city covered in lights below us.

"Do you think we will ever get out of here?" Reyna asked.

"I wouldn't count on it," Whitney replied. "Our lives are forever tied to this house, until our lives are no more."

"That is rather morbid," said Reyna.

"But likely true," I said and sipped my wine. "Unless I can come up with some way to get the plan back on track."

"Has he still said nothing to you?" Whitney asked.

"Nothing you haven't seen. It's as if that night never happened. I barely even seem to exist to him anymore."

"I am not a psychologist, but it wouldn't surprise me if Mr. Hammond was scared of his feelings for you. He is usually filled with rage, and greed, and has no idea what to do when he feels something else," Whitney offered. "He's probably just focused on damage control and once that is dealt with, he will come back around."

"I hope you're right. But if he doesn't, we need to figure out my next step. Have you spoken to Kevin?"

Whitney looked at her glass of wine, "I really wanted to, but when I finally got the courage I couldn't. All Kevin talked about was how we had to be extra careful, with Mr. Hammond being on edge. I'm sorry Liv, I couldn't risk it."

I was heartbroken but I understood. "It's okay. I get it. You and Reyna are the best things to happen to me in all of this. I wouldn't want either of you to get hurt because of me. We will figure something out."

"Given how much you brought in at the last party I doubt you are off the hook to work. Mr. Hammond would be foolish to have you not participate. I say, pretend you are really interested in one of the guests, genuinely interested, and see if that makes him jealous," Reyna suggested.

"I don't know, jealousy usually leads to anger. I am not the biggest fan of angry William."

They nodded in agreement as I topped up our glasses.

Reyna continued, "You're probably not going to like this idea either. But he is rather protective of you. I mean, some of us have been beaten before, and never has he shown the same attention he shows you."

"Please tell me you are not suggesting that I keep getting the shit kicked out of me?"

"Not exactly, but what if you get whoever you are with to be a little rougher, so that it leaves a few small marks. Nothing that wouldn't heal in a few days."

"Reyna could be right. It might work." Whitney said.

"Guys, I cannot keep getting hurt at each party. No matter how minor the injuries. I will just look like someone turning into a liability and not an asset." They looked like they wanted to protest but I continued "Yes, he seems keen to take care of me, but we need to find another way. If William is questioning his feelings, or trying to get away from them, another beating may be the excuse he needs to remove me from the house."

"I just don't see what else we can do." Whitney added.

"There's a way - we just need to think. Have either of you seen him get close to anyone before? Genuinely close, not just physically?"

"Not that I know of," Whitney answered. She had been here longer than Reyna and would have witnessed William's actions more. "However, I do sometimes see a wedding ring on his finger."

I was taken aback, "Wait! What? I haven't noticed a ring."

"Yeah, usually around Labour Day. I've only seen it a couple times. It's as if he forgot to take it off. He would go into his office or his room, come back out and it would be gone."

"Do you think he has a family somewhere?" Reyna asked.

"That would explain the weeks away. I just thought it was business," I said.

"So, did the rest of us," Whitney replied.

"But that doesn't explain why you only saw the ring during the holidays. If he was seeing a family more frequently, you would think he might slip up more," I suggested.

Whitney looked as if she had just solved the world's biggest mystery. Her face lit up, she got up from her chair and leaned back against the balcony railing.

"What if he *had* a family, not that he *has* a family. What if something happened to them around the holidays and he wears the ring as a way to honour their, or at least her, memory. He goes out a lot every year at that time, but always spends his nights here. If his family was alive you would think he would spend his nights with them too."

"This happens every year?" I asked.

"Every year I have been here. Now that I think about it, Mr. Hammond starts leaving the house more often sometime in the middle of August."

"That's only a few weeks away." Reyna stated.

I was starting to get excited by the progress we were making. "Okay. Let's say, Whitney, you are right. How can I use that? If I were him, I would want to shut myself away. I wouldn't want anyone around me during that time."

"I wonder if your trusted source would know what happened?" Whitney asked.

"The problem is I don't have access to that trusted source right now, and I don't know when or if I will again."

Whitney and Reyna looked at each other and I could tell they were putting two and two together. Whitney spoke first "So, it is someone who is no longer in the house then ," she stated, rather than asked.

Reyna added in her thoughts, "And the only people who have left were Adam and Smith, and we know Adam would not be going around telling you his dark secrets. At least not the real ones."

Whitney added, "And Smith would likely have been with Adam when Claire died."

There was no point in trying to hide it, "Fine, you're right, Smith told me about Claire." They both squealed, "Before you ask, I don't know why he told me. I think he felt bad about all the beatings Adam was giving me. Before Adam's and my last rendezvous Smith mentioned he was the one who got William to bring me here."

They both smiled and clinked their wine glasses together before taking a sip.

Reyna spoke first, "Smith is why you are here. Interesting. Anything going on between you two we should know about?" she teased.

"Ha. You're funny. No, there is nothing going on."

Reyna continued, "So, how do we get Smith back?"

"He has no need to come back. Unless maybe he needed to deliver a package from Adam. But how do we get him to do that?" Whitney added.

An idea came to me, "Maybe we are thinking about this backwards. What if we don't need to get *him* here. What we need is to get the *information* here."

Reyna and Whitney didn't seem to be following.

"What is our goal?" I asked

"To get you close to William," Reyna replied.

"Yes, ultimately. But what is our goal for Smith?"

"To find out what he knows about William's family life," Whitney answered.

"Exactly, or if he even had one. So, who do we know that would have access to us and to Smith?"

Reyna and Whitney thought for a moment but couldn't think of who had access to the houses that made up William's network.

"Dr. Boyden sees all the girls, does he not? So, if someone needed to see him, maybe he could pass a message on."

"Do you think we can trust him?"

"I don't know why, but I do." By their reactions I could tell neither Reyna or Whitney were skeptical.

"Since we don't want you to be the patient, how do we get him here?" Whitney asked.

I had an idea, "Reyna, if you pretended you were sick in the mornings, and a little throughout the day, maybe we could get him here to see if you might be pregnant."

"You were with Adam when he was here, so that would line up. Pretend your IUD might have been faulty," Whitney added.

"I can easily do that. But what do I tell Dr. Boyden?"

"If I can't be in the room with you, play on his feelings. Tell him that you are scared of what William or Adam may do if you are pregnant. I will give you a note and tell him you think Smith would be honest with you about Adam's reaction. You just want to prepare for the worst if needed. Now, as we need to get Smith's response, you will have to get him to say he needs to come back for a follow up. How does that sound?"

"If I can get Mr. C. to do what I want at a party, rather than what he wants, I can get Dr. Boyden to go along with our plan," Reyna replied more confidently than I had ever seen.

"You go, girl" I said and we all laughed.

Sitting on that balcony with Reyna and Whitney, I felt confident. These women and I were going to move the plan forward, and nothing was going to stop us. I looked at my friends and felt loved. I hoped they knew that ` I would do whatever I could to protect them and get them out of here. I only wished Claire could be a part of the dismantling of the system she had become trapped in.

CHAPTER FORTY-SIX

THE NEXT DAY, FAY SMUGGLED ME SOME PAPER, AN envelope, and a pen at lunch. She didn't say where she got it and I didn't ask. Sitting at the desk in my room, I decided to write two letters. The first one, I hoped, would bring me one step closer to William and then out of this place.

Dear Friend,

I have to make this letter short as I am rushed to write it, however, I wanted to thank you for your help the other day. What you have done for me deserves more gratitude than I could ever give. I hate to put you at greater risk, but if you are seeing this letter we have a mutual friend who wants a little bit of justice.

What I need to know is does W currently have a family? Wife, kids, anyone outside of A? Or has W had a family in the past? It has been noticed that during the holiday season W will sometimes have a wedding ring on. Please tell me what you can. The information could prove very useful.

I understand you may not be privy to this information, but I also know that you are a very observant man who has been employed by this family for many years. I am sure you would have noticed something. Every little bit helps.

You were one of the last people I ever thought would help me and I hope that whatever led you to do so continues to encourage you.

If ever I can do something for you, name it.

Please have a response back to the messenger ASAP and destroy this letter. In case we cannot contact each other again, know that I do not hold you responsible for C.

Your Friend,

O.

P.S I have included a second letter I was hoping you could get to a friend of mine. He will be very worried about my whereabouts. I am not looking to get you in trouble but I need my friend to know that I am okay. If you would be so kind as to email, hitchhiker2020@starnet.ca, the enclosed contents I would be forever grateful.

The second letter made me miss home more than I had up until now.

Joe,

I am sorry I haven't been able to get word to you sooner. I hope you don't think I left without saying goodbye. You know I would never do that. You must know that this email address is not my own and a friend of mine is sending this note on my behalf.

I was kidnapped outside Claire's and my old house. I don't have time to give you all the details but I am in a mansion somewhere in L.A. I can see over the city from the hill the house resides on. I am being forced to have sex with wealthy clients for a family who has run this business for over 20 years both in the USA and Canada. I would give you their name but right now I need to protect the people who are helping me. I am also close to getting the answers about Claire and don't need you running in here, guns blazing.

She was here, Joe. I was too late, but Claire was here. She was killed by the brother of the man I am being forced to work for. I am still piecing everything together and hope to understand everything soon.

Please don't come find me, no matter how tempting. You would only jeopardize the work I have done and then everything I have been through would be for nothing. I know you won't be able to just sit around so be careful, please don't come to L.A. If you must do something, go back to my old house and then walk north towards the bus stop. I know it's been months, but I dropped something when I was grabbed. A box. I don't know if it was left behind, but maybe there is something there that will help. They also use cell phones to bid on and pay for the women. I don't know what app they are using but maybe there is an angle there you could look at. The data has to be somewhere.

You have been an amazing partner and friend. Tell Sally and the kids I love them and I want both of you to know that I am fine.

Love,

Liv.

I put down the pen and read over both letters. I had been tempted to write most of Joe's letter in code, but feared Smith would get spooked and not send it. I really did want Joe's help, and hoped the clues I was giving him about the box and the app were enough to ignore my fake pleas to not come to L.A. If that didn't work, I was counting on Joe's stubbornness and loyalty to get him here.

CHAPTER FORTY-SEVEN

FOR THE REST OF THE WEEK REYNA PROGRESSIVELY GOT 'sicker'. She ran to the bathroom whenever William was around, especially when someone was cooking. We hadn't told anyone else our plan and everyone seemed worried about Reyna. She put on makeup to look paler than she already was and spent a lot of time in bed. I must admit, if I didn't know what she was up to, I would have been convinced by her performance.

Finally, on Thursday, William made an appearance at dinner. He was not inclined to look at me, or really any of the women. As he was in the middle of informing us we would have one large party before the annual New Year's Eve Bash, Reyna puked all over the floor beside her. We all stood up and stared, even I hadn't expected her to actually vomit. Whitney ran over to her, as Saria went to get the paper towels. As the women tended to Reyna, I went to William.

"She has been like this all week; do you think she could see Dr. Boyden?"

"Has anyone else gotten sick? If there is something going around before this party, I swear, every one of you is out of this house!" William pushed his chair back and left the kitchen.

Not wanting to waste this opportunity, I followed after him as he entered the foyer. "No one else is sick. Just Reyna. Adam spent..." William stopped in his tracks the moment I said 'Adam' and turned on me. His face was full of fury and exhaustion. I continued, "He spent a night with her when he was here, so maybe she. . . Maybe she needs to see a doctor." I looked at him pleadingly.

William looked at his watch and then looked back at me. "Fine, I will have Jack make the call. Just make sure she stays in her room. My men are busy, so have one of the other ladies watch over her. If it is contagious, I don't want you getting sick. You are not to spend time with her, understand? We have money to make this week, and nothing is going to stop that." He turned, and a moment later I heard a door slam.

Later that evening, Dr. Boyden examined Reyna. I didn't want to risk William learning I had seen Reyna, so I had Whitney give her the letters I had written for Smith, before the doctor had arrived. I trusted Reyna to do what needed to be done. I stood outside the bedroom with the rest of the women as we waited for Dr. Boyden to finish.

While we waited, Whitney and I quietly updated everyone on what was happening. After hearing concerns from others, I started to become nervous Dr. Boyden wouldn't go along with our request. Most felt we couldn't trust him and didn't understand why I did. They were scared I had risked their lives for a plan that wasn't guaranteed to work. Everyone felt they had a better solution, however, after hearing them, most didn't feel they would actually work. It was too late now anyways. The plan was in motion.

When Dr. Boyden left the room, his face had no expression. Sweat beaded on his forehead, which he patted with a handkerchief as he walked down the stairs. When he reached the bottom, he stood beside Jack and looked back up at us, "Keep her hydrated. I will be back in a couple of days with the test results and some pills to help her feel better." Then he nodded to Jack and left.

Jack went to update William, while the rest of us heaved a huge sigh of relief. It looked like Dr. Boyden was going to help us. I snuck in to see Reyna, while the others stood watch.

"He took the letter!" Reyna exclaimed.

"He said he would be back in a couple of days. What did you tell him?"

"The truth."

Shock covered my face. What was Reyna thinking? She could have just gotten us all killed. "What part of the truth?"

"All of it, how I was feigning being sick so we could get the letter to Smith as part of a plan to get us all out of here. How Adam killed your sister. Dr. Boyden remembered Claire, Olivia. I knew I had him when I told him that much. I could see it in his eyes that he could no longer deny what happens to us."

I couldn't believe she had revealed so much. I trusted Reyna and if she felt she had to tell Dr. Boyden everything I wasn't going to hold it against her. I sat beside her and took her hand. "Thank you. I hope this works." I gave her a hug.

"It will. Have faith."

Whitney poked her head in and said Mr. Hammond and Jack were standing at the bottom of the stairs, and wanted us all in the living room. Reyna was to remain in bed. I quickly hugged Reyna again, slipped out of the room and took my place at the back of the group of women crowded on the landing.

When we got into the living room, William was standing in front of the fireplace, impeccably dressed as always. Jack stood at the back of the room and against the bookshelves. We all sat around on the couches, which felt more uncomfortable than usual.

"Dr. Boyden called me after he left here," William stated sternly.

We all stayed silent and focused our eyes on William. Did Dr. Boyden tell him what we were up to? Was this it? Had I led these women to their death?

"It seems that, whether Reyna has the stomach flu, or worse, she has a problem that needs to be remedied. She will be confined to her room for the next week. None of you, and I mean none of you, are to see her. Jack will bring her everything she needs. We need to make up for the disaster my brother caused, and every one of you will need to work extra hard to do that."

We continued to focus on William and dared not show a sign of relief that he didn't know what we were up to.

"This means that each of you will be spending time with two guests at a minimum. So, make sure you are up for it. If I hear any complaints you are out. Got it?"

"Got it," we said in unison.

"Olivia, follow me," William ordered. I stood up and followed him out of the room, with Jack behind me. I kept repeating what Reyna said "Have faith, have faith."

Rather than take me to his office, we went out the front door and Jack opened the back door of an Escalade. William stood on the other side of the vehicle and motioned for me to get in. I hesitated, terrified I was being taken to Claire. My delay angered William, "IN NOW!" he ordered.

I climbed in and William followed suit. Jack got into the front passenger seat. The driver had already been in the vehicle and I recognized him as one of the many guards from William's last party. As we drove past the trees lining the long driveway, a range of thoughts went through my head:

I could jump from the car, but could I get away before being shot?

I could reach the driver's gun in his belt but Jack would have a bullet in my head before I could use it.

Were these the last streets Claire saw?

I wished I had said goodbye to my friends.

CHAPTER FORTY-EIGHT

THE VEHICLE STOPPED OUTSIDE A LARGE HOUSE ON WHAT appeared to be a wealthy suburban street. The houses were large stone structures with three-car garages and large yards. As I got out of the vehicle, dressed in black sweatpants and an oversized hoodie, I felt very out of place. There was an older neighbour tending her rose garden across the street. She looked up and watched us make our way up the front steps to a large oak front door. I could only imagine what she made of me.

A woman in a grey maid's uniform opened the door and we stepped into a foyer which seemed mediocre compared to William's. The walls were stark white and held what I am sure was some very expensive art. The main focal point was the scarlet carpeted staircase leading to the second floor. The woman led us into a large room covered in mahogany from floor to ceiling. The walls were wood paneled and the bookshelves brimmed with books. More paintings and marble statues decorated the room, along with a green leather couch and chairs alongside a beautifully carved antique desk.

Everything was very ornate. Although William's house was extravagant it was not as ostentatious as this one. I didn't know what I was doing here but I knew I didn't belong.

William motioned for me to sit on the couch, under the window, facing the door. I dutifully did and he sat beside me. Other than the forced confines of the vehicle this was the closest William had been to me since I bandaged his hand. I desperately wanted to ask what was happening but knew better, so I fiddled with my hands to try and quench the nerves. William noticed and put his hand on mine to stop me. I looked at him but he was watching the door. I thought about trying to show some fake affection by squeezing his hand but he quickly removed his hand at the sound of footsteps in the hall. I moved mine to either side of my legs and dug my nails into the leather of the couch as the hairs on the back of my neck started to stand on end. My gut was telling me something was wrong.

The door opened, signaling William to stand. I mimicked him. However, when Mr. Y walked into the room, my knees buckled and I fell back onto the couch. Why would William bring me here? Was the only way to keep Mr. Y away from the parties to bring the 'party' to him? At first, I thought I felt scared. Then I realized what I actually felt was betrayal and anger with myself. William had apologized for what happened to me and said he would protect us. I was stupid enough to believe him. I felt defeated and hated myself for ever thinking I could remotely trust William long enough to save myself and the others.

Mr. Y's voice brought my thoughts back to the room, "I have been known to have that effect on people Ms. Olivia," he said jokingly. A small but stocky man I had never seen before followed Mr. Y into the room, closed the door and stood guard.

I tried to get back up, "Please stay seated." Mr. Y sat in a chair opposite the couch and William retook his spot beside me. Jack stood behind the couch, hands folded in front of him. I could feel the anger building inside of me. I gripped the couch tighter as I looked to William for any sign of what we were doing here. I received no indication in return.

"Are we all set?" William asked.

"Straight to business I see. Yes." Mr. Y got up and went to the desk, where he unlocked a bottom drawer. He pulled out a case, opened it and turned to show the room's occupants the contents. Cash. My guess was hundreds of thousands.

Jack went over and inspected the contents. "It's all here," he announced, then closed the case and took it.

Mr. Y came back and stood in front of his chair. "I must say, Ms. Olivia, you drive a hard bargain." His smile reminded me of Adam.

I couldn't control my anger or confusion any longer. I pushed myself to standing, "WHAT THE FUCK IS GOING ON?" I yelled.

William calmly replied "Olivia, calm down, we are just settling some business."

"BUSINESS YOU NEED ME TO BE HERE FOR?" Mr. Y enjoyed my outburst and chuckled.

I looked from Mr. Y to William, who still showed no sign of emotion. I took a breath as I tried to assess the situation. I hoped the split second would calm me down but it didn't. I was full of rage. "Did you just sell me to this FUCKING ASSHOLE?"

I couldn't control myself and I lunged at William, knocking him into the side of the couch and onto the ground. He tried to get up, but I climbed on top of him and started to punch him as hard as I could. "How could you? After what he did! What kind of man are you?" My broken finger screamed in pain, but I wasn't going to stop.

I could hear Mr. Y laughing loudly now, and someone's feet shuffling behind me. Jack slowly pulled me off William and held my arms behind my back. My legs were free, so I got in a couple kicks before I was moved far enough away from William they would no longer reach. I couldn't hold back my tears and started to cry. The thought of spending one more minute alone with Mr. Y was enough for me to fight everyone in this room until I or they were dead. I glared at Mr. Y as he continued to laugh.

"I knew she was a wild one, William. Ha-ha. Got your hands full there."

William slowly got up from the floor, brushed himself off and straightened his suit. He tried to do up the button of the suit jacket and realized it had torn off in the scuffle. After he was satisfied he had put himself back together, he walked over to me "Are we going to have any more outbursts?" he asked sternly.

"Are you going to leave me here?" I replied curtly.

"After that, I should." William sat back down on the couch and looked for me to do the same. Jack let go of my arms and I reluctantly sat back down beside William.

"Mr. Y please continue."

"I would much rather watch another wrestling match, but alright." Mr. Y crossed one leg over the other and rested his hands on his knees. "Ms. Olivia, I understand I caused you some pain."

"Some!" I hoped my eyes showed Mr. Y just how much he repulsed me.

William placed his hand on my leg to signal I was not to speak.

Mr. Y continued, "Alright, more than some, and for that I apologize."

He sounded mildly sincere, but I didn't believe him. I doubted anyone else would either. Once again, I turned to William for answers. This time I got one.

"Mr. Y has agreed to apologize for his actions against you, and to pay me the revenue I lost while you were not working. He has also promised he would not harm another one of my workers again. Isn't that right?"

"Correct," Mr. Y said, with a smug look on his face.

Those of us who were sitting, stood up. William walked over to Mr. Y.

"There is one final thing we need to discuss," William said, and held out his hand to Jack. Rather than the case of cash, Jack handed him a gun. William cocked it and looked to the man standing at the door. The man promptly stepped out of the room. "To ensure no further incidents occur, and so you don't think you got off lightly, you will lose a hand." William moved the barrel of the gun between Mr. Y's hands. "You decide, right or left."

The smug look on Mr. Y's face had disappeared and was replaced by confusion and then fear. He looked like he might protest as he opened and closed his mouth a couple of times but no words came out. He regained some of his composure and said with a crack in his voice, "Left."

William fired a bullet into Mr. Y's right hand. Mr. Y screamed "I said left, fuck!" and he fell back into his chair.

"Oh, your left, not my left. Oops" William joked.

I couldn't help but smile a little. William looked back at me and pointed the handle of the gun to me. "Take it."

I didn't hesitate and grabbed the gun. It was heavier than I remembered. I stared at the power I now held in my hands. What I could do with it if I wanted. Were there enough bullets in here that I could kill the three men in this room and the guard? If so, could I find my way back to the house to get my friends? I was jolted from my thoughts by Mr. Y's incessant cries of pain.

William looked at me, "Your turn."

"My turn for what?"

"You get one bullet. Mind you don't kill him. Just hurt him. This man's death would cause more damage than you know." William stepped away from me.

Adrenaline ran through my body as I stared at a terrified Mr. Y. He looked at me with pleading eyes as he tried to stop the bleeding of his right hand. He, the chair and the expensive hand-woven carpet were stained with blood. It didn't take me long to decide what I was going to do. I looked angrily into William's eyes. I cocked the gun. And pulled the trigger without flinching.

Mr. Y fell off the chair in a heap of pain. Jack pulled him up and blood poured down the insides of his legs. Unless he got reconstructive surgery, he wasn't going to be enjoying himself with anyone ever again.

I gave William back the gun. As much as I wanted the men in this room dead, I wanted to do right by my friends, so now was not the time. Without instruction, I walked out of the room, down the hall and out the front door. Mr. Y's cries became more muffled the further I walked.

The neighbour who was gardening was gone and there wasn't a trace of life on the street. The driver was still in the car so I climbed in and waited. William and Jack weren't far behind me. As we drove down the street it took everything in me not to vomit. I had only used my service weapon twice in the line of duty. This was the first time I had ever used a gun with malice. I didn't like who I was becoming, but knew that if I wanted to kill Adam I would need to harden myself even more.

As we drove, the adrenaline started to dissipate and I was starting to go into shock. My hands were shaking, I was having a hard time breathing and I wanted to cry. I tried to get myself under control but the emotions were too much. I pulled my knees to my chest and cried hard. Who was I becoming?

William unbuckled his seat belt and moved to be right beside me. He handed me a handkerchief, wrapped his arm around me and pulled me into his chest. At this moment his touch did not repulse me. I didn't care who he was or what he had done. I just needed to be held as I let months of pent-up anger, frustration and grief wash over me.

No words were spoken during the forty-five minutes it took to get back to the house. William just let me cry as he held me tight.

CHAPTER FORTY-NINE

AS THE CAR DROVE UP THE LONG, WINDING DRIVEWAY, I pulled away from William and composed myself as best I could. I hadn't looked great when I left the house, but I knew I looked worse now. I ran my fingers through my hair and wiped away the last tears from my cheeks. William moved back to his seat, his blue shirt soaked through from my tears. He did up the one remaining button of his suit jacket but it didn't hide the mess I had made.

When we stopped outside the front door, Jack and the driver got out of the car. I reached for my door handle but, before I could open it, William took my other hand. "Are you alright?"

I wanted to explode with all the reasons why I wasn't, but instead said, "I'll be fine."

"I thought today would give you some closure, but maybe I was wrong to bring you along. I should have just handled it myself."

Why was he trying to have a conversation now?! I just wanted to have a shower and go to bed! I took a deep breath and knew I had to use this opportunity to keep getting closer to William. Fate was being very cruel today, but I would deal with her later. I sat back in my seat and turned to William.

"I'm glad I was there. It's just that it has been a very hard few months. Well, a hard few years actually. I guess everything I had buried came bubbling up today. I'm sorry if I ruined your shirt."

William's voice was calming, "I have more shirts. I know the transition into this life is never easy, but you have definitely had it harder than most. You feel trapped and don't want to be here. I don't blame you; I haven't given you much choice in the matter. But I do hope that we can stop being enemies, and, maybe one day, you will be content with your life here."

He kept a hold of my hand as our eyes were fixed together. He moved closer, leaned in and kissed me gently. His lips were soft and supple. As we parted, he lingered a moment and his eyes were filled with loneliness. William let me go, opened his door and stepped out. I sat frozen for a moment, looking after him through the open car door. I saw Jack open the large front door, and I could see all of the ladies waiting at the bottom of the stairs.

I crawled across the backseat and stood behind William. As we walked into the house, Whitney ran up to me, hugged me and stepped back, still holding my arms "What happened? You look like you've been crying. Where did this blood come from?"

I looked down at my sweater. I hadn't noticed the blood spatter. I didn't know what I was allowed to say, so I looked to William who advised the group, "Mr. Y will have a difficult time rising to the occasion from now on." William and I couldn't help but laugh. I thought I saw Jack smirk at the joke, but everyone else was confused.

William became more serious, "Olivia shot Mr. Y's penis."

Gasps filled the air. They looked at me and I shrugged and tried to lighten the mood, "Can you blame me?" Everyone laughed nervously and Whitney hugged me again. "At least he got some of what was coming to him," she whispered in my ear. I smiled and hugged her back.

"Ladies, I think it might be best if you go back to your rooms now. Olivia has had a long day, and although I am sure she appreciates your support, would rather be left alone. Whitney, why don't you grab a bottle of something. I am sure Olivia needs a drink," William instructed, and then headed in the direction of his office.

With the sun having gone down, there was a chill in the air, so I didn't feel like sitting out on the balcony. After I had showered and changed into my pajamas, Whitney and I climbed into my bed with glasses of whiskey as I filled her in on the evening's events. William may have instructed everyone else to stay away from me, but Whitney and I took his request for her to get me a drink as evidence she was excluded from the commandment. Whitney promised she'd fill in Reyna and the others, so that I didn't have to.

"He really gave you the gun?" Whitney was astonished.

"Yes."

"So, you could have shot William instead of Mr. Y?"

"Yes, and I wanted to. But Jack would have killed me within seconds, and then what would happen to all of you? Adam would reign with holy terror on this place."

"Oh God. Well, I guess thank you for not shooting him. But why would he give you that power? He must have known what you would consider doing. Why take the risk?"

"I have been trying to figure that out. He's a smart man, and everything he does is calculated. It wouldn't surprise me if there were only two bullets in the gun: One for him to use, and one for me."

"Limit the damage, if you did decide to go rogue."

"Exactly. William knew Mr. Y would think he was getting off light with an apology and some money. But William lured him into a false sense of security. Then he meticulously took back all of the power, and left Mr. Y terrified, in a pool of blood. I swear William even paid off Mr. Y's own man. One look and the guy left the room. What kind of man leaves their boss with men who aren't afraid to hurt people?"

"Maybe we are in over our heads here, Liv. If William has people in other crews, we are fucked." Whitney took a large mouthful of whiskey.

"Not necessarily. What if William was giving me an olive branch, as they say. Testing me to see what I would do. He must have known I would have thought I was being sold to Mr. Y, upon the money being exchanged. I am not sure he expected me to attack him. But even after that, he still gave me the gun. He must have known at that moment, I loathed Mr. Y more than him, and I wouldn't shoot him."

"Or maybe he just hoped you would," she quipped.

"I don't see William 'hoping' for much. Either way, how many of the other women has he allowed to shoot someone? Likely zero."

"None that I am aware of. Man, Kevin doesn't even let me near his pistol. What spell have you put on Mr. Hammond?" she chuckled into her drink.

"I haven't told you the most interesting part yet."

"More interesting than shooting a bastard's penis off? Well this should be good!"

By the time I had finished telling Whitney about the car ride and it's ending with a kiss she had finished her whiskey and was pouring another drink.

"Damn! That is some serious shit. Look at you getting close to the boss. This might be the drink talking, but how was it?"

"How was what?"

"The kiss. Is Mr. Hammond at least a good kisser?"

"It doesn't matter if he is a good kisser. Either way our plan is working." I took a sip of my drink as I felt my cheeks warming up.

"You are blushing! So, I am going to take that as a yes."

I couldn't contain the grin from spreading across my face. "Fine! He is a good kisser. Now, can we please get back to planning his demise?"

"Okay, okay. What's next?"

Whitney and I spent most of the night going through possible scenarios based on if, or what, we heard from Smith. Exhaustion, and half the bottle of whiskey, had us passed out in my bed by 1 a.m. My dreams were filled with scenes of Claire in the back of the van. Yelling for me to help her. Find her. Bring her home.

CHAPTER FIFTY

WHEN DR. BOYDEN STOPPED BY TO FOLLOW UP WITH REYNA, the appointment felt like it took hours. We all sat nervously in the living room waiting for him to come down. When he finally did, he walked straight to William's office. A while later he left the house, without so much as a glance in my direction, as I leaned against the door frame of the living room. We all stared at each other for a few moments while we waited to see if William, Jack or Kevin came out. When we were confident they weren't, we all went up to Reyna's room.

Reyna was propped up in her bed waiting expectantly with a smile on her face. "Olivia come here," she said sweetly, and patted the bed beside her.

As the others settled on Jessica's old bed, the floor, or leaned against the furniture, I made my way and sat beside her. She pulled a letter out from under her pillow and handed it to me.

My hands were shaking as I gripped the envelope tightly.

"Well, open it!" said Jessica eagerly.

I tore open the letter and read it to everyone.

Dear O,

I haven't been called someone's friend in a very long time. I don't even know if I deserve that title in this instance, either. I hope the information I provided about C gave you some peace. Even if the nature of the information was less than ideal. As for the questions you ask now, I can tell you this:

About 10 years ago, W had a wife and a little girl. This was before his father's death and W moving part of the business to L.A. I didn't know W well back then as I had always worked with A. Like now the two of them didn't get along. What I do know is that he adored his daughter. You wouldn't recognize him if you compared who he was with her, and who he is today.

A Labour Day weekend before W's father died, W was driving his wife and daughter home from a family gathering. There had been a large row between father and sons and W had stormed out of the party, furious. There had been an unusually early snow storm that year in Michigan and the roads were icy. From what A told me, W had been drinking. Next thing we all knew; W's car went down an embankment. Mother and daughter were killed and W woke up in hospital a few days later._

As you would suspect, he blamed himself and started drinking heavily. I don't know how, but W was never held legally responsible for the death of his family. A told me an investigation wasn't even opened. But W didn't need a jail cell to ruin his life. He took that upon himself. Making dangerous decisions with the business, drugs, women. He fought with A about everything. I remember one time at a barbeque, I overheard W yell at A "their blood is on your hands, not mine!" It was not my place to ask so I never found out what W meant.

W's life was falling apart, until his father stepped in and, on his deathbed, snapped W out of it. No one knows what was said between them, not even A. But after their father died, W was a changed man. A hardened man. He drank less, cleaned himself up and became who you see today.

I don't know if this helps you, or what you want to do with it, but I beg you to be careful. W may sometimes appear to be human, but I tell you, he can be just as bad as A. Don't let your guard down.

Your friend,

S

We all sat quietly and I read the letter to myself two more times so that I could commit it to memory. If I learned nothing else, I knew that William had a heart once. With that, and the little moments we have had, there was a small chance I could get him to open his heart to me. I folded up the letter and put it in the waist of my pants. There was no mention of Joe or if Smith had contacted him.

I got off the bed and kissed Reyna's forehead. "We all better get ready for dinner, before William notices where we all are." Everyone filed out of her room and headed to their own to change out of our casual clothes.

As I leaned against the back wall of the elevator, I couldn't contain my happiness. A smile spread across my face as I was starting to get excited. The pieces were starting to fall into place. As I walked into my room I saw William standing at the balcony door.

CHAPTER FIFTY-ONE

"HOW'S REYNA?" ASKED WILLIAM CALMLY, LOOKING OVER the backyard.

He knew I had defied his instructions by seeing her, so there was no point in denying it.

"Much better."

"Good. Have a seat." He pointed to the bed without looking back.

I walked across the room and sat on the side of the bed closest to him. I quietly removed the letter from my back waistband and slid it under the pillow closest to me. I couldn't get a sense of why William was in my room. He didn't seem angry, but he was a master at disguising it when he needed to.

"I wanted to see how you were doing after our excursion out of the house last week." He turned towards me and leaned on the door frame. "I am sorry I haven't been able to check in with you sooner. So much to clean up after Ad... my brother's debacle."

"I am fine. A few nightmares but otherwise, fine." My nightmares weren't about me shooting Mr. Y, but William didn't need to know that.

"If you want, I can get Dr. Boyden to give you something to help you sleep. I take something myself every now and then, when I need a good dreamless sleep."

"I would rather not take anything unless I absolutely have to. If I get to that point I will let you know."

"Fair enough." He stepped into the room, "Where did you learn to shoot?"

From the moment I cocked the gun I knew I would eventually be asked this question. "My father. He always went on about the world ending or another World War starting. He taught my sister and I to protect ourselves, just in case whatever country he thought was after us that week invaded. It was better to appease him than try and argue."

He latched onto the one point in my statement I hoped he would. "You have a sister?" he asked.

"What, you want her to come work here too? We are down a person." The comment came out snarkier than I had wanted and, by the look in his eyes, I could tell I may have pushed it too far.

"I will forgive you that comment, given what you have been through recently, but don't make a habit of it. The results won't be pleasant for either of us."

"I truly didn't mean it how it sounded. I'm sorry. Anyways, I *had* a sister." It took everything in me not to burst into tears or run at William and toss him off the balcony. My breathing had become heavy and I tried to slow it down but William noticed. He came and sat beside me on the bed.

"What happened?" he asked with no emotion, his hands folded together between his knees.

"She was killed by..." I didn't try to hide my tears. William reached out and took my hand.

"She was killed by a drunk driver."

William's shoulders slumped, but he didn't let go of my hand, so I continued, "The police say the guy was driving the wrong way down the highway back home. The driver must have driven down the off-ramp and into her lane, where she swerved to avoid him. She almost did, but he clipped her tail-end and she rolled over the edge of an overpass. They say she died instantly when her car landed on its roof on the cement of the highway below. But I think they only tell that to the family to make them feel better. She probably laid their screaming and crying until her final breath. She was a fighter. She wouldn't have gone that easily."

William cleared his throat, "What happened to the driver?"

"He continued to drive the wrong way and hit another vehicle, with a family in it. They managed to mostly avoid him. Then he drove head-on into a semi-truck. He ended up in a coma until he died a few weeks later."

I looked at William, who was staring at our clenched hands. He said nothing, so I continued, "I know you are not supposed to pray for the death of others. But I sat beside that man's bed everyday and prayed he wouldn't wake up. I knew, if convicted, he would only get a few years for killing my sister. As much as I would have reveled in his suffering, I doubted it would make a difference. Another would likely lose their life because of him."

"Some people change," William said softly.

"Maybe. But you take the only family I have left, and I am not giving out second chances."

"What was her name? Your sister?"

Shit, I needed a name. How had I not thought about this before? I wanted to shout "CLAIRE" but knew that, as soon as I did, he would see my resemblance to the Claire he knew and my plan would be over. I would be over.

"Joey. Well Josephine, but she went by Joey." Why Joe's name came to me at that moment I will never know, but I was thankful it did.

"I'm sorry she was taken from you," he said solemnly.

I gritted my teeth, "It's not your fault, but thank you."

I waited for William to make the next move. I hoped my story would make him feel the grief for his own family and open up to me. Finally, he spoke, "I'm sorry. I'm sorry." He kept repeating the apology. After he didn't stop apologizing I turned my body to face him and took his other hand.

"William, what's wrong?" I prayed with everything in me, to a God I hadn't really spoken to in years, to let this be the moment. Please have William give me more of the doorway to his heart that he'd shown me last week in the car.

Then the floodgates opened and William started to cry. He slid off the bed and he put his head into my lap and hugged my legs. He kept whispering "I'm sorry" over and over.

I wasn't expecting this. A man I had seen kill Jenna without any hesitation or emotion was weeping in my lap. I ran my fingers through his hair as I tried to simulate comfort.

We sat like that for the better part of an hour. I stared out through the balcony door at the city William kept me from. The sound of clattering dishes traveled from the kitchen window two stories below. Suddenly the "I'm sorry" William was repeating changed. I couldn't quite make it out as it was muffled by my legs. "I '____' her." It sounded like "I kept her?" and then I heard it, "I killed her."

"I killed her," William repeated through his tears.

I doubted he would get this upset about Jenna. Was he about to open up about his family?

"Who did you kill?" I asked quietly.

"I... I... No." He got up briskly and started to brush the wrinkles out of his suit. He wiped the tears from his face and straightened his clothes before he turned towards the door. I quickly got up and took his hand. I needed him to stay. I needed this to work. I needed in. He turned back to me so I spoke. "I am sorry for whatever happened. It must have been difficult, and I am sure you don't want to talk about it. But bottling up all those emotions can get a person in trouble sometimes."

I could see in his eyes I was losing him. I tried to turn the attention away from his issues to mine. "I mean, look at Mr. Y. Yes, he deserved it, but that doesn't mean I should have shot his penis off."

William smiled a little but didn't say anything.

"I'm just saying, unless you, Jack and Kevin sit around each night sharing your feelings..." William chuckled. Phew! I hadn't entirely lost him. "I am here if you ever want to talk. Just talk. No one needs to be the wiser."

William closed the space between us, kissed my forehead and then left the room without looking back. The scent of his cologne lingered. I knew I would forever associate that smell to hell on earth.

I stood as still as a statue until I heard the door on the other end of the hall close. I grabbed the letter from under the pillow, read it one more time and then tore it up and flushed it down the toilet. I made sure the last piece made its way down the drain. I took a pillow off my bed and laughed into it. My plan was working.

What I didn't know was how long the plan would take.

CHAPTER FIFTY-TWO

I DIDN'T WANT TO TALK TO ANYONE, NOT EVEN WHITNEY, so I waited until I knew they had all left the kitchen before I went down to eat. Kevin was cleaning up his dishes when I entered. Although he knew I was there, he didn't say anything, finished up, and left.

I put together a quick chicken salad, poured a glass of wine and headed back to my room. When I got off the elevator, I looked down the hall at William's door. Was he still in there? Wherever he was, what was he thinking? Did he realize he had said too much and closed himself off again? I considered offering him the dinner I made, but then decided against it. I didn't want to push my luck. I needed to ease into this 'relationship'. But I also didn't want to relax for too long. Every day I stayed here was one day closer to William learning the truth about my identity.

As September was approaching, the night air filled with smoke from a nearby wildfire, so I could not sit comfortably on the balcony. Instead, I ate at the desk and replayed the events of the day. From Smith's letter to

William's vulnerability. He was starting to let me in. Now the question was how do I get him to let me in more?

If I waited around for him to make a move, it could take months, if ever. It already took him a week just to see how I was doing after shooting Mr. Y and my breakdown in the vehicle. I definitely had to do something, but if I made the wrong choice, my whole plan would fall apart. I vowed my back-up plan would be to burn it all down, literally. But I wasn't there yet - even if the thought of watching fire rage through this horrible place filled me with joy and a sense of justice.

I always thought better when I paced around a room. I finished my salad and wine, then spent time going through the possibilities of what to do next:

Idea: Try and help William with the business and hope to work alone together
Cons: Highly unlikely Jack or Kevin wouldn't be around. It could take a while to generate vulnerability in a work setting.
Idea: As Reyna and Whitney suggested, provoke a client and become injured so William cares for me.
Cons: Always a danger of permanent injury or death. At some point William will see my injuries as a liability, and I won't be kept around.
Idea: Find a time when William is alone and try to seduce him.
Cons: He is rarely alone. The thought of his hands on me was repulsive. Sex doesn't mean he would talk.

I was frustrated. None of these ideas were good enough. Then it came to me! I would write a letter and slip it under his door. Unlike the office, I suspected Jack or Kevin wouldn't go into William's bedroom, therefore, no chance of them coming upon the letter. But would I be seen and someone think I was trying to break into the room?

I opened my door, leaned against the frame as if I wanted to stand there intentionally. Someone on the main floor would have to crane their neck to see movement on the third floor. I could only see a crack of the front door and would need to lean over the rail to see more.

I looked over to William's door. There was a camera above it. Not a problem. I was only delivering a letter. I closed my door and went back to my desk. I didn't have much paper left from what Fay had given me. I ran through what I was going to say a few times in my head, before I put it in writing. I wanted to make sure I sounded genuine. I wrote:

Dear William,

I am not too sure what to write but I knew that words would likely not be spoken about this evening. And that is okay. I just wanted you to know that what happened will be kept in the strictest of confidences. I suspect you would like to hold up the quintessential male persona to those around you. I get it. This place, and your role in it, doesn't really allow for a space of vulnerability.

If I am honest, it was nice to see a different, more human side of you. I mean, I do appreciate everything you have done when I have been hurt, but this was, well, more. I apologize if what I write is too personal or 'unprofessional'. Maybe I am just naive with this letter and it will cause more harm than good. But I think everyone deserves to have someone they can talk to, and I get the sense you are maybe a little more comfortable with me then others. Sure, Jack and Kevin are probably great conversationalists ;) But if you wanted a friend I could be that person.

I am not looking for anything in return and I understand my place here wouldn't change. I want to extend an olive branch to show you that we can be honest with each other. Here is my truth:

I often feel anger or resentment towards you for keeping us here. I had a life outside of all of this, a nice one actually. I would be lying if I said I didn't dream of going back. Even if it, or I, would never be the same. I didn't choose to be here, but rather was forced. Sure, you yourself didn't kidnap me, but your brother or the network you run did. So, I blame you.

But, on the other hand, I also feel grateful towards you. You pulled me out of the horrors of your brother's grasp. You continually care for me and, if truth be told, you treat the ladies and me more like humans than I ever expected. I am not condoning the business you run, but am generally conflicted regarding how I feel about you, this place and how I fit into it.

I suspect I am lucky if you have read this far, so I will stop. I don't expect you to reply or even acknowledge receipt of this letter. But should you want to talk, or write, I am here. (I mean, where am I going to go)

Olivia

I put the pen down, folded the letter and walked to my door. As I placed my hand on the handle, my heart skipped a beat. I willed away my fears about my plan not succeeding, and I opened the door.

As I stepped into the hallway, the silence filled my ears. With every step I could hear the floor creak under me, and prayed it wasn't as loud as I thought it was. When I got to William's door, I acted as if I didn't notice the camera. I took a deep breath and bent down to put the note under the door. I noticed the bedroom lights were on and also thought I heard the faint sound of music. Then I saw the shadow of feet stop behind the door. I froze. William knew I was there. What would I say if he opened the door? I pushed my letter under the door, got up and walked back to my room as fast as I could, while also trying to look normal.

I closed my door without looking back. I leaned back against the door and took a deep breath. I felt a sense of relief. This was it; if the letter didn't help bring William and I together, I would have to go with Plan B - burn this place to the ground!

I was suddenly stricken with a feeling of panic. Would William question where I got the paper from? Did I just endanger the people around me so that I could get revenge? I was hyperventilating so hard that my body was rejecting my dinner and I ran to the bathroom.

CHAPTER FIFTY-THREE

I PULLED MYSELF UP OFF THE BATHROOM FLOOR AND looked in the mirror. The bathmat I had folded up as a pillow had left lines on my face. If anyone asked, I would tell them I had too much wine and spent the night beside the toilet. As I stood there, I gripped the edge of the counter. I pulled the hand towel off the nearby rack, bunched it up in front of my mouth and muffled my scream. I told myself the plan was working, I needed to harden my nerves. I couldn't risk panicking in front of the others and especially not in front of William. I put the towel back and straightened it before leaving the bathroom.

After getting dressed, I made my way downstairs. No one else seemed to be awake, so I made a coffee, randomly grabbed a book from the shelves in the living room and sat down on the couch. As I looked at the cover, I realized I had grabbed *Anne of Green Gables*, by Lucy Maud Montgomery, and smiled. As a young girl, I read this book so much the pages needed to be taped back together. Based on the cracks in the spine, this copy appeared to have been read a few times. I opened to the first page of chapter one and made it to the end of the first paragraph, when I heard a door slam and William's angry voice coming closer.

"What the fuck does he think he is doing? Once again, I have to clean up his mess. I swear if he wasn't my brother..." he trailed off as he stopped at the front door, his hand resting on the handle, and looked over at me. I tried to give a nonchalant smile and pretended to go back to reading the book. I willed myself not to look up when I didn't hear the door open.

"Kevin, wait for me in the car." Kevin walked past William who had opened the door for him.

"Olivia," I looked up. William was stone faced. "I am going to be gone most of the day. Get the girls ready for tonight. I have invited very prominent guests and expect the best we have ever provided."

"Will do," I formally replied. I got up out of the chair and put the book back in its place on the shelf. I started to make my way towards the stairs and William walked out the door. Before closing it, he poked his head back into the house and advised, "Adam will be here tonight."

I stopped in my tracks. My heart didn't know whether to sink, or jump for joy. I wasn't ready yet. Adam knew I was Claire's sister, and was likely biding his time to release that information until it would cause the most destruction. Tonight, with all of the guests would be perfect. I couldn't hide my panic.

William walked back into the house, and over to me. He placed his hands on my shoulders. "You, and the others, will be safe. He will be kept in check and not be alone with any of you. Trust me. If I didn't have to have him here, I wouldn't. There is just no other way." William pulled me into his chest and wrapped his arms around me. I mimicked him. "I will explain more later." He pulled away without another word and left.

I stood there and stared at the door. I needed to get out of here, but how? I could see the guards through the sheer curtains on either side of the door. I knew there were more all over the grounds. I wouldn't make it five feet. God only knows if Adam had figured out I was a cop since we last saw each other. There would be no way he would keep that piece of information to himself for very long. If Adam wanted to get William out of the way, he could play to the guests that William doesn't know who he has working for him, so how could he be trusted? Or play the opposite card - William knew exactly who I was, but put the guests at risk for his own profit. They would turn on him and Adam could take over. My mind was racing. How was I going to make sure Adam didn't say anything?

I felt a hand touch my shoulder and screamed.

"Hey, it's okay, it's me."

I turned around and saw Whitney. I wrapped my arms around her, crying into her shoulder.

"I am sorry I startled you. We called your name but you didn't answer." The rest of the women stood behind her.

"Sorry. I just... I didn't."

"It's okay. We heard what William said about Adam being here tonight. We are all a little freaked out."

"Yah. I... wait, you heard that. Does that mean...?"

"We saw everything too," said Lily, with a hint of annoyance but mostly sympathy.

I felt my face get hot and was not sure why I was blushing.

Saria cut the tension when she offered to make breakfast, and everyone but Whitney and I headed towards the kitchen.

"Are you okay?" Whitney asked.

"I don't know. What if Adam tells William, or anyone, who I am?" The tears started again, as the reality of how much was at risk tonight sunk in.

"We won't let that happen."

"How?"

"Come on," she said cheerfully. "Let's have our pre-party meeting with the ladies now and make a plan."

With her arm around me, we walked into the kitchen.

CHAPTER FIFTY-FOUR

AS I SAT AT THE KITCHEN TABLE I REALIZED HOW GRATEFUL I was for Whitney. She was the one who pulled me through everything I had faced. Now, as she led the ladies in the conversation about what needed to be done tonight, I longed for our friendship outside of this house.

Eloisa leaned over and whispered, "Are you okay?"

I brushed the tear that was running down my face away, "Yeah. I just didn't sleep well, and the stress of Adam and all. You know." She hugged me and we turned our attention back to what Whitney was saying.

"Now that we got the formalities about tonight out of the way, there is another matter that we need to deal with. I know it is early but, Lily, why don't you grab us a couple of bottles of whiskey or whatever you can find. Fay, grab some glasses."

After each of us had a glass of whiskey in front of us, Whitney held up her glass and made a toast, "To not letting the bastard Adam hurt another one of us." We each downed our glass and passed the bottles around to refill.

Whitney continued, "None of us actually want to be here. Sure, some may have gotten used to it over the years. But none of us have ever gotten used to Adam. That man is a vile, sadistic, monster. We have all seen what he has done to Olivia, and I can bet you, given the chance tonight, he will do the same, or worse. I say we end his terror once and for all." She raised her glass and looked to all of us to raise ours in agreement.

I didn't hesitate, and when I raised my glass, she patted my leg with her other hand. Jessica and Eloisa quickly raised theirs, along with Saria, Reyna and Fay. Lily was the only hold-out.

"What's the problem, Lily?" Fay asked in frustration. "He hasn't exactly been nice to you either."

Lily hesitated and then said fearfully, "I know. But we all saw what happened to Jenna. If we make Mr. Hammond mad, he surely won't hesitate to kill us. I mean, Olivia is all close with Mr. Hammond now, but what about the rest of us?"

Saria stepped in, "But if we do nothing, then what? And besides, it's not like Whitney is suggesting we kill Adam." She chuckled nervously.

By this time, our arms had gotten tired and we had all put our glasses back on the table. We all looked to Whitney. I knew what she was thinking but no one else did.

Whitney drank her shot, "That is exactly what I am proposing."

Reyna and I smiled and held up our glasses. Everyone else sat in disbelief.

I decided I needed to speak up. "I know I haven't been here that long. You all probably don't fully trust me. I also know that, by doing this, you are all risking your lives for me. Yes, if this doesn't work, we could all end up dead." I heard some gasps and sobs. "But, as I look around this table, I see women who did not choose this life. Who have families and friends who don't know what happened to them. It is hard to hear, but the likelihood that any of us get out of here at all is pretty slim. So why not use what power we have to at least make a difference in this life? I am not as close to William as you guys think. In fact, absolutely nothing has happened between us. I consoled him once but that was it. If we do this, I am at the same risk as all of you. Besides, Jenna was closer to William, and she wasn't safe, was she?"

I needed everyone to agree to the plan, otherwise the risk of William finding out was too high. I continued, "Lily, we will only proceed if everyone is on board. If you are out, we are all out and we won't hold it against you. We are talking about serious action here. Now, you and I haven't always gotten along, and I am asking a lot of you. Keeping a secret like this will be hard, but I know you are strong enough."

Hands slowly raised their glasses, Lily's being the last one. Even then, she hung her head as we all drank.

Whitney took reign of the conversation again, "Now that we are agreed. We need a plan."

CHAPTER FIFTY-FIVE

WILLIAM DIDN'T RETURN UNTIL AN HOUR BEFORE THE guests were set to arrive. We were all getting ready, when we heard the booming voices of Adam and William in the foyer. Arguing as usual. I quietly made my way to the third-floor railing, but stayed back enough that I likely wouldn't be noticed. Based on the quiet footsteps and occasional creaking of the floor below me, the others had done the same.

"There is only one way you can cut me out of this business, and you don't have the balls to do it!" Adam yelled.

"You want to see balls? Just keep pushing me 'BROTHER!"

Adam laughed maniacally, "Bullshit. You are not fit to lead this empire, and now you are going to try and keep me from it. Ha! How many people have you actually killed little brother? A handful? A pittance compared to what I have done for you. Who are you going to get to do your dirty work if you send me away? Kevin here?"

"Get in the fucking office!" William instructed, and then pushed Adam down the hall.

Once the office door was closed, we could no longer hear the fighting, but we all knew it continued. I went back to my room and finished putting myself together. As I stared at myself in the mirror, I thought I looked quite pretty in a yellow sundress. I had never really worn yellow before, and kind of liked it. I smiled to myself as I twirled in the mirror, the bottom of the dress raising just a little. The smile quickly faded as I realized I was about to kill a man.

The ladies had come up with a pretty good plan, but it did rely heavily on the timing of all of the steps lining up. If one thing went wrong, it would not only ruin the party, but it could also be obvious what happened and who did it. William wouldn't hesitate to put us all down like sick dogs. Even though we went over the plan multiple times, I still wasn't sold on the fact William wouldn't learn the truth. I didn't think these women gave William enough credit, he was smart. However, based on the fight I just overheard, I hoped he wouldn't mind if someone else got Adam out of the way.

As the ladies gathered in the backyard, we quickly went through the plan once more. We had the backyard set up a little differently in order to help with its facilitation.

We wrapped up just as William, Kevin and Smith came out, with Jack staying at the entry gate. I was a little shocked to see Smith, but not completely surprised. It's not as if he could get out of this life either. We didn't react to seeing each other.

"Are we all set here, ladies?" William asked distractedly as he looked at his phone.

"Yes," Whitney said.

William looked around, "A new layout. Huh. I like it. Now, as you are aware Adam is here. I have asked him to remain in my office, however, we all know it won't contain him long." William put his phone away and massaged his temples. "I have also made it very clear that he is not to touch any of you, and that no one will be spending time with him. You are all here for the guests, not him. Guards will be practically handcuffed to him all night." He looked at his watch. "We are going to do things a little differently tonight."

I couldn't breath. What did he mean different?

"Rather than having each of you at a table, and the guests making their way around to you, I am going to have you all stand up front here." We walked over to the front of the patio stairs. The trickling of the waterfalls would have been soothing, had our plan not already started to go off the rails. William and Kevin moved us to different places in the line until they were satisfied. I ended up in the middle between Lily and Jessica.

"Kevin and Smith will stand on either side of the line and make sure no one gets handsy or tries to talk to you."

While William was talking, men were gathering up the name stands from the tables and replacing them with numbers. They also placed papers, pens and, from what I could see, what looked like a menu of our names with pictures.

"The guests will come in, walk past you and head to a table. They will then place a bid to talk to as many of you as they wish over the course of the evening. The order of the conversation will be determined based on their bid amount and ranking. Come 10:30 p.m., bids for two hours of your time will be placed as per the usual process. You could see two to three guests tonight. Any questions?"

Whitney stepped forward, "I just wanted to confirm, we will be the ones moving from table to table tonight? Rather than the regular process where the guests moved?"

"That is correct. Kevin and Smith will coordinate moving you between tables."

I felt my throat closing up. Reyna needed to be at a certain table for her part of the plan to work. What if the person there didn't bid for her? Would another of the women step in? The rest already had their assigned tasks that piggybacked off Reyna's. There would be no way they could do their part and hers. I looked to Whitney and could see the wheels in her head turning as well.

Smith came over and handed out shots. When he got to me I saw a smile try to escape the side of his mouth, but he caught it before anyone else could see.

Everyone held up their glasses and William said, "To a night to remember." Then we drank, him profiting off our bodies and the rest of us to the death of his brother.

CHAPTER FIFTY-SIX

AT 9:30 P.M., THERE WAS A STEADY LINE OF PEOPLE ENTERING the yard and slowly filing past us. There were many I recognized, and quite a few I did not.

Reyna did a great job of flirting with her eyes as each person stopped to look at her. When we had formulated the plan, she didn't hesitate to volunteer to complete one of the hardest yet most vital parts. Now she was doing everything she could to make sure she got to the table she needed to be at.

Once a young man had taken his place at what would have been Reyna's table we all looked to her. She winked and kept looking over at the table, flirting with the man from a distance. I must admit, she was really good. I swear I could see the man blush from the other side of the yard.

William took the microphone and the DJ lowered the music.

"Welcome everyone and thank you for being here tonight. You will find your bidding instructions and catalog in front of you. If you have not done so already, you have 20 minutes to submit your bids for the conversation portion of the evening. At 10:30 p.m. I will give you another 20 minutes to submit your bids for your choice of partner for the evening. The ladies are going to go take a break and look forward to spending time with you." He looked over to us, we smiled at the crowd and then William led us into the house.

"Great job ladies, now do what you need to do, as you may not have much time for a break throughout the rest of the evening." With that he left and everyone let out a large exhale.

"What are we going to do? Reyna might not get to her table," Fay asked in a voice not quite a whisper.

"It will be okay," Whitney responded "Whoever is at that table at 10 o'clock will have to complete the task. Are we all in agreement?"

No one hesitated to agree. Not even Lily.

Whitney continued, "Saria and Eloisa, are you still good to cause a distraction when we are ready?"

"All set," they said.

We all took another shot of whiskey. "To a night to remember." Nerves permeated the room as people paced, tapped toes on the floor, or fingers on the furniture. Jessica kept opening and closing the fridge so often, Lily had to drag her to the couch before one of us slapped her.

A while later, Smith came to get us and handed us little pocket cards. They reminded me of the dance cards my grandma had saved from school. There was a time stamp, table number and name. We didn't have time to compare our cards to see if Reyna would be at her place at 10 o'clock.

As we were led back out to the yard, we saw that Adam had made his appearance. He was standing with Jack near the entry table. I couldn't help but look at him. The anger on his face was palpable. Then a sly smile came across his face and he winked. I looked away and prayed he kept my secret a little longer.

I made my way to table four and spent 20 minutes listening to a man who I figured was in his late 20s to early 30s, talk about his job, money and plans to become a Senator. I was so stressed about ensuring the plan could move ahead, I was happy that he didn't seem to want me to respond. I just had to feign interest with a few "uh huh's" and flirtatious eyes, as I kept scanning the yard for any hints our plan would be foiled.

The time seemed to go by as slowly as possible. I couldn't recall the names of any of the people I talked to. Except Apolline. Who could forget a name like that. She was also very forward with her desires.

Just before 10 o'clock William announced the next rotation. I looked down at my card and saw table 15. I looked around and table 15 was Reyna's table. I would be the one retrieving the syringe. The plan was to keep me in sight the entire time to avoid immediate suspicion. Shit!

I confidently walked over to the table and introduced myself to the young man. He called himself Mr. F, was 27 and he had a thick southern accent. He asked me a few questions before he quickly turned the conversation to Reyna. I smiled and told him how she was a lovely woman, raved about by customers and, if he hurt her, I would kill him. He chuckled at that until he saw the seriousness on my face. I asked him if he wouldn't mind getting us a couple of drinks since I wasn't allowed to leave the table. He graciously obliged and headed to the bar. I made my way around to where he had been standing on the other side of the table.

We had picked this table as there were no others behind it and it had a good view of everyone. I saw William making his way through the crowd, checking in on the guests. Adam was still by the entry table. He was staring at me with eyes of suspicion. I stared back and, as hard as it was, I held his gaze as I reached under the table and retrieved a syringe of cooked down Oxy. We had used most of my stash. I was so nervous I dropped it under the table. Mr. F was making his way back so I broke my stare with Adam and bent down to get it. I didn't know where to put it without being seen. Thankfully, it was small and fit in the palm of my hand. When I stood up Mr. F was at the table.

"Everything all right?" he asked

"Yes. Just a rock in my shoe."

We toasted and continued to talk about Reyna until the time came for me to move on. I passed Saria, who quickly told me to put the syringe in my bra before someone noticed it. I wasn't sure how I was going to do that without being noticed. I tried to flirt with the couple at my next table, a Doctor and her shy husband. I ran my hand down the front of my chest but I just couldn't find a way to hide the syringe without being seen. I felt like all eyes were on me. In an act of desperation, I called Smith over to see if I could go to the bathroom.

"William isn't going to be impressed, but if you must."

"I am sorry Mr. and Mrs. K., everyone has been nice enough to keep me hydrated. I just need to use the little girls' room."

Mr. K laughed nervously as Mrs. K told me to hurry back. I got the feeling Mr. K wasn't the one who suggested they come to the party.

Smith and I didn't say anything as we made our way to the first-floor bathroom. Once inside I quickly positioned the syringe under my breast, resting on the wire of the bra. But the shape of it was visible. I hadn't really minded having small breasts before, but right now I wished I had a little more up top. I was starting to panic. I didn't know what to do.

Smith knocked on the door. "Hurry up. I can't have you gone more than five minutes."

"Almost done!"

I flushed the toilet and pretended to wash my hands. I was still holding on to the syringe when Smith opened the door.

"Look we have to..." he stared at my hand, then looked at me and back at my hand. He ran over to me and forced the syringe from my hand. "What are you doing? Are you trying to kill yourself?" He ran back to the door, looked out and then closed it.

"What? No! I wasn't going to use that on myself." The plan was teetering on failure, what did I have to lose? I would have to tell him the plan. He had been sympathetic to me before, maybe he would be again. "I was trying to hide it so that I could use it on Adam."

He was taken aback but quickly regained his composure.

"Exactly how were you planning to do that without being seen?"

"Saria and Eloisa were going to cause a distraction once I got close to Adam and then, well, I would stab him in the leg with it."

"And what is in here?"

"Oxy."

"How did you get that, and this syringe?"

"Dr. Boyden prescribed me Oxy when I first got here. I never took it. Jessica cooked most of it and put it in a syringe she had hidden away. She hid it under one of the tables in the yard before the party, as we couldn't risk it being found on any of us."

"I see. Where exactly are you planning on hiding it on yourself? You are not exactly the most voluptuous woman."

"I know, and no matter what I try I can't hide it well enough. I wasn't even supposed to be the one with the syringe. I was supposed to be seen all night and doing nothing to arouse suspicion. Now, I have had to come in here. This isn't going to work!" I sat on the toilet and started to cry. Everything was falling apart and we probably weren't going to get another chance. We lucked out with Adam being here tonight, and he wasn't going to be back again.

Smith held out his hand, "You better pull yourself together otherwise you *will* arouse suspicion." I gave him the syringe.

Looking in the mirror as I cleaned my face, I saw Smith put the syringe in his inside coat pocket.

As we walked back out of the house, every one of the ladies looked at me. I couldn't react as both William and Adam were also watching. William walked over.

"What happened? Why do you look like you have been crying?"

"Sorry, I just. . . well, Adam has been watching me all night and I let it get under my skin. I will be fine. Won't let it happen again."

"See that you don't. Now head back to your table. Smith, go keep an eye on Adam - I need to get the next part of the evening organized."

I walked away from the men and spent the next 20 minutes listening to Mrs. K talk about her desire to see her husband with another woman. I barely paid attention as I watched Smith. He didn't reach for his pocket the entire time. I was getting impatient. Would Smith help me?

"Darling, are you alright?" Mr. K asked.

"Oh, I am so sorry. I'm being a horrible hostess. I am just, well. . . I am just not having a great night. But I can guarantee that if we have any time together, I would be very attentive to your needs."

Mr. K blushed and Mrs. K replied, "That's what I like to hear."

Before we could continue our conversation, William called the ladies forward to once again stand in a line at the bottom of the stairs. Jack and Kevin took up places at either end. William instructed his guests to submit their bids. Whitney had positioned herself in the middle next to me. "What happened?" she whispered.

"Smith has the stuff."

"What? Why?"

"No matter what I tried, I couldn't hide it well enough. He caught me with it.

"What do we do now? What if he tells William. Or Adam?"

"I don't think he will say anything. He would have talked before now if he wanted to. Instead, he has helped us." I took a deep breath and continued, "Now, I think we just go about our night and forget the plan. It's over." All my hope and strength resided in that syringe and I had lost control of it.

"There has to be something we can do. Adam has been wearing a particularly evil grin all night. He has to be planning something."

"Whitney, it's over."

I looked out over the crowd. At William talking to his men. Smith looked as nonchalant as I had ever seen him. I looked at Adam. Whitney was right. He looked particularly vicious, which was saying something, as he always looked that way. He ran his finger along his neck like a knife.

This was it. He was going to end it here. Tonight.

CHAPTER FIFTY-SEVEN

ONCE AGAIN, MY MIND SPIRALED INTO WHAT ADAM COULD do to ruin me, and how William would react. I felt a sharp pain in my side, and realized Whitney had elbowed me, as William stood in front of me with his hand over the microphone.

"Are you okay?" he asked, for the second time tonight. This more caring side of him was a little off-putting, but if it got me and my friends through tonight I would keep up appearances.

"What? Oh yeah. Fine. Just tired and probably had too much to drink."

"Good." He uncovered the microphone and called Reyna forward. "Reyna here was very popular tonight, being in the top three for most of you. As is the way, only one of you had the highest bid. Mr. F!"

Mr. F came up and she escorted him to their assigned guest room.

William continued "Olivia here has become our most popular woman of late, and tonight is no different. I cannot say how pleased I am with the results. It's the highest bid we have ever received." The crowd cheered and I smiled in fake gratitude. "Without further ado, the gentleman who gets to spend an amazing night with her is Mr. G."

No one stepped forward. The crowd started to look around for the mysterious Mr. G. Suddenly maniacal laughter came from the entry table. Everyone looked over and saw Adam with a large smile on his face. He finished his drink, gave the cup to Smith, and walked over to William and I. The blood drained from my face and I felt like I was going to faint.

"I guess we shall be going," and he grabbed my arm.

Before he could pull me forward, William stood between us.

"Let her go," William said firmly.

Adam raised his voice, "You said it, the highest bid wins and I bid the highest. You wouldn't want to break your own rules now, would you?" He lowered his voice. "At least, not in front of your guests."

William retorted, "As you were not an official guest of this evening, but an obligatory one, you were not eligible to submit a bid. As such, the second highest bidder would..."

"Bullshit! I won your precious doll!" Adam yanked my arm so hard I toppled William to the ground and ended up on top of his back.

We both got up and brushed ourselves off. With Adam no longer holding on to me, William used his body to block me from him. William was no longer trying to play the genial host. "You are acting absurd, and this is not going to work, you worthless piece of shit. You were already going to be sent back home but now I am cutting you off. You don't have $200,000 to spend on a bid."

"Wow, cutting off your own brother." He picked up the microphone from the ground and addressed the crowd, "You see how he treats family. Imagine how he will treat you. Especially if you try to get close to his precious Olivia. I wouldn't be betting on her anymore if I were you!"

"That's enough! Smith, take him inside." Smith stepped forward and reached for Adam's arm, but Adam eluded his grasp. He now stood nose to nose with William. "Brother, if only you knew." He looked at me, "If only you knew what she really was. You wouldn't be so fond of little Olivia.

His sly smile filled his face and he made kissing gestures towards me. He went to step towards me but William kept him back. Looking over William's shoulder he whispered "It's all over now, you little bitch. You can't hide anymore."

He looked back to William. "This woman..." Adam's words started to slur together "of yyyyours ssshe..." he started choking as his eyes went wide and his face pale. His hands went to his throat. I moved beside William and saw his face had no expression as he watched his brother fall to the ground. I looked to Smith, who patted his pocket. I couldn't believe it, Smith had done what I couldn't. My crushed spirit was regaining some life.

No one was moving. Not even Adam. I knelt down beside Adam and as his eyes looked at me in terror, I whispered in his ear, "I did this. This is for Claire." Then I watched as life left his body.

I stayed beside Adam's body as William took the microphone from his hand. I didn't want William to think I was hiding something, so I looked to him. I noticed grief flash in his eyes. As quickly as it was there, it evaporated and he addressed the crowd. "Most esteemed guests. I apologize for the inconvenience my brother has caused. I understand if you wish to go, however, you are more than welcome to stay and continue as planned."

There was some bustling but no one left. He ran his hand through his hair, "Then, moving forward, Olivia will be spending the night with Mr. H. I have already set him up in a guest room, as he would prefer to keep his identity confidential." William watched Jack help me up. "Fay, you are with Mr. and Mrs. K."

William continued to announce the winners as Smith and some of the guards dealt with Adam's body. Jack took my arm and, for the first time, spoke to me, "Come along now. Let's get you inside."

Everything was a blur. Was Adam actually dead? Had we really succeeded? Did William suspect anything? Could Smith really be trusted? I was extremely nauseous. Jack took us into the elevator, but I couldn't tell you if we went up or down. We walked along the hallway and I needed both Jack and the railing to keep me on my feet. I felt as though all the alcohol I had consumed through the night was hitting me at once. I heard Jack pull a set of keys out of his pocket and then the click of a lock. He turned on the lights and gently sat me on a bed, took off my shoes and helped my lie down.

I could have sworn he said, "You'll be alright now," before I heard the clicks of the light switch and lock.

It was pitch black in whatever room I had just been put into. I battled hard to not let myself go into shock. I told myself the plan was always for me to watch Adam die. I had seen people die before in my job, but this was different. I couldn't put my finger on why I wasn't happier, but the only thing coming over me was a feeling of utter dread. Maybe it was because I knew my task wasn't complete. I needed to take care of William next and likely wouldn't have much help, if any.

With the state I was in, I had no sense of time. I could have been lying there for hours or minutes when the lock on the door clicked again. I stayed perfectly still. I heard the creaking of the door handle, and a shiver went up my spine.

I smelled a familiar cologne come closer to me. "Are you awake?"

My throat tightened, "yyyes."

"Good, we need to talk." I was blinded by the light being turned on.

CHAPTER FIFTY-EIGHT

AS MY EYES ADJUSTED TO THE LIGHT, THE ROOM CAME INTO view. It was stark white with minimalist contemporary furniture. A desk, dresser, bed and nightstands made the large room seem even bigger. The few art pieces on the walls seemed old and out of place. It reminded me of a Scottish painter my mom was obsessed with, Alexander Nasmyth. He painted Highland landscapes.

I sat up in the bed and noticed there was a walk-through closet to my left which led to a bathroom. I observed a folded piece of paper on the nightstand furthest from me. I found William standing, opening the door to his balcony.

"What happened tonight cost me hundreds of thousands of dollars. Not only because you are no longer being paid for, but the guests insisted I provide a discount on their bids, in exchange for their silence." He came and stood in front of me.

"Is there anything you need to tell me?" he asked.

I sat there looking up at him. I wondered if anyone had revealed the plan. Was this a test? Would I live or die based on my answer? I kept my answer vague while I tried to feel out the situation.

"I would be lying if I said I wasn't happy, or at least relieved."

"Understandable. Anything else?" There were no hints of tenderness in his words.

"Everything is still a little surreal. I don't even think I remember it all right now. Is there something in particular you want to know? Maybe that will jog my memory?"

He looked at me quizzically but thankfully didn't call my bluff. "What did you say to Adam?"

Crap! I had to make something up quick - "I told him that I was glad he was dying after what he did to me."

William went and leaned forward over the back of the chair and aggressively gripped it as he looked out over the yard. "He was a real asshole, and I can't recall a time where we ever got along. But he was my brother." He looked down at the chair then tilted his head to look at me. His tone became softer. "This is my fault. I knew Adam despised you, and yet I let him in here, without me, to watch over you. And I'm sorry I let you go with Mr. Y. I am sorry your time here has been nothing but pain. It is not what I wanted for you." William looked as though he was trying very hard to hold his emotions in.

The door to vulnerability had been opened. I got off the bed and walked over to him. "I know this is not what you wanted. You could have left me with Adam from the start. You could have put me to work whenever I was hurt, but you didn't. Would I choose to be here if I had a choice? No, of course not. But there are worse places I could be. And worse men I could be with."

I took his hand and looked into his sad eyes. I thought I saw the glimpse of a soul. He turned to look out the window, still holding my hand. We stood like that for a while until he let go and walked to the closet. He took down a small metal box from the top shelf, pulled something out and put the box back. He stood there for a while, looking defeated, and then brought it to me.

I looked down and saw a photo of him and what I presumed were his wife and daughter.

Before I could ask, William spoke, "This is my family. Or *was* my family."

"They are beautiful. Where are they now?"

Tears started down his cheeks. "They died."

I hoped I was convincing when I said, "Oh William, I am so sorry."

"It was my fault." He took the photo back and sat on the bed. I followed and sat beside him.

"I had been drinking and the roads were wet & icy. I swerved to avoid a dog and we ended up over an embankment. I was told they died instantly."

I placed my hand on his leg, "What were their names?"

"This is Sharon. She was the prettiest girl in high school. I am not sure why she chose me, but she did. And this is Penny. You know how they say you can't truly understand love until you have a child? Well, it's true. I never really wanted kids, but Sharon did so I didn't fight her on it. The day Penny came into this world was the happiest I had ever been. And the day I found out she was gone was the most devastated I had ever been." He put the picture on the nightstand and picked up the piece of paper.

"Is that where you got the scar on the inside of your arm. From the accident? I noticed when you served me breakfast that first morning."

William rubbed his arm and solemnly advised, "No. A few months after I killed my girls, the anger and sadness were too much. I tried to slit my wrist, but in the end, I failed at that, too. Jack found me and got me to a hospital before the worst could happen."

"I'm sorry you were in that much pain." I brushed his hair behind his ear.

He changed the subject, "I read your letter. I am sure it wasn't easy for you to tell me those things. Thank you for being honest. I don't get that a lot. Most people just tell me what they think I want to hear. But I am starting to learn you are different."

"You're welcome. And I am sorry about your family." I said softly.

William put the paper back on the nightstand and stood up, putting his hands in his pockets. He walked to his door and unlocked it. "It's getting late. We should probably try and get some sleep."

No! We were getting somewhere. Why did he always have to clam up? I understood that I couldn't expect everything to fall in place tonight, so I took the hint and made my way out of the room. As I crossed the threshold William said, "I will leave the door unlocked for when you come back."

I looked back at him and smiled. Then I turned back towards my room and heard the door close behind me.

As I walked into my room my stomach was rumbling with unease. I forced myself to throw up, as I didn't want William's inevitable touch to cause such a reaction. I made sure to hide the smell with many rounds of mouthwash. I changed into a silk silver night shirt which buttoned up the front and took a quick look in the mirror. I was cute enough. The last thing I wanted to do was have sex with William. But, I had already helped kill a man tonight, and if sex was what it took to finish off the plan to avenge Claire, then I would do what I needed to.

I popped one of my remaining Oxys I kept for just this occasion, and took a deep breath as I opened my door. And felt my heartbeat quicken the closer I got to William's room. My hand shook as I turned the handle. When I opened the door, William was seated at the end of the bed, clutching a drink in his hands. He looked up at me and smiled.

CHAPTER FIFTY-NINE

I SLOWLY OPENED MY EYES TO THE BRIGHT SUN SHINING IN through the balcony door and reflecting off of the opposite wall. My eyes focused on the shadow of a bird perched on the railing. I tried very hard not to move a muscle as I watched the bird's shadow walk out of view. I laid, unmoving, for a while, trying to get a sense of whether William was still beside me. I held my breath as I slowly turned onto my back.

He was gone.

As I stared up at the ceiling I could feel my chest starting to tighten and I fought back tears. I could still feel William's touch lingering on my skin. I felt unclean and my skin crawled. I got out of bed, turned back to straighten the sheets and froze as the scene of last night with William replayed in front of me.

When I had walked back into the room, William was seated at the end of the bed, his elbows on his knees and holding a drink. He had removed his suit jacket, shoes and socks. The jacket was neatly folded over the chair, and the shoes, with the socks stuffed inside, lined up nicely beside it. I walked over, finished the drink and put the glass on top of the dresser. I took a deep breath and emptied my brain of all thought, before I turned and walked back to him.

I stood between his legs, my night shirt grazing the top of his knees. Without looking up, William softly ran his hands up my thighs and under the shirt. His hands were cold to the touch and I shivered. I held onto his shoulders as he removed my lace panties. He started to unbutton my night shirt, as I ran my fingers through his hair and along his arms. The shirt fell to the floor and I stood naked in front of a man I loathed. He kissed my stomach before standing. I undid his belt and pants as he unbuttoned his shirt, tossing it onto the chair.

Even wearing a suit, I could tell William worked out, but I was not prepared to see him naked. His body was well kept and, in another life, I would have only been too happy to spend the night with him. As he stepped out of his pants, he lifted my chin so that our eyes met. I didn't know how, but he looked different. He wasn't the hardened man I had come to expect.

William gently kissed my lips, and then moved to my neck and collarbone. As he lifted me up, I wrapped my legs around his waist and he climbed onto the bed. He laid me down in the middle, and his lips continued their journey down my body. When he stopped at my breasts and gave them a little nip, I couldn't stop myself from releasing a quiet moan of pleasure. I didn't want it to feel good, but all the alcohol and oxy I had ingested were numbing reality.

William's lips and tongue continued down along my stomach and my inner thigh. William's hardened penis gliding down my body. I gripped the sheets and arched my back as William's tongue entered me. When he had me on the precipice of gratification, he stopped and traced his way back up my body, until we were face to face. He kissed me and slid effortlessly inside of me. My intoxication prevented me from registering if he had followed his own mandatory condom rule. He groaned loudly when he was deep within me. My fingers caressed his body as he thrust deeper and faster. We moaned with each movement of his hips until our bodies couldn't contain the pleasure any longer and pulsated together.

Afterward, William laid on top of me, his head buried in my shoulder, as we both tried to catch our breath. I stared at the ceiling, my arms wrapped around him as I tried not to think about what I had just done. When he finally rolled off of me, I sat up and the room began to spin. I put my head between my knees to try and stop the floor from moving. William got out of bed, walked around to me and passed me my night shirt. I avoided his gaze. I heard him turn on the shower and then he stood naked in the bathroom doorway.

"Joining me?"

Thankfully, he didn't have enough stamina for round two. We quickly showered with no words spoken. When he had dried off, he went back to bed while I remained in the bathroom. I closed the door behind him and I sat on the toilet. I tried to get as much of him out of me as possible, all while trying not to have a panic attack. The room was starting to spin again, so I laid down on the cool floor in the hopes it would make me feel better.

After a while, William called out, "Are you okay in there?"

"Yes, I had too much to drink and the room is spinning a bit. I should be okay in a minute, just need to cool down."

I used the counter to pull myself up, put on the night shirt, and made my way back to the bed. I stood watching William reading a book.

"Would you like me to go?" I asked.

William looked at me, "I... ah...you decide," and he went back to reading.

I was not expecting to have a choice. What I wanted to do was run. Run out of the room, out of the house and to Rice Canyon so I could find Claire's body. I wanted to run into the past, to a time when Claire and I were happy. Instead, I knew I didn't really have a choice at all. By going, I showed I was just another woman, looking only to make the boss happy. By staying, it might make him think I saw him as more. By staying, maybe I would be closer to knowing how William was involved in Claire's murder. Even if, as I stood there staring at him through the moonlight, all I wanted to do was take the bedside lamp and smash his head in with it.

I climbed into the bed, laid on my back and stared at the dancing shadows of leaves on the ceiling.

"I didn't expect you to stay." William said as he put his book down and turned on his side towards me.

"I can go if you want." I started to get up, but William guided me back down.

"I am glad you stayed."

We laid in silence for what felt like hours, although the clock told me it was only minutes. Then William spoke, "You are different. From the other women who have worked for me, I mean. You don't seem to be afraid of me like the others."

I was happy to know that I wasn't exposing the fact that I was terrified of him. Afraid I would reveal the truth, I didn't say anything and let him continue.

"I saw something in your eyes the day we met. I thought it was desperation, or sadness even. But our time together has shown me it was something else. I saw brokenness and yet determination. And I don't mean you were broken because of Adam, although I am sure he contributed. Rather, your heart had been broken and you were determined to mend it." He looked over at me and, when I said nothing, he added, "Then again, maybe I was projecting how I felt onto you. Maybe I was looking for someone to help me mend, given I can't seem to mend myself." William leaned over and traced my lips with his thumb, before he kissed me.

It was only when William turned off the light that I got the courage to speak. "You're right. I am broken. I don't know who I am without my sister, and my life has not turned out anything like I had planned. But maybe, we can be broken together and find a little bit of happiness."

William pulled me into his arms and we fell asleep.

A loud thud drew me back to reality. I looked around the room. No one was there so I left, for fear William would be back. I couldn't face him right now. As I walked down the hall, I listened over the railing to see if I could determine what caused the loud noise, but I couldn't hear anything. I was determined to have another shower and figured if I was needed someone would come get me.

I leaned my head against the shower wall as the hot water and my tears rolled over my body. I had a fight inside my head about whether I should keep playing this game with William. How many nights would I have to spend with him to try to learn the truth about his part in Claire's death? Did it really matter exactly what he did? Either way, it was his business that killed Claire. I could just kill him and get myself and the ladies out of here. I sat on the floor of the shower and brought my knees to my chest. I hated myself for enjoying being with William last night. If there was a next time, I wouldn't use anything to numb my brain. I would be fully present so that I wouldn't let myself get caught up in the moment.

When I eventually got out of the shower, my hands and fingers were shriveled. I was going to try and look a little nicer for William today, but then decided not to put in too much effort. Why change what was already working? Besides, the tights and sweater were more comfortable than anything else I had at my disposal. As I sat on my bed I prayed;

"God - if you are out there, I know taking another's life is not something you like. Hell, you wrote a commandment about it. Anyways, please give me the strength to get through today. Help me to help my friends and point me in the direction of how to get us out of here. I may not be someone you want to save after what happened with Adam, but please help me save them."

I patted the tears from my face and decided I better face the coming day. I couldn't hide in my room forever.

CHAPTER SIXTY

DARK CLOUDS WERE FORMING OUTSIDE AND CLOSING IN on the property, so I found all of the women gathered in the living room and watching a movie when I walked in with my tea. My hair was still wet from my shower.

"Oh, hi there, sleepy-head. Have a long night?" Fay joked and everyone laughed.

I smiled, walked past the bookshelf and pulled out *Anne of Green Gables* again. I sat on a chair in the back corner of the room. I didn't want to talk to anyone about last night and, given they had all turned back to the television after Fay's joke, I guessed they didn't want to either. I tried to read, but I was too distracted by the women in the room. Who would they be if they weren't here?

I pictured Fay as the CEO of a major financial firm mentoring other women in the male-dominated field. Whitney would be happiest if she had her own house with a large yard and a family she could love and spoil.

Jessica would be digging through some archives somewhere researching the lives of the people from hundreds of years ago, happily covered in dust as she revealed new knowledge of the past. Reyna was so young, she had her whole life ahead of her. I wasn't sure what she would be doing, but she had such a large heart, I am sure it would involve helping people. I knew she wouldn't go back to being a bank teller.

Saria had such an elegant and unique look about her, I felt she could be quite successful as a model. A couple of the guests had told her as much, and even offered to introduce her to some agents they knew, if she ever decided to leave this line of business. The day she told me that, was the day I realized the guests didn't know we were here against our will. Eloisa was another tricky one. After what she had been through here, I doubted she would want to return to the porn industry. She was a good cook, maybe she would try the culinary world. Lily could still have a bright career as a make-up artist and build a great life for herself anywhere in the world.

Each of these women were somebody's daughter, friend and neighbour. They laughed, loved and lived before this place and I hoped they would do the same after. I was going to do everything I could to get each of them back to their lives. How I was going to do that safely, I didn't yet know.

Jack came into the room looking as dominating as usual. "Ladies, please head into the dining room. Mr. Hammond is waiting."

Fay stopped the movie and there was some murmuring over what could be happening as we made our way. There wasn't a meeting scheduled for today, and we generally didn't meet in the dining room. Suggestions ranged from another party happening tonight, to someone leaving or a new woman finally replacing Jenna.

As I walked into the room, William's back was to me, so I was able to avoid eye contact for as long as possible. The floor length, vintage black floral lace curtains were open and I could see the ominous clouds had overtaken the sky. Someone had lit a fire, which was burning wildly, in the fireplace. The shadows it made around the room created a feeling of dread. I made my way to a chair away from William, took a deep breath and sat down without an expression on my face. After I got as comfortable as I could, I looked up at William and he nodded in my direction.

"Ladies, I know I usually give you the day after a party off, however, I wanted to inform you of the progress being made in the investigation into Adam's death." He looked at me. I could hear Saria, who was seated beside me, mumble she hoped Adam rotted in hell. If William heard he did not let on.

He continued and his voice became sterner. "Now, the coroner put Adam on the top of his list and has identified that he overdosed on oxycontin." William walked around the large table, stopped behind my chair and placed his arms on the top of it. "As a favour, the coroner is going to rule it a natural death, but now I need to know what actually happened."

I couldn't see William, but the terrified faces of the women around me told me whatever vulnerability he had shown last night had been replaced by the Hammond family trait of evil.

"Adam liked to dabble in drugs every now and then, but he knew his limits. Which leads me to believe he didn't know he had ingested it." I could hear William's nails digging into the wood of my chair as he tightened his grip. The sound made my ears hurt. "I know many people in this very room would have been happy to have Adam no longer around."

"But we were all with guests and then together by the stairs," Reyna said softly.

"Yes, Reyna, you were. But I know for a fact a couple of you were prescribed Oxy recently, and could have easily slipped something in his drink if you wanted to."

Whitney spoke up, "None of us were around Adam last night. And why would we want to be? Plus, who would be dumb enough to try and kill Adam, knowing they would be next?"

"You tell me." William let go of my chair and, as he took a seat at the head of the table, I looked to Whitney with fear in my eyes. He must know something. Why else have this conversation? Did Smith talk?

"This is what is going to happen. A friend of mine is going to speak with each of you today. If, in the end, he is satisfied that none of you were involved, I will drop the matter. If any of you resist his questioning it will only be worse for you. Each of you will be locked in separate rooms for the duration of the day or until my friend is done. Meals will be brought to you and Jack and Kevin will escort you to and from the bathroom as needed. You shall not speak to each other from this moment on. Understood?"

We all looked at each other and nodded.

"Get up when your name is called." Whitney and Reyna both looked at me, fear spread across their faces, but they each stuck out their pinky finger on the table to show they swore not to speak. I did the same.

After everyone else had been placed in different rooms, William and I sat in silence. The only sound was the fire crackling or footsteps in the distance. Then we heard a loud scream. William, who had been stone faced since the start of the meeting, flinched. He looked at me. "That will only happen if people don't cooperate."

I seethed with anger. I slammed my hands on the table, which shot pain through my broken finger and up my arm, but I pushed through it. I stood up, "So your plan is to torture each of us until you get the answers you want, rather than the actual truth, is that it?"

William opened his mouth to speak but I cut him off, "These women have been loyal to you, and yes, it is mostly out of fear but nonetheless, they know better than to cross you or make you angry. Yet you send them in there with your "friend". What kind of man are you? Why would you be so cruel to so many?" Tears had started down my face.

William walked over and stood in front of me. He placed his hand under my chin and lifted my face. The eyes I looked into were not the man who had cried in my lap or even the man from last night. I saw the man who stood in front of Jenna before he pulled the trigger.

"You can end it," he said calmly.

I didn't respond. "The rest of these women don't have to meet my friend if you tell me what happened."

I kept my eyes locked with his and stayed silent. William's grip on my chin tightened.

"There isn't anything that happens in this house that you don't know about. The women trust you, and talk to you. All you have to do is tell me who Smith was working with."

I couldn't hide my shock. My eyes widened and, even in William's grip, my jaw dropped slightly.

"Shocking, I know." William let go of my face and stepped back as he placed his hands in his pockets. "Adam and I trusted him for 10 years. His body was found this morning at the docks where we keep our shipping containers. He had shot himself and left a note taking responsibility for Adam's death. Apparently, he grew a conscience and couldn't take how Adam was treating the women. Then, likely knowing I would find out and come after him, took the cowards way out."

Previously when I didn't speak I was being defiant, now I just didn't know what to say.

Smith seemed to like you. I would catch him looking at you often. Is there anything I should know about you two?"

My mouth had gone dry but I mustered, "Not really. He was decent to me but he didn't stop Adam from hurting me. He even hurt me himself, under Adam's orders. Why would I have anything to do with that man?" I desperately wanted water but I was frozen in place.

I could hear whimpering in the distance as doors opened and closed. I heard Jack say, "Reyna, you're next," followed by footsteps.

My heart sank in my chest as I thought about what could happen to sweet, small Reyna. She was tough but would she be tough enough?

William continued. "People have made alliances with those they hate, when they share a common goal."

"What goal would Smith and I have in common?"

William had made his way around the room and was now on the left-hand side of me.

"You both loathed Adam."

Shit! Shit! Shit! How was I going to get out of this?

"Why would Smith loathe Adam?" my voice cracked and quivered.

"Why did everyone else hate Adam? Because he was a miserable bastard who enjoyed causing others pain and humiliation above all else. Including Smith."

"I... I didn't know that." I said honestly.

William looked at me as if questioning my response. Reyna's screams echoed through the house.

"Please don't hurt them," I pleaded. "They didn't kill Adam."

William didn't skip a beat and latched onto the meaning behind my words "Why are you so sure none of them killed him?"

I recovered quickly, "I just mean, well... as you said they trust me, and no one told me anything about trying to kill Adam."

"What about you? You of all people would have wanted Adam dead. Why should I believe you or any of the girls had nothing to do with it?" William was having a hard time containing his anger and I was having a hard time trying to figure out how to get out of this mess.

"Yes, I wanted him dead. Yes, I'm glad he's dead. I would do a happy dance right now, if it wouldn't get me a bullet in my head. But we had nothing to do with Adam's death. How in the world could we have helped Smith, even if we wanted to?"

My question gave him pause. Before he could respond, Jack was standing in the doorway barely holding up a badly beaten Reyna. A large bald man dressed in a black butcher's apron and covered in blood stood behind him. Jack had a gun in his hand with the grip towards William.

Reyna looked up at me and said, "I'm sorry."

CHAPTER SIXTY-ONE

"I'M SO SORRY," REYNA REPEATED THROUGH HER TEARS.

Jack let go of Reyna's arm, and she stumbled to the ground before shakily picking herself up, as she ran into my arms.

"I tried. I really tried but I couldn't take it. The tools..."

"It's okay. Reyna, it's okay." I whispered as I rubbed her back. She slid down my body to the ground and started sobbing.

I was scared to look at the three men huddling together by the doorway. This was it, if they believed Reyna - which, why wouldn't they? - they knew Whitney and I were the masterminds behind Adam's death. They knew the intricate planning and subsequent involvement of Smith. I dropped to the floor beside Reyna. "Do they know about Claire?" She didn't answer so I shook her gently. "Reyna, look at me. Did you tell them about Claire?"

She kept her head down "Yes." She whispered.

Fuck! Still bent down, I tried to look around the room for some sort of weapon. I doubted I was going to make it out alive, but I wasn't going down without a fight. There was a fire poker by the fireplace, but could I get over there quick enough? Footsteps started to make their way towards us and I knew I had lost my chance. Reyna and I were surrounded by all three men looking down at our huddled mass. It took all of the courage within me to leave Reyna on the floor and stand up.

Jack's face showed no emotion and the bald man seemed pleased with himself. When I turned around William looked as furious as I expected. Jack pulled Reyna off the floor with force and they left the room, followed by the bald man.

William stood there staring at me. The veins in his neck were throbbing. I was closest to the doorway, I could try and run for it. As if he could read my mind he said, "I wouldn't, if I were you. The front doors are locked, so you won't get out, and my bullets will run faster than your legs." His grip tightened on the gun which he now raised to the side of my face.

He was right. I gripped the chair in front of me and looked at my feet. William moved closer, until his chest was touching my left shoulder. He brushed away the hair that had fallen in front of my face and I recoiled.

"My touch repulses you, does it? It didn't seem to last night."

"I am a good actor," I said, with disregard for his authority. I wasn't going to play some meek, scared little girl. Everything was happening faster than I expected, but if this was the end, I wasn't going to roll over.

William chuckled "Yes, you must be. To think I was just starting to see you as someone other than a working piece of ass." His anger oozed out of him and I felt his spit on my face. I held my ground and turned to look into his hate-filled eyes. This was the monster I knew existed within him. The same monster that had resided in Adam. I had nothing to lose now so I asked, "What happened to Claire?"

"From what Reyna tells us, your friend Smith already told you what happened to her."

We kept eye contact, neither of us flinching. "Did you give the order for her to be killed?"

"Does it matter?"

"It matters to me!" I screamed. "It will determine how fast I kill you!"

"You're going to kill me?" he chuckled. "I am the one with the gun, missy." And he pressed it against my forehead.

I tried to buy more time, so I could formulate a plan. "Then I guess it wouldn't hurt to tell me the truth now, would it?"

William seemed to be contemplating his next move, so I continued, "What would Sharon and Penny want you to do? Provide closure, or be the monster I am sure they knew deep down you really were?" I knew bringing up his family would only provoke him, but I didn't care. I just wanted to use the only people he loved against him.

Flames of fire flickered in his eyes as William exhaled anger and grabbed my throat with his free hand. He squeezed hard and pushed me away from the table and hard up against the wall.

"My family's names are never to cross your lips!" he yelled. "You think I'm a monster? Well, a monster you shall get!" And he tossed me towards the fire.

Barely able to breathe, I got up and tried to reach for the poker, but William grabbed my hair and yanked me back towards him. I gave out a loud scream and kicked his legs out from under him. As he fell he let go of my hair. I quickly got to my feet and tossed a chair at William as I scrambled to the fireplace and grabbed the poker.

I heard William get up and cock the gun. I turned around, the poker at my side and stared down past the barrel of the gun and into his eyes, tears rolling down my face.

"Claire was a good person! All of these women are good people, and you turn them into slaves! You say your brother was a horrible person, but you are just as bad. You mask your evil behind the walls of a beautiful home and the money of prominent people. But you run this whole thing, so that makes you worse than Adam. So, go ahead and shoot me! What else do I have to live for? Even if I somehow managed to get out of here, you've ruined my life. You took the only family I had left, all because she caused you issues. Well, guess what? She had issues of her own! You tossed her aside like she was worthless. But she was worth something to me! At least when I tossed her aside I would go back and try to help her." I could barely catch my breath from the weight of what was happening. I wanted to keep yelling at him but I couldn't. I was exhausted.

William took advantage of my pause, "If you hadn't tossed her away, maybe she wouldn't be dead. Have you ever thought about that? It's not my fault at all. In fact, if you think about it, what is about to happen next isn't my fault either. If you hadn't come looking for poor little Claire, you wouldn't find yourself at the end of a bullet."

He took a step closer to me. I stood my ground and found my words, "Does blaming others help you sleep at night? We all make decisions that we don't always like. But when you decide to take a life - that is all on you. No one else. I will live with being a part of Adam's death for the rest of my life. And you will be accountable for the lives you have taken when their purpose no longer supported you..."

"SHUT THE FUCK UP!"

Startled by the yelling, I stopped talking.

"Don't pretend you fucking know me, you little bitch. Or that you know what is going on here!" He was visibly frustrated and roughly ran his hands through his hair. Then he stood tall, glared at me and said confidently, "Olivia Sophia Beaumont born April 15, 1991 and a member of the Toronto Police Service."

I felt as though I had the wind knocked out of me. I dropped the fire poker and fell to the floor.

He walked over to me, "I have known who you were since the moment you stepped on my plane."

I stared into the fire.

He bent down beside me, twirling the gun in his hand, "We do a complete background check on everyone who works here with me. Reyna isn't really Reyna from Delaware. She's Luanne from Ohio. It was only tonight, when my bald friend revealed my secret, that she learned just how far my reach went. I know everything about everyone here. Including you, little miss homicide detective. Conveniently suspended from your job so you could look for your sister."

My chest tightened and I found myself struggling for air. I had been here since the end of June, and the whole time he knew everything. Reyna hadn't actually told me who she really was. I had trusted her. Was everyone else lying to me too? I felt small and insignificant.

I didn't understand. Why would William protect me? Was he grooming me to trust him? If so, why? Why would he take me to see Mr. Y and then give me a gun? Did he want to see what I was capable of? What about last night, talking about his family. Tears washed over my cheeks as I realized William had been playing me like a fiddle the whole time. He let me think I had the upper hand, when it was him who was winning the game.

"Why don't you and I take a little drive? Maybe out to Rice Canyon. No sense in dirtying this carpet more than we have to. And, this way, you can have a little family reunion." He stood and held out his hand to me.

I looked at his hand and then the villainous face that looked down at me. I rubbed my hands on my pants as I looked into the fire. As the flames danced I saw Claire dancing around our backyard. I saw the two of us putting together the time capsule and digging up the ground to hide it. I saw us lying in bed talking all night. I saw Claire shield me from Dad.

I took a deep breath, got to my knees and took William's hand with both of mine. I used all my strength and tossed him forward. He knocked over the fireplace tools as he fell into the fire. He screamed and I scrambled to my feet. I grabbed the fire poker and hit him as he tried to crawl out of the embers, parts of his clothing on fire. He had dropped the gun, and I ran past him and picked it up. I turned around and pointed the gun at him as he took off his flaming suit jacket and tossed it aside.

William's face was covered in ash and burned, his pants continued to smoke as he stood there looking like something out of horror film. I pulled the trigger.

Nothing happened.

William and I looked confused. I quickly checked the safety was off, re-cocked the gun and tried again. Still nothing.

William started to laugh "The fucker gave me an empty gun." He turned away from me as he continued to mumble about Jack.

I took out the magazine from the gun and, sure enough, there were no bullets. I tossed the gun aside, picked up the fire poker and ran at William. Using both hands and all my strength, I stabbed him in the back.

He fell to his knees and then onto his side, still laughing. I stood over him, waiting for him to do something. He didn't move. I was about to pull the poker out of his back to use against the bald man, but noticed the other fireplace tools scattered on the ground. Rather than risk William refocusing on me if I removed the poker, I grabbed the shovel and was about to leave the room when I turned back towards the fire, still blazing. I used the shovel to scoop burning embers from the fire and put them by the curtains, the base boards and anything else flammable. William's jacket was still on fire when he tossed it aside and the carpet was starting to light. Now the curtains quickly engulfed in flames.

I stood and watched as the fire spread around the room. There was barely a surface which hadn't been tickled by smoke or flame. As I left the room, I heard William still laughing. There was no one in the foyer or living room, so I ran upstairs as fast as I could. Jack, Kevin and the bald man were nowhere to be seen.

All the doors were locked but the women were still inside. I used the shovel to bust the handles off. They stepped out of the rooms and looked at the mess I was in.

"We got to get out of here!" I yelled "The dining room is on fire." At the word fire they all ran down the stairs and stopped at the front door. They didn't try to open it, they just stared at it. Frozen. They could never walk out of it alone before. Would they be able to now? Smoke was starting to billow out of the dining room and the flicker of flames reflected on the walls in the foyer. I could still faintly hear William's laughter.

"Move!" Whitney yelled as she shoved people out of her way. She placed her hand on the doorknob, took a deep breath, turned and pulled.

CHAPTER SIXTY-TWO

THE COOLER AIR RUSHING PAST US THROUGH THE OPEN door gave us goosebumps, as it fought with the heat behind us. We all ran through the door and stopped at the fountain in the middle of the circular drive. The smoke alarms in the house had started going off, and I led the women down the right side of the driveway until we were safely away from the fire. We could have run, but instead turned around and watched the flames engulf the house. We silently agreed to watch the place, which had caused so much anguish, turn to rubble. The menacing clouds overhead offered no help to the fire, as they kept any rain they held to themselves.

We heard sirens in the distance. I tossed the shovel over the hedges and heard it trickle down the hill on the other side. I sat down on the curb and watched as a fleet of fire trucks and emergency vehicles pulled up to the house. Their lights reflecting off the house as pieces of it crumbled to the ground.

Paramedics came over with blankets and made sure none of us were hurt or had inhaled too much smoke. They spent time bandaging up Reyna. Afterward, they reported back to an officer, who then came over as firemen hosed down the house the best they could.

"Hi Ladies. I am Detective Teller. Can anyone tell me what happened here?" She had the familiar black notepad out, ready to document whatever we said.

We all looked at each other and I stood up.

"Ma'am, all we know is there was a fire in the dining room and we got out as quickly as we could."

"And how did the fire start?"

"Not sure," I lied. "We were upstairs when the alarms started going off. We ran down and saw smoke coming from the dining room. We got a safe distance away and waited."

"Which one of you called for help?"

We looked quizzically at each other. Someone called in the fire? I started to wonder if, wherever Jack or Kevin were, one of them was trying to help us. Jack had already surprised me when he provided William with a bulletless gun. Maybe he had been an ally all along. I answered, "None of us."

"Why not?"

I decided a partial truth would be easier to corroborate. "They didn't let us have phones, or any devices where we could communicate with anyone outside the house."

Detective Teller's facial expression told me she was skeptical of what I said. "Is that right. What kind of house is this?"

"Um well, it is, I mean was..." I didn't know what to say, but Whitney did.

"It was a whorehouse. Except more high class, but the workers were locked inside and forced to work."

Detective Teller's expression didn't change. "Okay. Was anyone else inside after you left?"

"William," I replied.

"And who is William?" she asked

"It was his house," Lily answered

"I see. Did any of you see if he got out?"

We all shook our heads. William's laughter still rang in my ears.

"Okay. I will have more questions for you once I get a better idea of what happened." She ushered over a couple of officers. "For now, these officers are going to watch over you until we can take you somewhere safe." Neither officer said anything but stood with their backs to us, as if they were guarding us from something that could crawl out of the house's ashes.

A while later, a small bus pulled up and a large disheveled man in a dark blue sweater stepped off and surveyed the scene. The lights from the emergency vehicles, along with flames, casted a shadow over his face. He spoke to Detective Teller and I figured he was obtaining instructions on what to do with all of us. I paid little attention as he made his way across the long driveway towards us until, through the bodies of the two officers standing guard, I saw that he was wearing a Toronto Maple Leafs sweater. I quickly stood up and saw Joe.

He was in disarray, with his hair and clothes a mess, but he looked like the most beautiful person I had ever seen. I pushed past the officers and ran over to him. I jumped into his arms and we both held each other tightly as we wept tears of joy.

"Oh my God Liv, what happened to you?"

I must have looked awful. My finger was broken, bruises were likely starting to surface from my altercation with William, and I was covered in soot and ash.

"Nothing good. I was so close, Joe, but I couldn't save her." My joyful tears turned to sorrowful ones.

He pulled me in close again, until Detective Teller bellowed for the women to get on board the bus. We were being taken to a hotel until we could be processed, questioned and sent home. Joe and I let everyone else get on the bus first, watching us as they passed, and then we followed. Before we sat down I introduced him to the group.

"Everyone, this is Joe. He was my partner at the Toronto Police Service." Other than Whitney and Reyna (who I still couldn't think of as Luanne) everyone else's jaws dropped. "I didn't tell you I was a cop as, to be honest, I didn't trust you with that information. In the end, William knew the entire time so I guess it wouldn't have mattered. What does matter is we are getting out of here."

Everyone smiled as best they could as we watched the emergency lights fill the sky above the rubble of a house which had once stood towering over the city. A place where dreams were made for those who could afford them and taken away from the women who were forced through the front door.

As the bus pulled out of the driveway, the adrenaline started to dissipate and tears started to fall. I sat comfortably in Joe's arms as I looked around at everyone consoling each other. Fay ran her fingers through Jessica's hair. Whitney and Saria cried into each other's arms. Reyna looked at me over Lily's shoulder, her eyes pleading for forgiveness. I wanted to walk over and tell her everything was alright and that I forgave her, but I wasn't sure if anyone else knew she had talked, so I felt it would be best for another time.

I turned to Joe, "How did you find me?"

"I have been looking for you since June. After you didn't return three of my calls I knew something was wrong. Sally may have told you to not speak to me for a while, but I knew you wouldn't just cut me off. We have been through too much for that. I went back to your old house but initially found nothing. I knew I was missing something, but it wasn't until my fourth visit that I found some letters under a bush along the sidewalk. They looked like an animal had ravaged them for food or tried to build a shelter. It took me a while, but I pasted the letters back together as best I could. Then I just kept digging and found out about the Hammonds, just as your friend Smith emailed me your note."

"He actually contacted you? Oh, thank goodness. I wasn't sure if he would. He was already risking a lot."

"After a little back and forth, he told me exactly where to find you. Sally dropped me off at the airport and I grabbed the next flight. I am sorry it took so long."

"Oh Joe, what would I do without you?"

He tried to loosen the mood, "Probably get fat eating take-out and watching reality tv."

We both laughed as the skyline of L.A. passed by the window.

"Will you do one more thing for me?" I asked.

"Anything."

"Help me get these ladies home safely."

"I will."

I smiled at him and laid my head on his chest. For the first time since that frightful night in May, I felt safe. I doubted the feeling would last, but for now I welcomed it and prayed the women around me felt the same way.

When we stopped at a red light, I saw what looked like the ghosts of Smith, Adam, and William all staring at me from the side of the road. Behind them stood Claire in a white sundress waving at me with a loving smile. As we continued driving their images evaporated.

It was over.

CHAPTER SIXTY-THREE

THE NEXT TWO WEEKS WERE A BLUR.. THE HOUSE FIRE, AND the nature of the business ran from it, were all over the news. I had paid attention to the first few stories, but I couldn't handle the images of the house, William, or Adam, and always turned the channel when they appeared. We had to have police stationed on our floor of the hotel to stop the attempts made by reporters, and interested citizens, to talk to us.

A well-known criminal attorney in L.A. met with all of us and offered to represent us all *pro bono* during the investigation and any trials that may take place. Like everyone else, she had seen the story on the news and said she felt compelled to help us. I was skeptical, and thought she wanted the potential notoriety that could result from representing us. However, as the other lawyers who visited came with a fee and much disdain, we agreed to her terms. None of us believed the others would have adequately represented us.

The LAPD used Smith's details about where Claire's body was buried in Rice Canyon, under a small mound of rocks for a gravestone, to find her. After a full day's search, a couple of empty holes dug, and the sunset imminent beyond the hills of the canyon, a young cadet found a pile of rocks with some fairly fresh flowers laid across them. Smith must have come to see Claire before he took his own life.

Once I got word they may have found Claire's grave, I paced around the parking lot and took small naps in the back of a police car as I waited to see my sister. Joe was with me and tried to distract me with coffee and talk about what we thought our lives would look like now. It took most of the night to unearth her body as meticulous steps were taken to preserve evidence. Finally, as bright stars hung in the sky, a stretcher with a closed shiny black bag on top was pushed along the pathway towards me. I had known what I would see come over the hill, and yet the site of Claire in a coroner's bag sucked out what little strength I had. I fell to the ground in a heap of tears. Detective Teller stopped the stretcher in front of me and slowly unzipped the black bag as Joe helped me to my feet.

Behind the dirt and the dark bruises on Claire's ghost-white skin, I saw peace. I had instinctively reached out to brush the hair out of Claire's face, but Detective Teller grabbed my wrist to stop me. She didn't have to say anything about compromising evidence. I understood and changed direction and reached for Joe.

It took a week for the Coroner and the LAPD to be satisfied they had all they needed from Claire. Joe and I had gone to the funeral home my lawyer had arranged, and saw Claire beautifully laid out on the embalming table. Her hair had been nicely curled, the bruises covered with make-up and a simple, yet elegant, light blue dress with small flowers covered the horrors done to her by Adam.

When Claire was first found, I thought I wanted to see what had been done to her, but after a couple of days, I decided I didn't want to know.

Smith had given me enough details to surmise what the coroner's bag covered up. I wouldn't be able to handle actually seeing the hurt I had been unable to prevent.

I had confirmed with Detective Teller that Claire's body wouldn't be needed for anything further, had her cremated and placed into a beautiful gold urn. The ladies, Joe and I had a short moment of silence for Claire in the hotel courtyard, followed by a rather somber celebration of dinner and drinks at the hotel bar. The hotel staff were nice enough to let us cordon off part of the room so that we would not be disturbed.

The next day, I went with an LAPD officer to drop Joe off at the airport. The Superintendent had extended his leave so he could spend the last two weeks in L.A., but Joe was needed back. The Superintendent extended my paid leave from the original three months, which had just expired, to twelve months. I was grateful and courteously accepted, but I was unsure if I would return to the Toronto Police Service.

We stood on the airport curb, wrapped in each other's arms. I had been lucky to have been partnered with Joe, and I thanked God for him. What friend would travel across the continent to find you? Joe would. We both hadn't wanted to let go, but finally we parted and Joe took his bag from the officer and headed inside. A small smile crossed my face. Claire and I would soon make our journey home together.

DETECTIVE TELLER HADN'T been convinced the fire was an accident. Although she had been getting push-back from high ranking officers to keep a lot of her findings off the record, Detective Teller didn't give up. She continued to investigate, no stone unturned, until she was satisfied she knew what happened. Detective Teller would come visit us at the hotel to ask more questions. Usually the same questions, but worded slightly differently. Our story never changed. I informed her of the bidding app in hopes she would track it down and could use the information to locate the guests who attended the parties.

After a few weeks, Detective Teller told us she didn't know how long the investigation was going to take. We had all been locked up long enough, before the hotel, and we all protested. After a short battle with our lawyer, Detective Teller informed us we could leave. None of us had been serious suspects, so she wouldn't be able to keep us in L.A. However, she had made sure she would always be able to contact us. She would call weekly, just to make sure the phone numbers our lawyer had arranged hadn't been 'lost'.

After most of us parted at the airport, I stayed in touch with everyone and checked in from time to time.

Detective Teller and her team located Reyna's family and got her back home to Ohio. Before she got on the plane, I hugged her and told her that her actions helped save everyone. She didn't believe me and continued to think she betrayed us. We haven't talked about that night since. Mostly, we texted each other cute animal pictures as a way to show we were still around.

Lily decided she would go to New York and try and get a job doing makeup on movie sets. A month after she moved, I received a call to tell me she had run into Victoria Steller and was hired as her personal make-up artist. I had no idea who Victoria Steller was, but Lily had been over the moon, so I was happy for her.

Saria found her way to Maine, where she got a job at a coffee shop right on the coastline. She told me it gave her peace to be able to see out over the water. The last time we spoke, she told me that one of her regular customers had asked her out to dinner. She had been hesitant. She wasn't sure if she would be ready to spend time with a man for more than it takes to serve them coffee. I told her to keep her options open, but to be true to herself first.

Fay remained in L.A. and helped Detective Teller as much as she could. The rest of us wanted to get away as fast as possible, but she was determined to get the story of what happened out there. She had put together a proposal to present to city council, to create a task force to help prevent and stop human trafficking. Fay was set to present it, with the backing of the Police Chief, in November. She said she had even been approached about writing a book about her experiences being trafficked.

Eloisa had been taken home to Texas, only to find her husband had remarried, had two children, and a new life after 6 years of her being away. The heartbreak had been too much for Eloisa, so one night she stepped off a bridge and washed up on the shore a few days later. No matter how far we had all gone, we had come back together for her funeral. Sadly, we had been the only ones there, besides the priest.

Whitney, Jessica and I found our own apartments within a couple blocks from each other in Toronto. I hadn't wanted to stay in my old place, as Claire had helped me pick it out and decorate it. Pieces of her resided all over that apartment. I had needed a fresh start. The new location had me closer to Joe and Sally, which had helped too. Us women had known we had to be on our own in order to move on, but we had not been ready to be completely apart from each other. We had weekly, if not nightly, dinners together. We supported each other through nightmares and panic attacks. We had grown closer over the months since leaving L.A. as the other ladies drifted away. Jessica and I had helped Whitney come to terms with not hearing from Kevin. Which, given her tenacity to 'get things done,' she appeared to do rather quickly, considering how long he had been a part of her life. We had originally thought Kevin may have been the one who had called the fire department, but with no word from him, we had become doubtful. Even after Whitney had appeared 'to be fine', I secretly believed that she wasn't over him, but I hadn't pushed her on it. She would handle the situation in her own way.

I had been happy to have Whitney and Jessica with me as I grappled with Claire's death and my role in the deaths of Adam and William. It would take a while, and lots of counseling, but one day, I would stop flinching when a man outside of Joe stood close to me. But for now, the three of us took small steps forward into each day. And each day we would become a little stronger.

EPILOGUE

THE TEST SAT ON THE BATHROOM COUNTER. I SAT ON THE floor and watched the timer on my phone count down. The tip of the test hung over the edge, taunting me. *You thought you escaped that life, escaped him. But what I will reveal to you will have you looking into the eyes of that world for the rest of your life. Every day you will see his nose, ears, or eyes.*

The timer went off, I silenced it and continued to sit and stare up at the stick which could change my future. Finally, I reached for the test and pulled it off the counter. I closed my eyes and said a small prayer,

> *"Lord, I know you have a bigger plan for me than I could possibly comprehend. I would respectfully request it does not include a child right now. But should you so choose may you give me the strength to love it, no matter who their father was. Help me to nurture it into the person you want them to be."*

I opened my eyes and, staring back at me, was a blue cross.

As if on cue, I turned to the toilet and vomited as I gripped the pregnancy test in my hand. I cleaned myself up and tossed the test in the trash. It landed on top of the other five tests I had taken this week. All of them had the same results.

I stared at myself in the mirror. I had barely slept in three months, couldn't keep much food down and, according to my psychologist, was suffering from Post Traumatic Stress Syndrome. How could I possibly take care of a child, especially William's child?

I had dismissed my missed periods to stress and the effects of what I had been through. I had not prepared myself for the possibility that I had been carrying a child inside me.

My phone rang. I looked down at it and saw that it was Whitney. I didn't really want to talk to her, but I knew she would keep calling until I picked up, so I bent over and grabbed the phone off the cold laminate floor.

"Hey. Can we talk later I..."

"Turn on the tv to channel 64," she briskly instructed.

"What? Why?"

"Trust me. Just do it." I could hear her sniffling through the phone.

"Okay, one moment, I have to get to the living room. Are you crying?"

Whitney ignored my question and changed the subject, "How'd today's test go? Get a different result?" she asked, partly joking and partly hopeful.

"Same as yesterday," I said disappointedly. I grabbed the remote and turned on the tv, switching the channel to 64. "What am I looking at?"

"They are about to provide an update on the fire," Whitney answered.

"I thought they had wrapped everything up. What more can they add?"

"I don't know, but Detective Teller called me to say they had an update and to watch. She said she tried to reach you but you didn't answer."

"Well, I would really just like to try and get on with my life. Here she comes."

Across the screen walked the assertive Detective Teller. She wore her dress uniform and stood behind a wood podium. Once she had settled her notes and looked into the camera, Whitney and I stayed silent.

"Thank you all for joining me today. As you know, on August 11, 2018 there was a fire which consumed the entirety of 1258 Holiday Drive. After further investigation, it has been discovered that this house was an unlawful brothel which trafficked women and forced them to perform sexual favours for wealthy and powerful people across the city. We will not be releasing the names of those individuals at this time; however, we are in the process of speaking to many of them right now. Charges are pending for some, based on what we found during our investigation. Once charges are laid, their names will be released. The operation was run by a large organization, with William Hammond at its helm."

My legs went weak seeing William's picture pop up on the screen. As I sat on the arm of the chair closest to me I could hear Whitney pacing in her apartment. Her heels were clicking on her hardwood floors.

Detective Teller continued, "We previously reported Mr. Hammond was in the house at the time of the fire and died. However, after further examination of the scene the Fire Marshal has concluded there were no human remains on site."

My heart stopped. "What did she just say?" I asked Whitney, still staring at the television screen.

"They think William is alive, but that can't be right. Can it?"

Detective Teller continued, "If anyone sees this man, they must not approach him but call the police immediately." Detective Teller instructed, "He is considered armed and dangerous. I will now take questions." Reporters lobbed questions at her but I was too busy staring at William's picture on my tv screen, so their voices became muffled.

"Whitney, he was still alive when I left him. Maybe he left out the back of the house? Fuck! Just when I thought things couldn't get worse." I was nauseous again and put my head between my knees.

"It's going to be fine. No one knows where we are." The crackling in Whitney's voice told me she didn't believe what she was saying.

"Reyna knows, and she turned pretty quick last time," I said in a panic.

Whitney didn't respond right away. She knew I was right. "Okay this is what we do. We get you out of town as soon as possible, change your number and we don't contact any of the group again. We can't create any trace between us and them, alright?"

"Right." My voice was starting to tremble. Would William's torment never be over? Would I ever be able to live without looking over my shoulder?

"Start packing now! I am going to make a few calls and see if I can find us a place to stay. Once I have a place, I will come and get you. We will leave your car behind, ditch mine when we are on the road and get a new one. Any questions?" Whitney always sounded so sure of herself when she made a plan.

"I don't know if I can do this. I had to be so strong for so long, I don't know if I can do it again." I started to cry.

"Olivia, everything will work out. I will be there with you. We will find a nice house in a nice town and live out the rest of our lives as two crabby old women with an adorable baby okay."

"The baby, oh my God. What if he finds out about the baby! Whitney, I am freaking out. Please hurry up and come get me."

"I will. Talk soon." I heard the beep of the call disconnecting.

I noticed missed calls from Jessica, Saria, Fay and Lily. I ignored the notifications and grabbed my suitcase from the front closet. I struggled to get it out, and ended up falling hard onto the floor after I got the suitcase unstuck. My phone went flying into the living room.

There was a knock on my door. I used the suitcase to prop myself up, rubbing the bruise that was sure to be forming on my ass. Jessica lived down the street and likely came over to check on me after she couldn't get through.

I opened the door and a familiar cologne filled the air. I froze. It wasn't Jessica in front of me. It was the face that haunted my dreams every night. Instead of the evil red eyes, and torturous grin, the face was calmly smiling as if his presence was the most natural occurrence in the world.

"Hello Olivia."

ACKNOWLEDGEMENTS

First and foremost, to my editor and friend Lisa Klemmensen. The guidance and support you provided gave me the strength and courage to actually turn words into a book. Your patience with a 'new' author was incomparable. Thank you for your candid discussions!

To my brilliant Pastor and friend, Preston Pouteaux, for your wisdom on becoming a published author. Without hesitation you shared your experiences and, with your encouragement, helped me see that I, too, could make my dream come true.

To my many friends, whose support and championship helped me to conquer my fears, be myself and share that self with the world. There are too many to name, however Megan Desplanque, Carol Whyte, and Wendy Hobbs and Ryan Schriml- you all pushed me to keep going when there didn't seem to be an end to the road.

To my family, who recognized my strengths before I did. My Dad, for instilling in me that it is never too late to go after what you want. My Mom, for being my first promotor to the world even before there was anything to promote. My sister, for the childhood late night conversations as we laid in our bunk beds to those over a cup of tea around a table. No matter what life throws at us, nothing will keep us apart. To my mother-in-law, for making sure I never went hungry during a two day visit! To my sister-in-law, Candice, your excitement and feedback propelled this idea over the goal line.

To Brian, my loving advocate, for being a sounding board. For embracing my crazy and being the puzzle piece that fits just right.

ABOUT THE AUTHOR

N.L. Blandford has entered the literary world with her debut novel The Perilous Road to Her. Her poetry was first published when she was 13 and recently her drabble titled "Love of a Lifetime" won the Arlene Duane Hemminway Unconditional Love Drabble Challenge. She resides in Calgary, Alberta where she has built a life of dream exploration with her husband, mild mannered dog, Watson, and stubborn but loveable cat, Sebastian.

Human Trafficking and Sexual Exploitation Resources

Note: The following information was obtained through open source searches and does not represent an endorsement of the identified organizations.

The United Nations defines human trafficking as "the recruitment, transportation, transfer, harbouring or receipt of people through force, fraud or deception, with the aim of exploiting them for profit." (United Nations. https://www.unodc.org/unodc/en/human-trafficking/human-trafficking.html)

The extent of human trafficking occurring in your country and around the world is unknown. This is due to:

- The hidden nature of the offenses,
- Reluctant of targets (victims) and witnesses to come forward to law enforcement.
- Difficulty identifying targets in practice.

"It takes an average of three years and seven attempted interventions to rescue a victim from a life of exploitation." (Not In My City. notinmycitylearning.ca)

To help stop human trafficking become knowledgeable about the issue and take action. There are extensive resources available. Below is only a selection.

Learn More

United Nations -Office on Drugs and Crime (https://www.unodc.org/unodc/en/human-trafficking/what-is-human-trafficking.html)

Canada

• Not in My City (https://notinmycity.ca/)

• Timea's Cause (https://www.timeascause.com/)

• Government of Canada - Human Trafficking (https://www.canada.ca/en/public-safety-canada/campaigns/human-trafficking.html)

• Public Safety Canada (https://www.publicsafety.gc.ca/cnt/cntrng-crm/hmn-trffckng/index-en.aspx)

• Canadian Human Trafficking Hotline (https://www.canadianhumantraffickinghotline.ca/)

United States of America

• Rebecca Bender Initiative (rebeccabender.org)

• The Polaris Project (USA) (https://polarisproject.org/)

• U.S Department of Homeland Security ((https://www.dhs.gov/blue-campaign/what-human-trafficking)

Reporting/Get Help

If you have been a victim, or might know a victim, of human trafficking please contact:

• Local law enforcement

• Social Services

• Licensed mental health practitioners

• In Canada, the Canadian Human Trafficking Hotline at 1-833-900-1010

• In the United States of America, the U.S. Immigration and Customs Enforcement (ICE) Homeland Security Investigations (HSI) Tip Line 1-866-347-2423

CPSIA information can be obtained
at www.ICGtesting.com
Printed in the USA
BVHW070032190621
609671BV00001B/4